AGE OF
ATHERIA

AGE OF ATHERIA

A Novel

by

JENNY MCCLAIN MILLER
& GREGORY JOHN MILLER

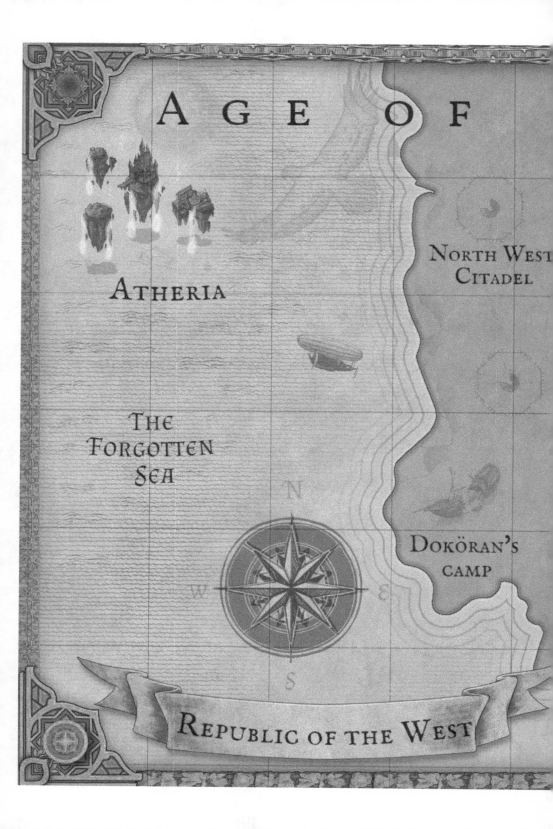

AGE OF

ATHERIA

NORTH WEST
CITADEL

THE
FORGOTTEN
SEA

DOKÖRAN'S
CAMP

REPUBLIC OF THE WEST

ATHERIA

BASILICA

NORTH EAST
CITADEL

LOWER WEST
CITADEL

DEATH VALLEY

PALMETTO
PUBLISHING

Charleston, SC
www.PalmettoPublishing.com

AGE OF ATHERIA

First Edition

Hardcover ISBN:979-8-88590-133-8
Paperback ISBN: 979-8-8229-0180-3
eBook ISBN: 979-8-88590-860-3

Edited by: Ciera Horton McElroy
Map illustrated by: Jenny McClain Miller
Cover design: Palmetto Publishing

www.ageofatheria.com

To River and Ryder,

our source of inspiration

and

to Skylar,

our very own Archlight

Behold, a day will come when there is great weeping, great pain. Whole cities will burn in great fires. A new Babylon will arise from the ashes, wicked and dark. The darkness will no longer hide in the shadows. They will strike like iron snakes in the night. But this will not be the end of all things. Disciples of the Light, a place is waiting for you – cloaked within the clouds, where the trees tower high and provide shade on the warmest of days. The water that falls will fill you. The flame that burns will ignite you. What has been foretold will come to pass. A great multitude will arise, anointed and beautiful in the eyes of the Light. The ancient words will illuminate their way. Together, they will awaken. Together, they will rise.

THE BOOK OF LIGHT, 2:8-10

ADY

Footsteps pound through the night like thunder in her heart. Each step he takes brings her closer to that world. She cannot see his face, covered by a hood, yet he feels so familiar. His breath becomes louder, like a whisper in her ear. He runs. Fire erupts around him. He makes it to the top of a grand staircase. He reaches for something in the night. A door? Yes, a door. He drives his fist onto the wood, knocking three times. As it opens, he quickly enters. And then—darkness.

The bell breaks the silence and cuts through the darkness like wildfire. Ady jolts and gasps for air. She keeps her eyes closed, searching for the cloaked figure. Where was he? *Who* was he? She attempts to retrace his steps in her mind—she could sense his urgency, his fear...smell the smoke that filled his lungs. The burning light of day scorches her sun-kissed skin as if she could feel the depths of the fire within her bones. It is high noon in the desert heat. She feels the hot concrete bench beneath her; it is almost nauseating, returning from a dream like this. Steadying her breath, she opens her eyes as the bell continues to strike.

These dreams, they have been coming far too often. Sometimes, in the slightest glimmer of light, they are good dreams. More often than not, they are crippling with fear and darkness—but it's always an escape from the Republic. At least there is the garden, a place to escape within the Citadel. Here, there is life. Here, she can be alone and allow her mind to wander freely. As she takes a slow breath, something in the sky catches her attention.

A hawk soars over the Citadel walls. She has never seen a bird like him. He glides on the wind, hovering above—almost watching. His feathers amber and gold. She watches this, his effortlessness—what freedom he must feel. His shadow crosses the sparse plants and flowers in the garden.

Again, the bell. If only she could skip lecture. After all, she has nearly memorized all the Speakers tell them. Even as she thinks this, she knows she cannot. In eighth form, Eagan was whipped with a rod for sleeping through exams. This is the Lower West Citadel. There are rules to be followed.

With a sigh, Ady gathers her journal and satchel, plucks leaves for pressing, and hurries to the central courtyard, past the scent of the wildflowers that grow amongst the concrete. The high wall circumference provides little shade at this time of day. The moment she is back in the courtyard, she is confronted by smells of sweat and pewter, clanging from the blacksmith's shop, smoke from the bakery that sells only rye. She knows every stone in this place, every misaligned brick. It is so dreary at midday—the sameness, the sounds of the rusted swinging shop signs, the faded fabric of uniforms. Black for men, shades of gray for women and children.

Ady has lived in the Citadels her whole life: first in the North East, before her mother died, and now here, in the desert. Within *those* walls, memories contained her mother and brother. Within *those* walls were the memories of being ripped from her brother and brought here by orphan transport. Alone.

Here, she knows every square inch within the Citadel circumference. Here, she has made new memories and precious few friends. There—across the gray quad— are some of the forgotten rooms, the doors barred off and sealed. There, above the girls' dormitories to the southern wall, is the rampart walk that encircles the entire perimeter. Should the Raiders of the Rebellion attack from the Wasteland, she is to flee to the rampart, Eagan tells her. Though, how they would escape, she has no idea. But he will meet her there. She also knows how to find water in case they are under siege (there are stores hidden beneath the mess hall).

But the Citadel guarantees protection. The guards at every gate are proof of that—though the West Gate is the only one that opens, the only way in and out.

Ady presses through the burgeoning crowd. The lecture hall is near the library, her second favorite place in this mundane world.

Today, the market seems especially busy. Merchants push carts through the rickety rows of canvas tarp booths. The marketplace is full of contrasts, many from different walks of life, descendants from the Old World: young and old, dark and light, some speaking hybrid languages. An old peddler touts a filament lightbulb while the medicine women sell aloe water. A pregnant girl displays rationed bread on a kerchief, hawking to trade for fruit or juice. Overhead, the Redcoats roam the rampart, marching between the columns that support the bulwark. Their gold insignias, stitched into their tunics, catch the strong sun. They are to protect from any threats outside the walls, always watching and training. Below, amongst the citizens, are the Bluecoats. They keep order and enforce the laws of the Republic.

As Ady dodges market carts and pickpocketing children, she hears her name.

"Ady! You're going to make us late!" Grenn stands outside the lecture hall, up ahead. Her arms are crossed, holding books against her chest.

Typical Grenn. She is always punctual, the first to arrive at the sound of the bell. Her long blonde hair is neatly braided. Ady prefers to push the limits. She prefers her thick chestnut hair in a mess of waves, anything to be different from everyone else's uniformity. Eagan loves this about her, says she's like the North Star, bright among the sea of others.

"You don't have to wait for me." Ady shifts her satchel.

"Don't tell me," Grenn says, opening the door behind her. "A little midday meet up with Eagan?"

"A few minutes alone in the garden. He's still at training with Tiri, you know that."

"He likes to break away and see you any chance he gets," Grenn reminds her, smiling.

"True," Ady smiles back.

The girls enter the lecture hall. Most seats are already full, so they slip into a back row. Ady drops her satchel and swivels the rotating desk forward.

"Did you finish the reading?" Grenn whispers. She lays out the textbook and a notepad. "Because I found Chapter Twelve confusing."

"I didn't even start it." Ady revels at Grenn's shocked expression.

She doesn't tell Grenn that she's been reading another found book: a novel called *Hello Earth*.

Grenn does not approve of Ady's exploring. Sometimes, before curfew, Ady slips through the Citadel's dark corridors—past the lecture hall and the grounds where the Redcoats train, past the closed market shops. She clings to the shadow of the high stone walls. She wants to know what is in the forgotten rooms. Republic officials send Bluecoats as valets to fetch buried supplies, and the forgotten rooms are opened, even for just a few hours. This could cost her twenty rod thrashings if she was caught inside one, but to her, it's almost worth it. What are they hiding? The doors are locked from the inside, and steel rods bar the entrance. Grenn is convinced that exploring is dangerous. "If there are things we shouldn't know, then there's a good reason not to know."

Ady isn't convinced. If there was no one alive who remembered the Great War anymore, how did they know what really happened? Books of the Old World are rare discoveries these days: but occasionally, she will pry open a forgotten cabinet, find an unlocked closet and discover a random assortment of treasures: small cards with numbers and faces, tiny hearts and diamonds. And, beautifully, books. Just yesterday, she found a new room unlocked. It was in her dormitory basement. She assumed the Republic had been using it for food storage since it smelled faintly of spoiled fruit.

"What if there's a quiz?" Grenn hisses.

Just then, Speaker Monroe enters the hall from a side door. Conversation dies instantly. His black cloak is too long, and it gathers around his ankles. A white sash rests across his shoulders, the Republic symbols standing out in blood red.

"Morning, class."

"Morning," they say in unison.

He discards his books at the podium, then raises his arms. Everyone stands. Ady places her hand on her heart and recites the Chancellor's Pledge beside Grenn:

To our great and mighty Republic

We pledge allegiance to Thee

Mother of the land

Father to the lost

Home where we are free

We hail our great and mighty Republic

They settle in their seats again.

"Today we are discussing national security between the Citadel quadrants," says Speaker Monroe. He adjusts his half-moon glasses. "We'll pick up at the end of Chapter Eleven."

Grenn's pen is already poised for taking notes.

Why even lecture what they've been learning their entire lives? Ady slouches in her desk chair. She knows what's coming: a history of the Great War, shrouded in a vague veil. Explosions and bombs that consumed the world. Technology shot and people stranded, the Republic rising, gathering survivors in small communities. Citadel walls went up around what surviving structures remained throughout the region. Storehouses filled with supplies and the gates closed to the outside. But there were early dissidents, rebels. Those who questioned the Republic from the early days, refusing to live by the new laws and within the walls. They withdrew to the barren wastelands to start anew, even though riddled with bones and debris. They became lawless. But there was more. Rumors had recently circulated that there were others sent to the Wasteland: the sick. Anyone who'd been exposed to the black rain, the deformed and dying, were banished from the Citadels, deemed unclean. Was it any surprise they'd all become godless? Known now for their savagery, their violence, their raids?

They're getting closer, Eagan told her just last night. A raid was imminent. Another Citadel just fell by the hands of the Raiders only a few months ago.

"The Rebellion is made up of guerrilla fighters, which is an old-world term for hit-and-run warfare," says Speaker Monroe. "Or tactics like sabotage, ungodly violence. Unlike the Republic, they are disorganized—"

Grenn takes notes. Ady props her head on her wrist. Already, she wishes for the garden.

She has found things there—secret things she doesn't dare tell Grenn or even Eagan.

Once: her journal fell, and she knelt to retrieve it. She saw the letters G+J '18 etched into the bench's underside. Another time: her heel knocked a path stone out of place. There, in the dry dirt, was a black canister. A label had peeled off, but inside she found a tiny paper scroll filled with initials and dates. People had lived here before the Great War. She's found other things, too: rings and keys to nothing; coins with a bird crest.

Sometimes, when she sits in the garden alone, she can almost feel it. The light and life that once lived here.

"Let's talk about maneuver warfare," Speaker Monroe says as pages flip throughout the lecture hall.

Ady raises her hand.

She hears more than feels herself speak: "Speaker, is it true that the Republic exiled the sick?"

He looks up and blinks. His lips narrow to a thin, tight line.

"The Great War killed most of the world's inhabitants. Resources were scarce. The Republic had to protect survivors. You know that."

"But not all survivors." There is a ripple through the lecture hall, as students shift in their seats and glance back at Ady. "Is it true that we sent out people who were exposed after the bombs? When they were just victims first?"

"The early days were dark times," says the Speaker with a sigh. "Dark, dark times. It is not our responsibility to question the founding leaders, who made difficult decisions to keep all of you and your families safe."

He smiles a toothy smile.

"But—" she begins.

"Ady, I suggest you keep your questions specific to the material at hand."

"This class is History, isn't it? And isn't that part of our history?"

She knows it is: the Great War is always lurking in the corners. It is hidden in the young children's rhymes, folded into the old women's legends. Bombs that fell from the sky—a sickness that came from the heavens. The lucky ones living in underground bunkers until it was safe to return to the air.

"If you'd like to discuss this during office hours, I suggest—"

"But I don't want to discuss it during office hours. I want to discuss it now."

Speaker Monroe surveys the class and grips the podium. Even from the back row, she can see his knuckles are white.

"The ice is thin, Ady—"

"You told us the Republic built the Citadel. Didn't we learn that a few weeks ago?" She nods toward Grenn's textbook. "How the stones were carted in from the quarry and the ruins, and there was this big assembly line? People working together, up from the ashes and all that. But we exiled innocent people from here, didn't we? People who now want to kill us?"

"The Republic fortified what was left after the War between the nations, yes."

She feels Grenn's grip on her arm. If she goes much further, she'll get a thrashing on her palms. But why is no one else curious? The other students sink into their seats and stare at the Speaker. A moment passes. Then, he clears his throat and continues with the lecture: "We must identify their weaknesses, find where they are vulnerable."

The Citadel walls are supposed to bring protection, keeping out the Rebellion. Eagan says the rebels are wild and rabid, deformed and sick. He says they are coming. And he would know—he's been training to fight with the Redcoats his whole life.

But then again. Who knew what was true?

EAGAN'S VISIT

Night falls over the Citadel. Through the narrow dormitory window, Ady can see the sky darken to indigo as shadows lengthen over the dunes in the distance. Curfew has begun.

Her room is small, minimal. There are only the bare essentials, just enough to live. But it's hers and full of treasure: found books beneath the floorboards, silver coins and rings tucked into her wool socks in a small drawer. Her favorite book—a slim tome with lyrics and strange capitalizations, the author named e.e. cummings—is wedged beneath the bunk. The walls are bare gray stone, cold to the touch. She keeps a little cup of milk on the window for the stray cat.

It's well past curfew now: the Redcoats will be making their rounds of the perimeter walls. The citizens will be in their dormitories. A room over, Grenn has probably begun her homework for the next day's lesson: a chapter reading about the Eastern Alliance and a hand-drawn map of the regions beyond the Republic. And three flights of stairs below, the forgotten room will be open—unless a Bluecoat discovered the error and barred the door again. Sometimes, those little mistakes happen. Last night, by the light of her single flickering candle, she saw the depressing tomb: boxes with damp and stained sheets, faded furniture and smashed bottles, little shards of broken glass, half-melted cards, names barely legible, images erased. What more could she discover?

It's time to find out.

Ady stands at her desk and fills her satchel: one wax candle, flint, journal and charcoal, and a scarf for her face in case of heavy dust.

Her mother was the one who taught her to explore forgotten rooms—back when she lived in the North East Citadel. Her mother Laylia, with the same thick dark hair yet pale skin, with a voice that could spin the most beautiful lullabies, would sometimes wake little Ady. She'd hand her a candle, signal to be quiet, and take her through the darkened hallways. Once, they discovered a room full of small lockboxes and numbers. "This is how they used to send letters," Laylia said, pointing to the slits in the walls. "Before the Swift birds." Laylia was always serious during these excursions. She would grip Ady's shoulders and say, "You must remember what it was like. You must know." All of this changed so quickly. One night, Republic officials carted Laylia away to the medical ward, saying she was *contagious* and *infirm*. Dangerous. She had seemed fine to Ady and her brother—she can still remember that pale hand reaching toward her from the stretcher. The next she saw Laylia, she was dead and thin as bones.

Outside now, there is the sound of footsteps and faint voices. Probably guards on the rampart walk. Ady halts, waits ten seconds to be sure, then buckles her bag.

Next, she stoops and removes her boots. Wool tights are quieter, less risk of being heard on the stairs. Her room is at the end of the girls' hall, six doors down from the community bathroom. If the others are asleep or working, she can slip out unnoticed and take the outer staircase to the basement.

Another sound, this time closer. A soft creak, the rustle of fabric.

Eagan—she doesn't have to turn around to know it's him in the room, his presence calms her. She can smell the sweat and iron. His hands graze her arms. She catches her breath and turns toward him as he removes his hood. Even in the darkness, she can make out the hardness of his chiseled face.

"I didn't think you were coming…" She reaches for his cheek and feels the softest scrape of blood. "You're hurt."

"We train with real swords," he says. "You know that."

"Was anyone else hurt?" She can feel the worry tighten in her chest.

"Just a few scrapes and bruises—this was just from a quick spar."

"I hate that. I don't like you guys fighting each other." She struggles to keep her voice low. The walls are listening.

"Well, you know we'll be facing the real enemy soon," he says. "We have to be prepared."

They kiss softly, briefly. The Republic bans meetings after curfew. They look down, too, on couples they did not match themselves.

"What really hurt was the extra sprints, full gear," says Eagan, rubbing at his shoulders through the cloak.

"Any wall miles?"

"Just a few, not bad. We were all trying to keep up with Ito, he's faster than any of us." He looks around. "Do you have any more barley tea?"

"Not made."

Eagan has a habit of dropping in unannounced through the window. Sometimes, he even sneaks away from his occasional nightwatch on the rampart. He always slips in quietly, skilled at moving around the Citadel after hours. Once, he arrived while she sat on the floor reviewing her garden finds, trying to determine what "geocache" meant on the little scripted scroll. When he asked what she was doing, she scrunched the cache in her palm. "Oh, nothing," she said. It was a reflex, she claimed. But this was what he hated: the reflex to hide.

As if he doesn't do this, too.

"What about you, your day?" he asks.

"Lecture was—you know. The same." She sighs and rolls her eyes in mock annoyance.

Eagan sits on her bunk, keeping his boots on the ground. "My father would have hated all this: the waiting. We've been working harder than ever, and we're still just here. Just sitting here like birds about to be shot. The Commander says the Raiders are headed this way, no doubt this time."

Ady starts at the mention of Eagan's father, James Alexander. He'd been like a father to her, as well, before his violent death just a few years before. He'd taken her under his wing after she was transported here, separated from her brother. Sometimes, when she catches sight of Eagan from across the courtyard, at just the right light, she thinks, for a moment, that he is his father, returned.

"But how does he know?" she manages to say.

"How do they know anything? Envoys. Stealth airships. They have their ways, Ady."

"At least you get told *real* things," she says.

Sometimes—rarely—she is envious of Eagan. She will be leaving lecture and will catch a glimpse of the Redcoats on the training grounds. Their swords emanate the desert light. They are pristine, precise in their red tunics. They know how to strike. And at a moment's notice, they have the chance to leave beyond these walls. Without her.

Eagan leans forward, his hands crossed. "In for the night?"

Did he watch from the window as she packed the candle and flintstone? She tries not to glance at her bag. He knows her too well. He will read through every small movement.

"Oh, you know," she shrugs.

In years past, before James' death, Eagan explored with Ady. They pried open cupboards; they wondered about the switches on the walls. Once, when Ady was twelve and Eagan fifteen—when they were still just friends—they climbed through a broken window into a forgotten room. And what magic they found! Little triangles that made sound, great beauties of black and white. That day, they discovered music. That was also the day they were caught: someone must have heard the sound as they experimented with the instruments. Ady received ten rod strikes; Eagan received twenty. He should know better, the officials said. He was to be a Redcoats recruit. Not even James, the Captain, could keep them from their public punishment.

It isn't that Eagan likes the Republic or even agrees with their methods. She knows this. She loves this about him. But he does fear for her, which is wonderful, but also stifling. The weight of someone else's love can be a heavy thing to carry.

"Why don't I make some of that tea?" she says.

Ady turns from Eagan and retrieves a mug from her desk drawer. It's one of her found artifacts, discovered in the pantry of the dormitory kitchen. It says *The Big Bang Theory*, which she thinks is a funny name. The theory of what? The barley, she keeps in a brown bag and scoops to steep for tea.

As she pours water from the pitcher, she feels Eagan approach from behind once more. His arms encircle her waist. She breathes deeply and leans back into his chest.

"You know I just want you to be safe, right?" he says. "You don't know what they're capable of."

"Yes, I do," she bites back.

"Fine, I won't—I'm not trying to tell you what to do, just—I don't even want to know what you're doing, so if I'm ever asked, I can genuinely say I don't know."

She turns around, places her palm on his cheek.

"I'll be okay."

Even as she says this, she is unsure. The Raiders are coming. They have never been this close to the Citadel, have always remained in the netherworld, in the Wasteland, which seemed so far away it was almost unreal. They dwell in the outskirts of the region, where the most significant destruction occurred, where the oceans vanished, and whole cities crumbled. Any day now, Eagan will be leaving with the Redcoats into battle. He will venture beyond the Citadel walls—and what will he find?

Be safe, she wants to tell him. But she knows that's an impossible request.

"I'll see you tomorrow," he says and kisses her.

Then he detaches from her embrace and returns to the window. Before she can say anything else, he leans onto the sill and jumps over the ledge. Ady stares out after him as she sips the barley tea.

CHAIN OF COMMAND

Morning in the Citadel: low desert clouds screen them from the sun. The sky is dusky gray. In the training grounds, the Redcoats are practicing. Their iron swords clink and clatter.

Captain Ellington stands on his balcony and overlooks the soldiers. They have done well. It's not yet time for the midday meal, and already they shine with sweat, their muscles long and lean. On one side of the training ground, men stand in lined ranks, practicing their shield wall. They are a moving red quadrant, each step in unison. Across the grounds, the foot soldiers are fencing. Ito spars with a double-sided spear.

"Do you think the Raiders will be merciful?" Ellington bellows. "Do you think they will leave survivors? No—this wall will not hold, but we, men, we will hold. Only the strong survive."

Ellington adjusts his red and gray sash. The gold insignias have lost their glimmer, but still, he wears them. Once, he would have been down there lunging with them. He would have demonstrated the proper grip on a gladius. He knew how to thrust a sword between rib bones. He knew how to balance a javelin.

His men have not yet seen battle, but they are as prepared as he can get them. They run miles along the rampart walk, carrying each other. They have practiced going days without food or water. They know how to make their own knives.

Beyond the training yard, high above the rampart, large red sails billow in the wind. Docked just outside the walls, the Republic's Army has a fleet of six airships. The ships are powered by heat and lifting gas, rising on the wind like majestic warbirds. Ellington rarely sets foot on the fleet, though—it's reserved for battle. Or the higher-ups, even higher than him.

"Let your blood and your scars remind you of the pain. Death is worse. Far worse. We build up a tolerance. We build up endurance. The Rebellion takes no prisoners."

He has fought the Raiders only once, when they neared the Citadel's region. This was long ago, during the famine years. Rations were strict inside the Citadel walls. (Still are, really.) They ate whatever they could find: alfalfa and small sprouts, potatoes, the occasional nectarine. Scouts had long since scavenged through the outer abandoned settlements and brought back any cans, bottles, and boxes containing edible food. It began with signs of hunting in the outer perimeter—an arrow that was not theirs. Blood trails they would never leave. Citadel sentries discovered and reported this to the Republic Commander. What followed was a brief and brutal skirmish: an attack in the darkness as the Redcoats descended upon them in the outer lands. There were only a few wild ones, hardly even a camp, and the death toll was still heavy. They fought with rough and ragged tools, hatchets and machetes, guns without bullets, hacksaws.

The sentries say there are hundreds now—and coming.

"They hunt to kill, to feed," he continues. "We must always be prepared to look death in the eyes and win."

"Easy to say off the battlefield."

Ellington turns in recognition.

"Commander Cayhill," he says and lowers his head. "We did not expect you."

"I prefer surprise inspections," says Commander Cayhill. His voice is gravelly. He steps to the balcony's edge and surveys the training grounds. With his sculpted white hair and broad shoulders, he carries himself like an ancient founder of the Republic itself.

"Men, lower your weapons!" Ellington cries. The sounds of steel on steel cease.

The Commander shakes his head. "Don't stop on my account. I'm here for them."

Ellington raises his arms, and the men continue.

The Commander rarely makes inspections: he is one of the few who travel between the Citadels to meet with the Republic officials. He answers only to the

Chancellor of the Republic, the supreme ruler that Ellington has never seen in person. He governs from a distance, in his Basilica halfway across the continent.

"Will they be ready?" he asks.

"We are always ready."

Ellington's grandfather was a small boy when the Great War erupted. He was an early survivor who escaped one of the large cities and hid in the underground bunkers. Then he became a settler. He'd helped build the Citadel walls, clear out the remains. "The bodies," he used to say. "So many. Some no longer looked like people. I still see them at night, when I'm dreaming." The horrors of those first days, mass graves and strict rations. Fear of sickness, the black rain, fear of the deformed and exposed ones, fear of the traitors, praying for the clouds to shrink and the sun to shine again. He became an early founder of the Redcoats. He knew firsthand the importance of keeping the community safe from invasion.

Commander Cayhill clasps his arms behind his back. His breastplate is newly shined, and it catches a slight shimmer of sun. A scar runs down his left cheekbone, thick and prominent.

"Have you been keeping an eye on him?" he asks.

The Commander does not have to specify who "him" means.

"He fights through any pain. He is one of our strongest."

"Let's hope it stays that way. I'd hate to lose one of our best men."

Ellington finds Eagan among the throng. He is with the foot soldiers, dueling with Tiri. Both men have been training for years, both muscular and athletic. Tiri could kill a man with his stare—but there is something to Eagan's agility despite his hulking height. And something to his magnetic air. So like his father.

There is the slightest twinge of guilt.

Had Ellington done the right thing in reporting James Alexander all those years ago? He'd heard only rumors, the softest of whispers among men. He'd noticed small group huddles, sudden silences when he approached. Treason was always a threat. And James had grown too powerful, then Captain of the Redcoats. He could have so easily turned the soldiers on the Republic.

"We will not lose him," says Ellington. "Sir."

His eyes have not left the ensuing duel. Ellington watches as Eagan nicks Tiri's shoulder. As Tiri winces, Eagan disarms and lands him on his back. Eagan's blade lightly grazes his neck but does not draw blood. Then they stand, shake hands. A pity they must practice so violently. But it's necessary, Ellington knows. Wounds are a sure way to become stronger.

Besides, these men have not seen what he's seen. Not yet.

SEEING THINGS

A dy had half a mind to skip lecture altogether. If only she could go to the training grounds and watch Eagan practice. There is a water barrel near the shield trough where she can sometimes perch unnoticed during the dueling matches. She can study every movement as though practicing herself.

But last time she missed lecture, she faced the rod as punishment. After her ten lashes—she counted to keep from crying—Speaker Monroe upped the threat.

"Next time," he swore, "both you *and* your friend will be punished."

Secretly, she doubts he would follow through on this threat. But she cannot do that to Grenn.

After bowls of hot cereal and sunflower seeds, she and Grenn settle into their lecture chairs. The other students trickle around them. There is a general hush around the Citadel today. The rumors move person to person, and Ady picks up only snippets: *the Raiders kill men but eat women ... they take babies for ransom ... they drink warm blood.* Not that anyone has proof for these claims. Still, unease catches like a struck match, and she notices how more students enter with stooped shoulders. Some bite their lips. Others have new nervous ticks like fidgeting at their desks.

Speaker Monroe arrives. Class begins.

Already, she knows what her day will be like. Lecture, meals, then chore brackets. Today she is on slop duty, so she'll have to report to the Citadel cook and gather the composting waste. Potato peels and carrot skin, pomegranate shells. Everything will pile into her pail, which she'll lug to the West Gate. (She has seen it open a few times, only ever to let the Redcoats in and out.) There, the land tenders monitor the growing plants. Right now, there will be a few green tomatoes, perhaps an eggplant, some radishes. Slop duty is at least better than seamstressing, needling thread in a dimly lit room. At least she can be outside, her hands in the dirt.

Beside her, Grenn takes furious notes. Speaker Monroe has begun a history of the Eastern Alliance and Republic's trade agreements.

This is when she feels it: the pierce of someone's gaze. Heat knives across the hall. Ady freezes. She then turns—and there, to her right, stands a man against the far wall. He wears all black, but these are not garments of the Citadel. His arms cross over his chest. He's staring straight at her.

"Grenn," she whispers.

Grenn only elbows her to be quiet. Speaking out of turn can lead to demerits.

Ady raises her eyebrows at the man. His expression does not change—he seems calm but focused. The hair rises on the back of her neck. Is he looking at her? Really *at* her? She returns her gaze to Speaker Monroe.

"—And what we must remember is that the trade coalition began out of necessity to facilitate an exchange of crops—"

When the Speaker looks up from the podium, he scans the student hall. If he notices the man in black, he does not let on.

Ady glances to her right again. But the man has vanished.

Grenn tears out a page from her journal and slips her a folded note: *You're acting strange, you ok?* But Ady just shakes her head. Speaker Monroe continues the lecture.

Sometimes Ady sees things.

It's like dreaming. She'll be alone in the garden, her palms on the concrete bench. The hot stone will take her somewhere. One moment she breathes the desert air, she hears the Redcoats train in the distance. The next, she walks among trees taller than the Citadel walls. There is water, the sound of rushing wind. The ground beneath her feet is green beyond green, and flower stalks reach to her waist.

Once, she saw a tall being with white cascading hair, a figure who floated among the trees. The being touched the dull bark of a dead tree, and suddenly light emanated along the branches. Leaves sprouted, flowers bloomed. Breathing new life.

Mostly, there is a stillness when Ady has these dreams—like magic, like slow-moving clouds.

Eagan says she has such a deep imagination and appreciates that about her. To Ady, it feels like being lifted from this dull reality, even for a few moments. Her daydreams are precious retreats.

Is this what makes her yearn to leave the Citadel? This aching belief inside her that there is more beyond these walls? That there is still civilization somewhere, past the Wasteland?

After lecture, the students disperse, some to their chore brackets, others to complete homework. The Citadel echoes with the clash of swords from the training grounds, and the air is thick with stewed-smoke from the mess hall. Ady waits for the others to leave and then sits on the lecture hall steps.

"What is it?" says Grenn, sitting beside her. "What happened in there?"

How to describe what she saw? Grenn would just say she'd seen ghosts.

"I thought that—" Ady's voice trails off. She'd noticed so many details. Surely this was not her mind playing tricks. She saw the vibrant green of his vest, the stubble that peppered his face. He was older than Eagan, younger than the Speaker. She'd never seen him before. "There was someone in the lecture hall."

"What do you mean?"

"Someone not from the Citadel."

Grenn blinks, then nods slowly. "Okay," she says. "Well, I didn't see anything."

"He was by the door." Her voice rises as she can tell that Grenn does not believe her. Grenn cannot hide her emotions: she has a face of glass. "He was—I could swear he was watching me."

Grenn places her hand on Ady's arm.

"Listen, you know that's not possible. Nobody comes in or out, unless you're a Redcoat or Commander Cayhill. You're just going to work yourself up."

"I know what I saw, Grenn."

"Hey, I'm just trying to look out for you. You sound paranoid. Are you drinking enough water?"

"I'm fine."

"Let's go to the mess hall, let's get you something—"

"I said I'm fine." The moment the words leave her lips, she regrets it. She can hear the sharpness in her own voice. Grenn wilts visibly but then straightens her shoulders. "I didn't mean it like that," Ady says more softly. "It's just. He was there."

This was not a dream. It couldn't have been. He was only a stone's throw away. He cast a shadow.

Grenn stands and dusts off the seat of her tunic.

"Alright, well, I'll catch you later then?" she says.

Ady nods and watches as Grenn walks toward the dormitory alone.

DREAMING

arkness—dim and heavy. It is colder than well water, colder than night. Ady moves slowly, one foot before the other. Ahead, the world is blacker than a moonless sky, than the interior of a forgotten room. She raises her hands, reaching for something, anything. There is only more darkness, more silence. This is when she feels the light, a soft glimmer behind her. Is her own skin glowing softly? Or is there something pressing against her back, something bright and pure and beautiful? The light provides her only guidance as she feels compelled to walk forward until her bare feet reach the water. The water moves beneath her as if inviting her in. With an apprehensive step, she feels the cold as it sends a piercing shock up her body.

The Citadel's sounds still trickle through the window—Eagan's breath warms her shoulder as she longs for his touch—and yet, she is somewhere else entirely. The string keeping her tethered to the Citadel is taut, tight, slipping. She moves through the sable dark, alone.

Ady sits up in bed. Her face is slick with sweat. Loose hair strands cling to her skin. It was so real, the darkness, the water. She surveys her dorm, from the satchel to her pitcher, to the gray tunic puddled on the floor. A new find from her evening explorations—a small black plectrum that says *Fender*—sits out conspicuously on her desk. But she'd left this place. She *had*. Her feet are still cold and wet. Ady shivers under the bunk blanket as Eagan stirs beside her.

"Hey," he says. His hand reaches for her cheek. "What time is it? Are you okay?"

"Still night," she says. "And no, I—" How to describe the feeling? The sudden, unexplainable tightening in her chest? These dreams that are both peaceful and panic-inducing? "It keeps happening," she says.

With more and more frequency, she doesn't add. Light vanishing in the garden, the man at lecture, these dreams that wrench her awake. She bursts from them, shocked to be in her own bunk, startled to find that nothing had happened. But they felt so real, more real than life, every sensation heightened.

"Tell me," Eagan says and sits up, too. He runs his fingers through her hair. Pale moonlight from the window catches his face, and she smiles at him.

"It'll sound silly," she sighs. "I'm walking somewhere dark. But it's not like night. It's not like anything. It's like a big black cloud. And—" she moved her hands as though parting water "—there's something beneath me. Like I'm walking into water."

As she says this, she can smell it: the damp stone.

"Are you alone?" Eagan asks.

"I'm not sure. I feel alone. I feel cold. It's like I'm the only person on the planet. I feel lost, but I'm not."

He kisses her shoulder, but she flinches slightly.

"There's more," she says, hugging her knees to her chest. "Today, there was a man in our lecture."

"What do you mean?"

"I don't know. He was on the side of the lecture hall, just standing there, against the wall. Watching us. Watching me."

He raises his eyebrows in concern.

"No one else saw him. Only I saw him."

Again, that darkness—and what was she searching for? Where was she headed? Through the water that smelled like the desert after rare rain, wet and heavy like wool. What awaited her after the darkness?

When she meanders between tree trunks, when she can pluck flower petals for her hair, when the ground is soft moss beneath her feet—those sights she loves. But these night dreams—this half-waking half-sleep—, they send a jolt of nerves through her like an electric storm.

Eagan looks at her long and hard. If he wonders why she didn't bring this up earlier in the evening, he doesn't let on. Just hours ago, they sat by her window and watched the sky turn from gold to indigo. They waited for the stars to appear, hardly talking, content to name the constellations.

"You'll be okay," Eagan says at last. "Nothing will happen to you. I promise."

She knows he cannot promise that. Even so, she leans and presses her forehead to his.

"I know," she says.

They lie back again, burrowed against the cinderblock wall. Eagan's breath eases into a sleeping rhythm within minutes. But Ady just stares out the sliver of a window. She counts the stars.

THE BOOK

At noon the next day, Ady sits at a library desk. Beside her, Grenn unfolds a sack lunch from the mess hall: two mealy apples, oatmeal, and dried jerky. Grenn offers an apple to Ady, but she refuses. Ever since her dream last night, she has felt nauseous and almost feverish, unable to eat.

Lecture ended early this morning. Exams are coming, and that means extra map work and recitations from the Trinity Convention. *All signatories, out of respect for the international community, dedicate to repatriate prisoners and uphold a permanent ban on weapons of mass.* The agreements are long and wordy, thousands of pages, and every year they study new elements of convention protocol. Last year in eleventh form, she studied *ratification*. The Republic is not new to bans. They have all but abolished religion, doing away with every sect from the Old World.

Grenn removes a set of charcoal pencils from her leather knapsack.

"How do you pronounce this word?" she said, pointing at her unfurled map of the Old World.

Mojave.

It was not far from where their Citadel resided as a black flag on the Republic maps.

"I have no idea," Ady shrugs. She flips through her own open journal: she was supposed to be copying portions of Trinity Convention charter two *Jurisdiction*. But all she has been able to write today is a memory of her dream. The way the water brushed against her feet. The way her hands seemed to wade through the darkness.

"I think it's Mo-Jay-Vee," says Grenn. "Doesn't that sound right?" She shades in the desert.

From the far side of the hall, the librarian gives them a loud *hush*. She is small, beady-eyed, her face tight with sharp angles. She knows little about the books themselves (Ady asked her once about a plant section, and the woman had no idea where it might be), but her desk is raised on a small platform. She is more lookout than librarian.

Ady twiddles a pencil in her palm. The words on the page run together—

And this is when she feels it again. That burning stare, the goosebumps trickling up her arm. She follows the feeling and glances past Grenn to her right. There he is. She almost screams at the sight of him—whether from shock or relief, she isn't sure. The man from the lecture hall stands tucked between two racks of books. He's real, in the flesh, in that green vest with the tousled hair. His mouth curls into a faint smile. As they lock eyes, he turns on his heel.

"I'll be right back," she whispers to Grenn, who hardly looks up from the map.

Ady weaves through the other desks, mostly empty, past a few other students with open books, food beside them in tied handkerchiefs. She steals a glance at the librarian, who seems to be engrossed in a filing system—and onto the bookcases.

The row where he was standing is now empty. Ady ventures forward. Surely he wanted her to follow him?

Around her, the books are bound in blue. But she knows there are different covers beneath, that there used to be something more. She's found only a few books in forgotten rooms, including a thick heavy text called *Religions of the World*. How many forms of spirituality existed in the Old World? She learned of a man named Jesus who died on a cross, a Buddha who meditated, an "eternal way" called Hinduism. How confusing it must have been to live in the Old World; how could you pick what to believe? The Republic has chosen for them. There is one religion for all, and it is the way of the Republic.

As she walks, she runs her fingers along the book spines. Same, same, same, that soft staticky linen. And then, something gleaming and cold. She stops and examines the shelf. There, jammed between the dusky blue bindings, sits a metal-bound book. A book unlike anything she has ever seen. She has walked this aisle countless times. She has explored here with Grenn looking for *anything* interesting to read, she has even snuck secret kisses with Eagan between shelves, just before he became a recruit. How had she never noticed this?

The book, though heavy, comes smoothly into her hand. In the now-empty gap, the man watches her. Ady gasps softly.

"Who are you?" she asks quietly. "I know you've been following me."

"Keep it safe," he whispers back. "Tell no one you have it."

"Where did you get this?" She examines the book by running her hand across the cover. Her fingers trace the engravings along the cool metal. Looking closer, she sees geometric patterns, circles upon circles. She tries to open it and is stopped by a clasp along the outer edge, locking its contents.

When she looks up again, he is gone. Ady clutches the book to her chest, trying to quickly conceal it. How could she? It radiates with the muted sun coming through the windows. It almost vibrates against her chest.

Back at her desk, Ady slides the book quickly into her satchel under the table.

"Find something interesting?" says Grenn. Her attention is on the map as she adds pointed trees in the upper left quadrant.

"What do you mean?" Ady snaps.

Grenn hesitates. "Nothing? I just meant, I don't know, did you find what you wanted?"

Ady casts a glance at the librarian, who's watching them again. "Oh, you know, was just browsing. For our final."

Grenn narrows her eyes. "Right. So what'd you get?"

"Just something on the Eastern Alliance," says Ady. She stuffs her journal and pencil into the satchel. "Look, I'm not feeling well, I'll see you later."

"You were fine a few minutes ago."

"I know, but—"

The librarian sends them another *hush*, and this time smacks a ruler on her desk.

"I'll see you later," Ady whispers. She can feel Grenn's gaze following her out of the library.

She'd expected the peaceful monotony of the Citadel. Women pawning hand-stitched towels and head wraps—men scooping coffee into tin cups—the sounds of the Redcoats at training. But instead, there is a commotion from the central courtyard. Students and merchants crowd around one of the raised watchmen's stations. A woman screams, then a child. Ady elbows her way through.

A woman—Marta, Ady recognizes—kneels in the dry dust, her hands clasped to her breast.

"Please," she pleads. "It won't happen again. It was his first time—"

"There should never be a first time."

"But he's six, please, he's only six. It was just three potatoes, not even a whole day's—"

Ady retreats as if in slow motion. She has seen this before, too many times. Once, a girl her age was caught sneaking oranges from the mess hall, and her whole family went without rations for an entire week—even the grandmother, who was already frail. The Bluecoats have been cracking down on theft more and more. Perhaps they fear a shortage should the Raiders attack and siege the Citadel. Usually, they focus on general peacekeeping, disputes between merchants, enforcement of chore brackets, curfew, rations.

But this? This is a small boy. Ady watches him even as she tries to vanish into the crowd. His ribs show through his tunic. Dirt streaks his cheeks. He is too young, yet, to be in lecture, to be assigned a rank. He is left to wander the Citadel, assist with chore brackets, probably look after younger siblings while his parents work in the marketplace. Is it any wonder that he slipped food? He looks so tiny on the watcher's block. The Bluecoat on duty, gruff and raggedy with an unkempt beard, grips the boy's wrist and unsheathes his sword.

The crowd gets restless. Some men cry out to stop the guard, others shrink back in fear. Ady notices other mothers cling to their own children's hands, some turning them away, shielding their eyes from the ensuing horror.

Marta stays on the ground, clawing at the dirt. She is sobbing now.

"That's enough," cries a Redcoat soldier, Thomas, approaching from the training grounds.

At first, the voice sounds like Eagan, warm but firm. It isn't. Still, she recognizes the man from the falcon training grounds. He is always so patient with them, teaching and meticulous. She has long wanted to speak to the birds the way he does, with heart and valor.

"Let him go," Thomas orders.

The Bluecoat pauses before he reluctantly releases the boy, who runs crying into Marta's arms. The crowd sizzles with tense energy. The two officers speak in a hushed rage to each other before the Bluecoat turns to the civilians and barks to return to their business.

Ady does not hesitate. The dormitory is just ahead, and she walks straight, eyes on the ground. The book seems to burn in her bag—what would happen if *she* was caught? Not only with this, which was surely illegal, but with all the other treasures in her curio-filled room? Would she be considered a traitor? Wasn't her secret life worse than stealing rations? And if so, what punishment would they save for her?

GRENN

Grenn stares at the Old World map. She has just shaded the Mojave desert terracotta red. Next, she will fill in the forests to the north, mountains to the east, and waves to the west, where water once lapped at the shore.

But she cannot concentrate.

Why has Ady been so cold to her, so strange? Sure, Ady is always off exploring. Always late, always *elsewhere*.

Grenn remembers when Ady first arrived from the North East Citadel. They were the same height, both in fifth form, and Ady was assigned to Grenn's dormitory for single girls. Like many of the other convoys, this one was full of orphans. The youngest were adopted into family units, but the older ones received the standard smock, moccasins, lecture primers, and room number. Grenn was there when Ady first entered her cinderblock dorm. Grenn brought her fresh pomegranate juice, warmed from the sun, a rare treat from the mess hall. And friendship bloomed from there. Grenn recognized something kindred in Ady, even then. They both wanted something more. For Grenn, this meant a room to share with someone else, a family to grow. She could remember her own parents, but briefly. Her mother, with that same tawny hair and willowy figure, starved to death—self-induced, Grenn later learned, secretly passing off rations to her baby girl. Her father had been a Bluecoat before a civilian skirmish left him weak and wounded. He died when Grenn was six.

She and Tiri can get there, she knows—the couples' wing. She could petition for a private herb box on her window where she could tend rosemary, thyme, marjoram. Maybe she will be one of the elite seamstresses, sewing tiny beads and patches on the Redcoats' uniforms. So she will wear the gray wool, she will study the texts. She will fill in the maps, land by land, recite the charters, and memorize the pledges—she will do her chores and will not talk back. This is how to avoid trouble, Grenn knows.

But Ady arrived feisty. She brought no personal belongings, not even a knapsack of spare clothes. Immediately upon arrival, she wanted to scout every inch of the Citadel, like a bird hopping around every rung on a birdcage. For years, the Redcoats kept falcons, and one of Grenn's chore brackets was cleaning the pen. Little Ady would sneak leaves from the garden to press; she'd collect falcon feathers to weave into her hair; she'd sometimes try to sneak to the garden after curfew to count the stars. And hadn't Grenn loved this? Hadn't she, even, felt envy along with fear?

"The Bluecoats have their watch stations, but they change them up some-times," Grenn said once over a meal. "So one day they'll be by the South Gate, and the next they'll be right outside the marketplace."

"So what?" Ady shrugged.

"So don't assume they aren't watching."

What she didn't say: she once saw her own father slap a pickpocket, younger than her, across the face. She was always trying to warn Ady, trying to keep her safe, even as she, too, marveled over the treasures that began to accumulate in Ady's room.

But now? Something is shifting, and she can feel it in her bones—like the soft rumble of the earth that sometimes shakes the Citadel walls. She'd always hoped that Ady would settle out of her restlessness. That she and Eagan would also share a couple's dorm, that she would tire of exploring forgotten rooms and leave the past to die. Why disturb the things of the dead? Why stir up trouble? Grenn stares at the library door, where Ady has just vanished. She wonders if she should follow and demand to know what's wrong.

The librarian catches her eye.

Grenn snaps to attention and focuses again on her map. *Sonora, the Sonora*, she thinks, and takes up another pencil. But from the corner of her eye, she sees the librarian approach.

"Ady certainly raced out in a hurry, didn't she?"

The librarian smiles. Her teeth are yellowed and long. Grenn scrambles to remember her name: is it Olive? Bertha? Nan?

"Yes, ma'am," Grenn says. She keeps her eyes down.

"And what's this?"

"A map for Speaker Monroe. It's the Old World."

"So, Ady. Why did she leave so soon?" The librarian nods to the open kerchief of food. "Two rations. She didn't eat?"

"No, she was—" Her mind races for something, *anything.* "Not feeling well. It might be, you know, her time."

Grenn hopes the woman will catch her drift. But doesn't buy it. "Ady borrows a lot of books from this library." The woman drums her fingers on the desk. "She didn't register any with me today."

Grenn says nothing.

"Why did she leave, Grenn?"

A student at a nearby table looks up, blushes, and averts his eyes.

"I don't know, really," Grenn says. She starts to roll her map, but the librarian places a hand on the scroll. "Seriously, she didn't tell me. Ma'am. She had this book with her, I don't know."

It had been just a glimpse, but she saw the shining cover and saw the knife-gaze from Ady saying *Don't ask.* She hadn't. But she'd never seen a book like that, not here. All books, Republic-printed or Old World recycled, were covered in dusky blue.

"It was different than any book I have ever seen. Silver, I think, and she put it in her bag," Grenn says, the words slipping out. "And she just walked out." The librarian stiffens, as though a string pulls her head taut. Her lips tighten, and she looks away from Grenn, back toward her risen desk. A long moment passes, and Grenn braces herself for a slap.

"Attention," the librarian calls, so loud that Grenn jumps in her seat. "The library is now closed, please return to your dormitories or report at once to your chore brackets."

There is the silent shuffle of students packing their bags. Some form a line at the desk as the librarian returns to her post. But Grenn only sits and stares at her map, at the blank place where the Citadel should be. She traces Ady's steps in her mind, out the library, across the quad, to the dormitory, that book in her bag, whatever she was hiding. Grenn bites her lip to keep from crying.

What have I done? she thinks. *What on earth have I done?*

REDCOAT ORDERS

A low ram's horn sounds the alarm at 1400 hours. The civilians do not notice. To them, the blast is merely the sound of the Redcoats, some signal from the training ground. They heckle in the market and grind herbs into tinctures in the medicinal ward. But Ellington knows. He is seated at his desk in the high-rise office. He hears the short, musical bursts, followed by silence as his men slowly lower their swords. For the first time in days, the training ground goes silent.

Ellington breathes deeply. Spread across his desk are the names of everyone in his ranks, nearly nine hundred—that and a tactical map of the Wastelands. He has been studying the topography, what little they know of it, and reviewing the Raiders' possible routes. His shoulders tense. He wants to stride out on the balcony and demand that the men pick up their swords, get back to it—he did not tell them to stop! But instead, there is only the still hum of murmuring voices.

Minutes pass. He watches wax trickle down the taper candle on his desk. He listens for the piercing cry of the falcons, uneasy from the sudden shift in the air. They are not used to this—have not yet seen war. Not these birds, they are young, but their ancestors were fighters. Now, most fly only when hunting for the rare small game beyond the Citadel. *Poor birds*, he thinks—*poor scared little birds*.

Then his door creaks open. A young officer, thin as a whippet, enters the room. He pants and sheens with sweat.

"Captain," he says. "A message from the Commander."

From his hip pouch, the man retrieves a folded piece of parchment. Ellington holds out his hand. He feels a slight twinge of resentment at the charade. Couldn't the Commander have deigned to actually come in person or summon him for something this important?

The note is curt and simple and not even in the Commander's handwriting. Ellington reads it once, twice, three times, and folds it neatly into a little square.

"The men know, don't they?" he asks and then adds, "They know that it's time."

The officer awaits a command, and his chest heaves with shallow breaths. Ellington stares at the folded square note for a good minute.

This job has become more than he bargained for.

This used to be Captain James Alexander's office before. This desk was his. The bookshelf, refurbished from a forgotten room by one of the Citadel carpenters, also his. The maps and blue-bound books and even the lapel on his breast, all last owned by a dead man. By a traitor. Sometimes, when Ellington stands on the outer balcony and watches the men practice their duels, he feels that Alexander is here beside him, watching. The hairs stand on the back of his neck. His arms tingle with goosebumps. It's true that he'd been jealous of Alexander's standing in the Republic, jealous, too, of the way the other soldiers looked at him—not with fear but with regard. That was a commodity rarer than extra rations. But sometimes, if he's honest, he misses the anonymity of wearing the Redcoat himself, wielding the sword instead of the orders.

The scout must have seen smoke, he thinks. Only that can explain the ram's horn. A breeze has entered through the terrace, colder than usual. The wind must have blown smoke from the Raiders' camp, which means they must be close enough to smell and see.

Ellington looks up, remembering himself. The officer still stands before him, the sweat now cooled.

"What are you waiting for?" Ellington barks, his anger surging.

The man pales and bounds to the door.

"Wait—" Ellington says then. His mind races with all that needs to be done. There are hardly enough hours left. "Send for each of the cohort lieutenants."

The boy disappears.

Ellington is alone again with the charts. One of the open books is a history manual, saved from the Old War library: *Militum.* They follow Roman tactics. It was the only military strategy approved by the Trinity Convention and by the

Republic. Their army was not large enough for a Legion, but he had cohorts and centuria, they knew how to walk in Testudo formation. Ellington stands, adjusts the insignia on his vest. He must roll his shoulders back, must look firm.

West Gate 0800 hours, the note said. That was all.

He knows how it will happen: they will gather by the West Gate, the only one that ever opens. They will march in tiered processions. The citizens will wave and throw scrapped handkerchiefs. His men will leave the safety of the Citadel, head west.

What would that bastard Alexander do? For years there has been only training, only a long wait. Many of his men have never seen battle, including the late Captain's son, Eagan. They are still mostly children.

The door swings open again, and a cluster of men enter. Captain Ellington straightens and feels his features harden. He scans them quickly and recognizes the lieutenants' faces—Eagan, Lucius, Galin, and others. He strains to remember the names of his own men, and even that seems distant, like impossible and forgotten knowledge. The lieutenants stand at attention, legs wide, hands clasped behind their backs. They stand shoulder-to-shoulder in the crowded office, but they remain silent. Still, outside, there is no telltale sound of clashing metal.

"There's news," says Captain Ellington.

GOLDEN HIEROGLYPHS

A lone in the dormitory, Ady slides her wooden chair to jam the door. There are no locks, but this will hold for now. She drops to her knees and releases the satchel from her shoulder. It burns from the strap and heaviness of the book—it slides to the floor.

She picks it up and feels that it is still so cold, even though it's been in the heat of her bag. She runs a hand—slowly, firmly, like stroking one of the feral cats in the Citadel—across the cover over the embossed details. This is when the shimmer appears. Is it a trick of light? She leans closer. The geometric patterns of circles and elaborate symbols become laced in shining threads of light. They glimmer like the stitching in the Redcoats insignia, but silver instead of gold. She snaps her hand back, and the illumination fades. It then disappears.

The sounds of Citadel life waft through the window. A few shouts, perhaps still from the marketplace skirmish. Footsteps thud overhead as a Redcoat strides along on the rampart walk. Ady glances back at her locked door. She has a feeling Grenn will be along soon to demand answers. But what can Ady say? How can she possibly describe what just occurred?

With a deep breath, Ady follows her fingertips along the outer edge and finds the metal clasp. With a click, it unlocks, and she opens the cover. The book pulses with light, as though distant stars are hidden within the pages. She looks closer. And yet, to her surprise, the pages are empty. When Ady's fingers brush the light-colored parchment, that light appears again. But there are no words, no illustrations. She'd expected runes, perhaps, ancient letters she could not decipher. This seemed like an empty journal. But something important nonetheless.

He'd said to keep it safe. To tell no one she had this. Why the sleight and secrecy when there are no contents inside? Since she saw the man in the lecture hall, she'd clung to the secret hope that he *was* just a vision, that her dreams were simply slipping out of sleep and into this, the world. But this book in her hands is real. As was Grenn's glimpse of it, the way her friend's eyebrows arched in question.

There's a rustling from the window—the whisper of soft tread and murmur of a cloak. With a jolt, Ady shoves the book back into her satchel, just as Eagan's boots appear on the ledge. He climbs in, and the bulk of his shoulders block most of the afternoon sun. A chill is already settling in the air, a sign it will be one of those cold desert nights.

Her heart pounds, and her voice feels shaky, high.

"You're early." Ady stands to greet him. "Why aren't you at training?"

Suspicion flickers through her. Had Grenn run to tell Eagan what she'd seen? Had she asked him to check on her? Eagan stands unmoving by the window, his hood still shadowing his face. Ady reaches for his hand, but he stiffens at the touch.

"What is it?" she says. "What's wrong?"

He lowers his head, and she can see the exhaustion in his face, feel the weight on his shoulders. Before he says anything, she knows why he is not in training until dusk today. The men must be sent to pack, prepare. To say goodbye. The Raiders are coming. The rumors are more than rumors, the attack must be imminent, must be close. She imagines Tiri looking for Grenn, off to share the same news, and she feels a slight twinge of regret at the way she'd swept from the library.

"How soon?" Ady says when he doesn't offer anything.

"First light tomorrow," he says, at last lowering his hood.

She wants to take his face in her hands, whisper sweet prayers, and tell him— oh, but what? Her mind darts from thoughts of Eagan in the Wasteland, asleep under a strung tarp, awakened to shouts and fire and blood splattering across his cheek, then back to the Citadel. She sees herself, alone now truly. She will be in bed, alone, wake up to those dreams of endless water, and hear blasts from the West Gate. There are only what, she counts quickly, a hundred Bluecoats? What happens to the Citadel without its warriors here to protect them?

"I wish you could stay," she says simply. There is nothing more than that.

"It's not my choice, you know that."

"I know, I know—"

Ady steps away from him, afraid she might cry if she doesn't. She turns to pace the dorm and slides her foot to nudge her satchel under her bed, the book tucked neatly inside. She moves to the desk and pours two tin mugs of water, hoping Eagan doesn't notice her chair locking the door. If he does, he says nothing. He only sits on the bunk, his arms resting on his knees. She joins him. He takes the water gratefully.

"You remember where I told you to go if a raid does come?" he asks as he runs his fingers through her hair, gently placing loose strands behind her ear.

"Yes."

"Good," he pauses. "There's something I want you to have."

From his hip pouch, he retrieves a golden pocket watch. His father's. It was a rare heirloom that survived from the Old World, passed down from Eagan's great-grandfather to his grandfather to his father. She has seen it many times. Often, as dawn rosied the sky, Eagan stirred beside her and lifted the watch to cast a slant of light. She'd seen his father wear this years ago. This watch was a connection to his past, something his family loved enough to keep safe throughout the early settlement years. And secretly, she'd always envied this. She owned nothing that once belonged to her mother Laylia, nothing from the former Citadel.

As she looks closer, she can see faint words inscribed on the metal: *You are my North Star.*

"I saw one of your books, poems about the stars, and I have always felt like you are my North Star," Eagan says, his voice hardly higher than a whisper.

"I didn't know you ever read them."

"I couldn't sleep one night, and I read some." He places the chain in her palm.

She shakes her head as the tears threaten to stream down her face.

"I need you to take this," he says. "I need it to be safe. And I need you to be safe. And know wherever you are in the world, I am always with you."

"Don't talk like that." The watch is cool in her palm, and the chain snakes down her wrist.

Eagan downs the water and sets the cup on the floor.

"I wish I could stay longer, but I can't raise suspicion. I have to gather my things." He raises the hood again, but not before kissing her lightly. "We're going on foot, so there's not a whole caravan. Then we have a final call-out." She nods and slips the watch gently over her head. It feels heavy, out of place. "But I'll be back, okay? I promise you that. I will be back for you."

THE BRUTALLION

Eagan moves down an unlit corridor. It is well past curfew as he weaves from the mens' dormitory, past the lecture hall and Ady's garden. He maneuvers within the shadows and keeps to the dark alleys between market shops. He stops at a wooden door and checks over his shoulder. The alley remains quiet and vaguely lit by moonlight. There's no sign of having been followed. A Bluecoat officer is patrolling the courtyard from a distance, his back turned. Eagan knocks as a barred window slides open.

"Pro societate secreto?" says the voice.

"Justitia," he says.

The door unlocks, and Eagan steps through. The stair shaft is ink-black. He blinks as his eyes adjust, and follows the other man down a winding flight. The steps open into one of the basement cellars, long abandoned. This used to be a cannery in the early days of the Citadel, when there was food to spare and save for winter. Now there are only overturned crates, a few metal shelves with empty jars. A handful of candles light the room, resting on makeshift benches. There is the faint hum of conversation and hushed, uneasy laughter. Eagan surveys the room, his eyes greeting the gathered men. Ito and Tiri, his dearest and oldest friends—he would trust them with his life. There are Thomas and Felix, the falconers—Magnus and Howe, and the many others. They look so tired. Some rub at their sore shoulders, others sip from the leather pouch at their hips. Ito stands, long and lean, in the far corner, his arms crossed.

The men quiet to a silence. Eagan lifts his right arm and makes a fist. The men mirror him, then together bring their fists to their hearts.

"My brothers," Eagan says. He tries to keep his voice steady, to will away the angst. "I think we all know why we are here." There is a soft murmur among them. The candles flicker, casting shadows on their taut faces. "The rumors are true. The time has come. The Rebellion is moving in from the Wasteland. Our scouts have already seen smoke from their encampments. The Captain has announced that we are to lead the front lines of the Redcoats at first light."

Even as he says this, he feels anger knot and twist in his chest.

"What I don't understand is, why call us outside the walls when we could protect ourselves here?" Tiri's dark skin shines with sweat as he shouts this out. He is the strongest of the men, but as clever and perceptive as Grenn. "They could never sustain a long siege."

Eagan can see right through Tiri's stony expression. He is thinking of Grenn, alone in her dormitory. Left to wait here like Ady.

"Ambush," says Eagan. "Commander Cayhill wants us to ambush their camps before they even have a chance to reach the Citadel."

But the Raiders are smarter than that, he fears. What if they wanted to be seen? What if they knew the Republic would attempt a preemptive attack, leaving the Citadel practically unguarded? The Bluecoats aren't warriors! They're local crime patrols. They're the Commander's private squadron. They have not trained with swords and spears, they do not know how to fall into rank at the sound of snare. He tries not to picture it: the Citadel asleep, half empty. The canons and shields and falcons gone with the Redcoats, the best scouts sent as sentries to survey the camp. Ady is still awake, perhaps, returning from her explorations, from wherever she goes, bringing back whatever she finds. Would the Raiders take advantage of the women, kidnapping them and their children out of the Citadel walls? Would they slaughter everyone, claim the Citadel? Or would they leave it all to burn? Fury seethes in his gut. But to deny Captain Ellington outright? They'd call him a traitor like his father. They'd hang him in the square before first light.

Still, he knows it could all be a ruse. A great trick—an empty campground, lit embers, and nothing else. A circumvented trail, a trap. Perhaps his father knew they would need the Brutallion for a time such as this. He'd laid the groundwork, a brotherhood that began with only a handful of loyalists. Usually, their meetings were quick and furtive, small gatherings every fortnight. But Eagan knows what his father knew: when the fight arrives, the Bluecoats will not protect them. They need a secret militia for the people. His father had been a good man, if distant, if always working—in his own way, he'd been protecting Eagan and Ady, too, when she arrived.

Eagan steadies his own breath and places a hand on his sheath.

"Listen, men," he says. And his voice drops to his usual tenor. "We've known this day would come. Haven't we? Isn't this what we've been preparing for, all those hours of training. And for what? I know some of you have been in this fight for longer than I have been alive." His eyes rest on the older soldiers. They sit in the corner, hunched over their knees. Their skin is hard-baked like earthenware pottery. One man, Cassio, lost his tongue years ago for voicing allegiance to James Alexander, just after the allegations of treason. "My father sacrificed himself so we could continue," Eagan says, turning about the room. "He never once allowed the Republic to intimidate him." There are grunts of approval, a few nods. "Tomorrow, we leave at 0800 alongside the rest of the Redcoats. We will prepare for battle— and for a quick retreat."

Ito locks eyes with Eagan and stands a little taller. He is the best runner. He can outrace anyone, even with weighted sacks during long wall miles in the hot sun. He can run a mile in four minutes. Ito also, usually, marches in the back ranks.

Eagan's plan is this:

When the Redcoats reach the dunes, the farthest western point visible from the walls, then Ito is to fall back. No one will notice. All eyes will be trained on the flanks ahead. He is to hide in one of the dune caves and watch the Citadel, wait for any sign of danger. Should he see the faintest tendril of smoke or a lookout emerge from the outskirts, he is to start a fire signal. The Redcoats are not traveling far. The light will carry into the Wasteland. And if it does, if they see the smoke, the Brutallion will detach from their legions and return. They will meet Ito back at the Citadel, near the South Gate. There is a secret entrance, Eagan knows, built into the outer colonnade comprising the bones of the Citadel. One of the columns that support the rampart walk conceals a spiral staircase, fifty flights up, around and around in a tight coil. His great-grandfather helped build the compartment as a secret escape route, but it was mostly forgotten as time passed since the Great War. He has climbed it only once, as a small boy, following his father by torchlight as he learned the hidden door on the rampart. At the time, it was a game, an adventure—he could never guess that his father was showing him a covert way out. The Brutallion will use this entrance to return to the Citadel. And if any Bluecoats are on patrol? Well, they'll deal with that later.

Eagan raises his fist once more. He watches as the men follow suit. Tiri and Ito smile as if to say they are with him to the end. He sends a small prayer to the heavens that this, this would be enough. Then they all lower their fists to their hearts.

THE WEST GATE

Light floods the Citadel. But this morning, there is not the quiet stir of dawn—the soft flutter of the falcons and the early risers warming oats in the mess hall. Today, everyone is awake early. The dorms are empty. Breakfast, too, is forgotten. Instead, crowds press to the West Gate. Commander Cayhill stands on the rampart wall and watches as the gate rises with a thunderous grumble. The Redcoats are lined up in formation. Their shields catch the golden glint of sunrise, and their cloaks are a rich red.

Ady elbows her way to the front, desperate for any last glimpse of Eagan. All night she hardly slept. She longed, even, for those dreams of walking through water, anything to escape the weight of the Citadel walls around her. Eagan did not come back all night. She kept slipping into some fitful state and then shivering awake. She sat up and scanned the room, certain she was being watched, certain something was wrong. But no one was there. The chair still guarded the door. The pocket watch still rested against her heart. The mysterious book was still under her bed. Eagan was still gone—she was alone. When morning dawned, finally, she threw on her tunic, pulled back her hair. She ran to see them.

Now the Redcoats march in orderly rows, a sea of crimson. She scans each face, every scar and sharp chin.

Around her, the people are quiet. Why aren't they screaming? Why don't they cry?

Some of the Citadel orphans wind and loop through the crowds and Ady can feel them, their soiled skin, as they graze her. They reach the front of the masses and wave at the Redcoats, probably hoping for any nod or smile.

— 44 —

Ady strains her eyes, searching. They all look the same in their uniforms, their swords sheathed around their waists—spears in their right hands, shields in their left. There are so many, some she recognizes from lecture, before they enlisted. Others had been assigned to her chore brackets. And some she knew from the hours she'd spent watching practice. She knew their skills with the sword but not their names.

Then—there Eagan is! Opposite her, in line with a row of men, a new cohort. His face shows no emotion, his eyes are trained on the road ahead. But she sees his strong gait and reaches to feel the watch chain hidden beneath her tunic. *Be safe*, she thinks, she prays. *Be safe, be safe, be safe.*

Once, while stargazing through her dormitory window, Eagan asked, "Why do you think the stars glow?"

Contemplating her response, she stared into the abyss of the night. "I think each star has a great power, in which they are all connected somehow. I think their light lights our way."

"Like a North Star," Eagan whispered. He smiled and kissed her forehead.

She never knew if this was true, but she loved the thought of it. Stars reflected the hidden light. She watches Eagan pass from view, concealed now by the others, rows upon rows of more soldiers. And she thinks that Eagan has been like this. He has reflected her hidden light, everything the Republic has tried to extinguish inside her. Both he and his father saw through the brokenness when she arrived orphaned and alone—they recognized the tender parts of her and accepted her anyway. The pocket watch vibrates softly as it counts the time, second by second, minute by minute. He is *her* North Star—and she needs that light to live.

Ady wills herself not to cry. Someone jockeys for a better view in the crowd, bumping her, and she steps back.

Everyone she's ever known is here, hunched together, smelling of sweat and sleep, agitated with nerves. Ady notices Grenn, across the way, crying softly into a small knit kerchief. Grenn catches her eye. And what they share is not a smile, not really. They nod, knowing. The men might never come back.

THE GARDEN'S LAST NIGHT

Trees tower high above. Sunlight trickles through the leaves, glistening on her skin like small rays of light. There is a faint breeze, then the sound of waterfalls from a high depth. She takes a deep, slow breath. Through the trees, there moves a flash of white. She looks closer. The stark white of fur passes between the treeline. She follows. Something—or someone— calls to her. Searching, she sees a man beyond the trees, gleaming amongst the sunlight. His brown hair is a mess, and he has the chiseled features of someone she knows but can't place. The cracking of a twig wakes her.

The garden is empty when Ady opens her eyes. She sits at her favorite bench and now watches as the sky darkens. Already, the earliest stars begin to appear. The moon is a crescent sliver.

All day she has felt numb. She's had no appetite, no hunger to scope out a forgotten room. She sulked through the lecture and avoided the library. She avoided Grenn, even choosing a different desk. She spent hours among the plants in the vegetable plot outside the marketplace. She volunteered to help the cooks peel yams for supper. The hours seemed hot and slow and sluggish, she did anything she could to distract herself and pass the time. But all day, in the back of her mind, there was this: Eagan marching into the Wasteland. And the book hidden within her satchel all day. It was safest with her, she thought.

Now, she relishes the cold stone beneath her, her safe place within these walls. The bugs have begun to hum, blanketing the garden in a soft white noise. Above, late shadows have turned the walls from beige to orange to dark gray. The occasional Bluecoat strides by, high above her, making his rounds along the rampart, taking the place of a Redcoat as lookout.

When the scout is out of sight, she removes the book from the satchel, unlocks it again, and thumbs through the pages. Still, there is nothing.

Ady sighs and places the book on the bench. She breathes deeply, and the air is thick and heavy. She closes her eyes once again. Where is the water? The smell of a world she didn't know? She longs to return there, to that place of stillness. She wants to feel the coolness of the waters upon her feet, anything to send feeling back to her body. She wants to venture deeper into the dark. Or to where the trees tower high, offering shade and protection. Who was that man among the trees? The white fur? Her thoughts leave her dreams. Instead, all she can see is Eagan's silhouette as he vanished out of the West Gate.

Please come back, she whispers. *Please, please come back.*

She's lost everyone she ever loved. The memory of her family has faded to distant voices and shapes. Her father died before she was born. She only knew of him from the stories from her mother. And Laylia—Ady could never forget the color of her eyes, the same cerulean blue...or the tenderness of her touch as she led Ady through the dark passages of forgotten rooms. And her brother, who had he become? Did he join the Redcoats as a young recruit within the North East Citadel? Was he even still alive? Her earliest memory of him was hiding beneath the tables of vendors in the marketplace, pretending they were being chased by the Bluecoats, although they'd never stolen anything. He always encouraged her adventurous streak.

Her last memory of the North East Citadel was the painful goodbye to her older brother and the seemingly never-ending caravan ride to the Lower West. The numbness she felt during that long ride reminds her of the numbness she feels now. When she arrived, Eagan's father took her in as best as he could. She sat with him and Eagan at meals in the mess hall, she listened to his stories about the Old World, passed down, he said, from his ancestors. Though he was the Captain of the Redcoats, he was gentle when others were harsh. Once, he caught her showing Eagan a pouch she'd discovered in a forgotten room: inside were little silver treasures, a miniature dog, shoe, wheelbarrow, and a thimble, along with others she couldn't decipher. The thimble was too small to fit on her finger, much smaller than the ones in seamstressing. She and Eagan froze when James entered the dormitory, certain he would lecture them—or worse. Instead, he just smiled and said,

"You must have found a game." James raised a finger to his lips and left them in peace. She loved this about him, and she grieved his death for weeks with choking sobs in her pillow every night.

Ady stirs on the bench as thunder grumbles in the distance. A storm is coming.

The now-familiar sense of being watched sends a chill up her spine. Ady opens her eyes to meet the gaze of the man from the library, just a few paces away. He stands just inside the garden's archway, concealed from the gaze of anyone in the central courtyard.

Ady stands cautiously. She grabs the book and clutches it to her chest. "Why are you following me?" she says, willing her voice to sound strong.

The man clasps his hands behind his back and steps toward her. In the dusky light, she can just make out the scruff on his face.

"I told you to keep it safe," he says. His tone is soft but ragged, as though he's gone hours without water.

"It is." Ady glances around to see if anyone else is nearby. But the rampart walk is empty above them. "Who are you? And what do you want?"

"My name is Edgar."

"And what do you want with me? And this book? Why do I need to have it?"

The man offers a faint smile and tosses back his disheveled hair.

"Any questions you have will be answered in that book."

Ady scoffs. Maybe this man is actually crazy—doesn't he know there is nothing written in the book? She wraps her arms tighter around it and tries to keep the rising panic from her voice.

"It's blank," she says.

"So, you opened it?" He takes several steps forward at this.

"Please, stay back." Ady retreats behind the stone bench. "Haven't others seen you? You're not from this Citadel."

"You're right. I'm not. But there isn't time to explain." He tilts his head to the night sky as if searching for a sign or signal. "It's time to go, Miss Adylyn."

Time slows—and for a moment, Ady thinks she's been here before. Or that she's heard this man's voice, these words, in a dream, or a memory. She blinks and feels as though she's hovering above the Citadel, above the garden, watching herself back away from this stranger who knows her name. She feels the distance between her and Eagan, the miles from here to their camp, feels the darkness that controls the night. She stands here in the farthest reach from the main Citadel market, this small enclosure tucked against the rampart. Would anyone hear her scream? Would anyone even know to look for her? And yet there is something soft in Edgar's eyes, not threatening. He does not step any closer. He holds his hand out as if to reassure her, as if to say, *you can trust me.*

All she says is, "How do you know my name?"

But he doesn't have time to answer.

The ram's horn sounds throughout the Citadel, followed by a loud blast. Ady gasps at the sound as the walls seem to ricochet. The blare is chased quickly by a distant clamoring of shouts from within the courtyard. The sky warms to an unnatural orange. Smoke enters the air. Edgar looks over his shoulder with an odd sense of composure.

"Miss Adylyn, we have to go *now.*"

Startled, she ignores him, throws the book in her satchel, and runs past with heavy steps. She emerges from the stone archway and hurries toward the courtyard.

She finds chaos: the marketplace is on fire, each of the canvas tarps and pitched booths. The library, too, is engulfed in flames. People run in disarray—some stand in complete shock, paralyzed. Her first thought is that a fire started from the mess hall. Someone was shaping flat loaves for tomorrow's midday meal, and a candle knocked over, or coal fell from the oven. But no, this is more than that. She can tell by the fact that the flames have spread so quickly. The whole courtyard is ablaze, hot and red and suffocating. Her mind flashes to her dormitory, all the collected treasures shoved in drawers and under floorboards. All those treasures from the Old World will perish forever.

This is when she sees them. This is when she remembers Eagan's warning, *Get to the rampart.*

They run amongst the citizens of the Citadel, wielding torches, bearing weapons she's never seen. Razor edges and serrated axes and long metal rods. Some wear leather sashes across their bare chests, thick and muscular. Some wear the aged furs of animals across their leaner frames. Black boots lace up their shins. Streaks of red and black run down their cheeks, as though their eyes are bleeding. The Raiders are here. Inside the Citadel.

LOOKOUT

Ito blinks the sweat from his eyes. The sun sinks toward the hills on the horizon. The last of the Redcoats have slipped from sight, becoming only a cloud of dust and smear of red in the distance.

Outside the Citadel, the desert flattens to a valley, once filled with saline lakes and basins. What's left is a craggy slope on the outskirts of the Wasteland. Ito crouches by one of these ridges, speckled with dead tree skeletons. His Redcoat cloak is under him like a blanket. His shield is abandoned in the sand. He watches the Citadel as it changes colors in the dimming light—first stone gray, then briefly, a resonant sandstone gold. He feels the setting sun bake into his arms. His skin is beginning to peel. He takes a sip of water from his canteen, only half full.

They marched all day with their slow and even pace, one foot in front of the other, but it seemed like they only covered a few miles. They stopped once, at noon, for a brief midday meal. Bread, dried meat, and hard cheese, coated with a sheen of desert dust.

Ito tried to keep his mind from wandering. He focused on waiting for Eagan's signal.

"Strange, isn't it?" said the man beside him as they marched into the afternoon.

"What?"

"Being outside the Citadel. It's so dry."

They passed faded metal signs, bent and collapsed. Tires, too, and broken-down vehicles, the color all but faded. Ito had forgotten that many, if not most, of his fellow soldiers had never been outside the walls.

The plan worked seamlessly. The man directly in front of Ito—Thomas, one of the Brutallion, the trained falconer—arched his shoulders as though adjusting the weight of his spear. Then he raised his right fist to his left shoulder. And Ito simply stopped walking. The ranks continued without him in their neat and orderly rows. Ito had to think fast, had to find a place for shelter. Keeping his gaze on the Redcoats, he stepped backward. Would someone see him? Would a page boy notice he was missing and sound an alarm? He'd say he was stopping for a piss, he'd claim an irritable stomach. Anything. His mind raced with possibilities as he gripped his spear and continued the silent retreat. But no one so much as looked back. And when the men were a slingshot's distance away, Ito turned on his heels and ran back toward the dunes.

He's still a good few miles from the West Gate, and the Citadel is as wide as his thumb from here. He can still remember how small this place seemed at first. He arrived as a boy, exiled from the Eastern Alliance in one of those sorry cavalcades, full of other exiles, refugees, orphans. He'd never seen desert like this, hues of brown and clay among the weathered rocks, emanating heat off the horizon. In his land, there had been ponds, still, and brightly colored fish. As a boy, he held his thumb up to the Citadel as they approached and watched it grow and grow until the walls absorbed them. He found his people, Tiri and Eagan—that was necessary to survive, he knew. Finding brothers who would give their lives for you. Even as children, as they roughhoused and admired the Redcoats, the other boys marveled at his speed and flexibility. Where Eagan was firm and sturdy, Ito was lithe and limber. Where Tiri could beat a man to a pulp with brute strength, Ito could execute a mean high kick. But give him hand-to-hand combat, and he can level someone twice his size.

Now, he feels the exhaustion of the day in his muscles. But he continues to watch the horizon for any sign of trouble.

Eagan clearly believed the Raiders wanted the Redcoats to attack, leaving the Citadel vulnerable. But secretly, Ito wonders if this is true. Captain Ellington is surely gruff and obsessive—but is he also that dense?

Ito adjusts his position on the rocks and leans over his knees. His calf muscles are sore from walking, and he massages them softly.

The sky paints itself a rich blue as the sun deepens to an evening red. Ito's gaze moves from the Citadel to the sunset, and this is when he sees movement. At first, he thinks it must be a straggling animal. A ram perhaps, or mountain goat? Perhaps a flock, if flocks still exist. But no, they are taller than that. They are men.

Ito drops to his belly, flattening himself as much as possible. Was Eagan right, after all? The light is fading, but he can make out a cluster of men, hardly taller than his fingernail in the distance. They approach from the northwest. Ito blinks and tries to focus his gaze. He counts ten, twenty, thirty—more than fifty. He continues to scan the number of men approaching. There must be close to a hundred. They are not advancing toward the Citadel gates, though. Why are they walking in this direction?

Ito tenses and reaches for his spear. There's rattling in his brain, and he can't tell if it's from a snake somewhere or if it's his own fear—excitement—shock! The Raiders have stopped some two hundred paces away. He cannot make out their words, but the husky grate of their voices travels on the desert winds. He watches as they kneel and seem to slide open a grate in the ground. His first thought is that they have buried ammunition to batter the Citadel gates.

Brilliant bastards, he thinks, panic rising in his gut.

But instead of lifting supplies from a hidden cellar, they descend into the ground, one after another. Then, just as swiftly as they appeared, they vanished.

Ito stays frozen, his eyes still trained on where they disappeared. Is it possible that the Raiders had built a tunnel that leads to the Citadel? Had they been planning for just such an opportunity? An unsuspecting Citadel emptied of its warriors. A night unguarded. Ito thinks of all the people in the Citadel. They would be cleaning up from the evening meal, drawing water to bathe their children, mixing yeast for tomorrow's loaves. Quick, breathing deeply, Ito rises to his knees and retrieves the flintstone from his pouch. Eagan had said to leave a smoke signal. The Redcoats couldn't be far ahead. They would have stopped to camp for the night or rest for the evening meal. Ito strikes the stones, cursing under his breath as he imagines the Raiders getting closer and closer to the outer wall. He calculates that he has what, twenty minutes? Maybe thirty before they're inside the Citadel walls?

At last, there is a spark. It catches on some tumbleweed beside him. The wind blows smoke into his eyes, but the fire catches—small at first, then ravenous. Ito jumps to his feet and races to tear branches off the dead trees. The dry wood takes quickly, and the little fire casts smoke into the night.

Eagan and the rest of the Brutallion will be back soon, he knows. But Ito cannot wait for them. Eagan will understand. Abandoning his spear, canteen, and cloak—extra weight—he straps his sheath to his waist belt and takes off toward the Citadel, as fast as his legs can carry him.

The remaining miles feel like a breeze. His body pulsates with adrenaline and energy, every step like lightning kissing the ground.

As he approaches the towering wall, he heads for the South Gate. He counts out loud to himself, moving his eye-line one by one. There is no time. He has to run directly to the correct column, as they are hundreds of feet apart. As he approaches the southernmost column from the West Gate, there is no time to catch his breath. He searches around the base, groping in the dark, remembering Eagan's instructions. Then he feels it—a large smooth stone. But it's clearly been moved, since behind it, catching the moonlight, is the wooden door. He enters the column. Inside, there is a staircase wrapped along the outer wall. Ito rises through the darkness, one foot before the other.

THROUGH THE FIRE

The smoke stings and Ady blinks to keep from crying. She moves through the courtyard as the main buildings catch fire. One of the nearest Raiders plunges his hatchet into a woman's chest, and her screams rise above the crackling flames. Ady recognizes her. They'd shared a chores bracket for years. She is only a few years older than Grenn. *Grenn*, she must find her.

Ady thinks she might vomit. She grasps the satchel and tries to shield her eyes from the smoke. It is a thick haze now, and the Raiders fade to murky figures, obtuse and dark. There is a roar and the crackle of thatch and wood. Ady turns to the sound and knows instinctively that it's the library. The roof has given in.

She must remember Eagan's instructions. She must get to the rampart walk. The closest entry is by the South Gate. If she keeps to the wall, she can avoid the chaos in the central courtyard. Ady continues, crouching in the shadows—but she's only gone a few steps when she hears her name through the tumult. She knows that voice anywhere. Grenn hobbles through the smoke, crying and soot-stained. Dark liquid streaks the tunic along her stomach, and blood drips down her shins.

"What happened to you?" she cries, taking Grenn by the hand.

But there is no time to answer.

One of the savages has ventured nearer the wall. He spars with a merchant, who defends himself with a barrel lid. But the Raider's brute force is too great, and he breaks the man's shield like snapping a stick.

"Come on," Ady hisses, looking away from the slaughter to come.

She runs with all her might. Her lungs burn, and her skin pulses from the heat. Tiny flecks of ash land on her skin and singe her hair, but still, she runs. There is nothing but this—she tethered to Grenn, fleeing for the rampart walk, fast among the falling cinders, past screaming children and abandoned carts, and water barrels, past bodies, too, still breathing, still bleeding. Some reach out for her, beg for help, but what can she do? Behind her, Grenn sobs and pants, near breathless from fear. Ady clasps her hand tighter. She can feel Grenn slipping in her sweaty palm as her breath becomes sporadic.

"We've got to go!" Ady urges. For a moment, Grenn's grip loosens, and her body feels like dead weight.

"I can't—keep up—" she cries.

They near the mess hall. There's a cellar behind, where officials keep the refuse until workers dump the remains over the wall's edge. The Raiders don't seem interested in the food supply because it's less populated here. Ady leads Grenn behind the mess hall, where they collapse out of sight.

"We're going to fix you up, okay?" Ady rips the end of her tunic into two long strips. "What happened?"

"I went looking for you," Grenn says. Her tears leave little lines down her darkened face. "I've wanted to talk to you all day, ever since—"

Two men run by, and Ady stiffens. She slams her hand against Grenn's mouth, and crouches lower, behind the refuse bins. But they're just Republic officials. She loosens her grip when they pass.

"Never mind that, we've got to get this bleeding to stop," says Ady. The stab on Grenn's stomach is deep, and the gash on her leg runs to the bone. But it is also clean, like a sword and not a rough-hewn weapon. Ady deftly wraps the first piece of fabric around Grenn's waist and another tied around her leg. She applies pressure to stop the bleeding on her stomach. Grenn grimaces in pain and grits her teeth.

"How did you get this?"

Ady looks over her shoulder at the open stretch of the Citadel. No sign of Raiders. "Grenn, listen to me. Did one of the Raiders get you?" Grenn presses her hands to her eyes and shakes her head.

"It was a Bluecoat."

"A Bluecoat? What do you mean? Why?"

"They were in your room! I went looking—and they were there. They saw me. It's all my fault."

Ady's chest tightens, and her heart seems to skip a beat. They were in her room? All her found things! All the treasures from the forgotten rooms. Every key and coin and scrap of the Old World that she'd hidden in a private menagerie. Had one of them seen her in the garden with Edgar? Had she been spotted on her last excursion to the forgotten rooms? But why would they be searching her dorm now, of all times?

"It *isn't* your fault," says Ady. Grenn's face is paling, and her skin is already clammy. "We need to get you out of here."

Ady crawls from their hiding place and looks right and left. The flames are concentrated in the central courtyard, and most of the fighting is there, too. There is a quiet pocket here, but not for long. The Raiders will surely raze every building, uncover every stone. Some Citadel civilians congregate at the closed gates, pounding their fists into the wooden doors. Where are the Bluecoats? Why aren't they fighting back? She has seen none of them, not even the usual wall patrols.

But entry to the rampart walk is not far now. Less than a simple sprint—they can make it if they focus, if they rest for a moment.

"We'll need to run," Ady says, turning back to Grenn.

Ito crouches and scans the lower courtyard for any sign of them. He reached the Citadel just as flames leaped to consume the makeshift buildings. He watched as tiny, sporadic fires appeared from various points, as though lit from within and not from one attacking source. He saw the Raiders emerge from a door near the marketplace, from a building he'd thought was a forgotten room, barred off and sealed.

The Brutallion cannot be far behind him.

Now the desert wind is dry and strong, lifting ash and cinder from one building to the next, like a floating current of stardust. Ito watches, cringing at every body that falls. Then he sees them, running toward the mess hall in tandem, connected like a braid. Agile over fallen stones and toppled crates, the debris of the falling Citadel. He knows it's her by her hair, loose in the wind.

Ady tugs Grenn from their hideout. The shouts are approaching from all sides. Soon, too soon, even the rampart entrance will be impossible to reach. She has never actually walked the wall, only seen the Redcoats on patrol or logging miles, but she has always longed to join them, to prowl the circumference and see the highest vantage point. But never under these circumstances. Her mind leaps and bounds ahead of her. How will they get down from the wall after reaching it? Can Grenn even climb the stone steps with injuries like hers? But they must press on, through the smoke and clamor, past their lecture mates, who run in clusters now before them, all going somewhere. But where? To hide, to lock themselves in dormitories, to the gates?

A heavy hand lands on her shoulder and Ady screams, throwing it off.

"Ady, Ady—it's me, it's Ito—"

He steps around to face her, and she could almost cry at the sight of him. His skin shines from sweat, and his black hair clings to his forehead. She is about to throw a barrage of questions—*is Eagan with you?*—when Grenn goes limp and collapses beside them. The guttural cries of the Raiders are nearer. Somewhere, a baby wails. A man howls with animal anguish. An explosion rattles the mess hall and sends shattered glass like rainfall. Ady screams and shields her head, but tiny slivers slice the skin of her arms.

"Come on," Ito says. He kneels and lifts Grenn as easily as if she were made of woven thread.

ON THE RAMPART

Every muscle aches. Every part of Eagan's body wants to drop his shield and sword and collapse. They have finally emerged onto the rampart walk. His shoulders strain, and he blinks furiously to keep sweat from blurring his vision. Smoke clouds the rampart walk. But all around, there is the roar and riot of the ensuing chaos.

This was the last place he saw his father alive. He stood on the rampart just days before his execution, wearing his Redcoats uniform. His father warned him of a raid. Warned him to get to the rampart and to always protect Ady.

Ady. There is only Ady. She knows to wait for him on the rampart, but can she get here? Will she make it?

The Brutallion streams around him from the spiral stairs. Their feet pound the stone. Some throw themselves over the wall, landing on building roofs before they tumble to the walkways below. To his right, Thomas stands behind a battlement. Magnus sends arrows into the Citadel like fierce falling stars. He staggers, struck from behind, and Eagan leaps to his defense—his sword lodges firmly between the ribs of a Raider. Below, there are various scuffles around the Citadel, skirmishes and fires spreading. Eagan leans through an open embrasure and watches in horror as a Raider hacks at a woman's bloodied arm. Bluecoats enter the rampart now, up the courtyard steps. His first thought is that they are coming to help, to send arrows over the wall at the Raiders. They have come to claim higher ground. But Eagan watches, stricken, as the first Bluecoat removes a dagger from his belt and strikes at Magnus. The archer is quick and dodges the next blow, but blood trickles from a gash in his side now. Something lights inside Eagan, and he springs forward, enraged. With a swift slice, he disarms the Bluecoat, sending the dagger clattering to the stone steps, before he hurls the man over the rampart wall.

His plan ran smoothly until it didn't.

The smoke signal arose above the Joshua trees like a faint trickle from a pipe, a little tendril that reached the graying clouds. The Redcoats had stopped to set up camp and prepare the evening meal. Ranks broke and dispersed. Men lowered their gear, dribbled water over their sun-scorched skin. The falcons fluttered in their cages that Thomas set up on the camp's outer edge. The dunes now rose above them, stark and rugged, with footholds only an agile mountain goat could manage. A few page boys carried pigskin sacks of now warm water, and they made figure eights through the men, offering refills. Eagan perched on a dusty rock and pulled rations from his belt: salted meat and hard cheese, a casing of nuts.

As much as he and his men had prepared, a part of him held tight to the hope that he might be wrong.

But there it was—the smoke, the sign.

Just as he'd hoped, the few Redcoats who noticed the smoke signal assumed it was from the Citadel and ignored it. But the Brutallion knew. Minutes passed, and Eagan's men ventured closer, each trying to appear busy. One removed a flint and took to sharpening his sword. Another man sat on his shield and massaged his calf as though working out a stubborn knot. Thomas poured water into the falcon trough, then cautiously unlocked their cage door.

But Eagan braced himself. He tensed as he ate and scanned the throng for any sign of Captain Ellington, but he was likely at the front flanks, perusing a map of the Wasteland.

Darkness was near. And clearly, Ito had seen something imminent. The Citadel was in danger.

Pages pitched tents, and the Redcoats stood and dusted themselves off, stretched, and removed their gear for the evening. Amid the shuffle, Eagan stealthily turned and crept due East, toward the darkening sky and Ito's smoke signal. His men, one by one, slowed and broke from the camp. Thomas called a faint whistle, and the trail of falcons emerged from the edge of the camp. Trained and silent, they disappeared into the night. Within seconds of rounding the first dune, Eagan was out of earshot, concealed among the many uneven rocks of the landscape. He waited and counted heads as the men appeared. A hillock separated them from the rest of the Redcoats, who milled about with all the night watch preparations. Eagan raised his right fist silently, and the motion rippled through the cluster of men, like light following a fuse. Then, he reached for the gold stitching of the Redcoat insignia on his tunic. With one swift tear, the patch tore off, revealing the Brutallion crest. Three interlocked bands—Borromean rings—like a bond of brotherhood. The other men followed suit, and there was the gentle rhythm of tearing fabric.

We must go fast, Eagan thought. His heart pounded, and he could almost feel the blood course in his veins. *We have to make up lost time before they notice we're gone.*

"Hey!" The voice was crisp and clear, someone young. Eagan turned sharply, and in the dying light, he made out the faces of two new Redcoats recruits. They were in Eagan's command. The shorter one, Ivan, had a slop of reddish hair. He was good at fencing, a decent runner, thin. The taller, Seth, was dark and lean. His hair was cropped short, as though sliced with a single razor across his scalp. But they were *not* part of the Brutallion. Eagan watched as Magnus plucked an arrow from his quiver and drew his bow. Tiri clutched his mace and stood battle-ready.

"None of that," said Eagan, but his worries were already in the Citadel walls, with Ady. They didn't have time for a holdup—or for the Redcoats to come after them. What good could Ito do alone without reinforcements? "You two, what do you want? You broke rank."

The boys looked stunned. Seth stepped back, his grip tightening on his spear.

"Us?" he spat. "You did! You're our commanding officer. We followed you."

Eagan's men began to stir. Some scuffed their feet into the ground, sending a little cloud of dust into the air. Magnus kept his bow aimed at the boy's tender neck.

"Look, what's going on? Are you...deserting?" Seth stammered and stepped back again in disgust.

"We're going back to the Citadel," said Eagan simply. "There's danger there."

Ivan looked over his shoulder, back to where the Redcoats milled around the campsite. Seth said nothing. His sword was sheathed, but Eagan noticed that his hand was on the hilt.

"You can now either come with us, or—" Eagan grimaced, but pressed forward, "—or we will have to kill you."

The boys stared back for a long moment. Eagan studied their faces, willing them to follow. Ivan was sweating, and his chest heaved. But Seth's hand was still on his hilt, still poised to fight.

The moment passed. Panic erupted on Seth's face, and he turned to flee. Eagan sighed and watched him shrink into the darkness. He heard the scream as Magnus's arrow struck him in the back.

Ivan just stared, blank and unmoving. His mouth chattered as though he were cold, but he said nothing. Eagan gestured for him to come. And as the Brutallion began the trek back to the Citadel, Ivan was now with them.

"Go, go—" Eagan cries above the roar of the crackling buildings. An eruption blasts from somewhere, and tiny droplets of glass sear into his cheek.

He needs to find Ady. She is the one who must escape. Everything depends on it.

Around him, the Brutallion fights as best as they can. Thomas lifts his right arm and throws it down forcefully, letting out a barbaric scream. The falcons descend from the sky like warbirds and plummet into the sea of Raiders. Magnus's arrows and the birds' force cascade upon them, taking out a front line in the courtyard below; Felix throws daggers like perfect silver slugs through the air. Two more Raiders have nearly reached the rampart, scaling a courtyard building and leaping from the roof. Their blood-stained hands grip the sandstone. Eagan hacks them down, a clean cut at their wrists.

To his left, Tiri rages through the mass of Bluecoats that continue to stream toward them. His muscles strain through his cloak, thick and hulking. He crushes the skull of a Bluecoat officer with a single blow of his mace. There is the spine-tingling sound of cracking bone and the remaining officers back away from him. Eagan watches, bewildered. Why are they fighting their own men? Don't the Bluecoats recognize them? How could they possibly attack Republic soldiers—even rogue ones—while Raiders infiltrated the Citadel?

But there is no time to dwell on that.

"Look out—" The warning is from Ivan, a sharp and clear tenor. He stands beside Eagan, his own spear outstretched. Another Raider has managed to reach the wall. He swings a spiked club, but Eagan ducks and plunges his own sword through the savage's barrel chest. Up close, the Raider looks almost inhuman, his teeth, bared in pain, look sharpened somehow. He falls backward, over the wall and into the smoke below.

Eagan shoots a smile at the young recruit. The boy's face is speckled with blood freckles now, and he looks fazed, as though sleepwalking.

Suddenly, there is a gasp from Tiri. Eagan follows his gaze into the smoke-blurred ground.

"It's Grenn!" Tiri cries. He runs, leaping over fallen Bluecoats bodies, to the rampart entryway. Eagan follows blindly. Grenn is the only one who can soften Tiri, like warmth to butter. Her voice, her gentleness. He caves to her, and Eagan knows this feeling. How love can make you desperate. And where Grenn is, Ady will be, too. He runs behind Tiri, coughing now. The smoke thickens, and he can barely make out the shapes below, except for silhouettes in the smolder. Tiri ducks his head as he stoops into the rampart corridor and down the many steps. They have practiced these routes hundreds of times with weighted packs, sometimes carrying each other across their shoulders. They have logged miles on the uneven stone, even up and down these very stairs, but never like this, thinks Eagan as he follows Tiri into the dim corridor. It's hotter here. The smoke funnels up the stair shaft and fills his nostrils. He coughs and keeps one hand out for Tiri's shoulder in front of him.

At last, they reach the Citadel grounds. The heat is enough to scorch his skin. The wind lifts burning flakes from the far reaches of the courtyard. There is the distinct and revolting smell of charred flesh.

But there, finally, is Ady. She holds Grenn's pale hand to her face, and she cries out something indiscernible. Tiri drops to his knees. Grenn looks so tiny beside him, like a broken bird in the shadow of a mountain. Ito and another Brutallion soldier spar with three Raiders. It's so strange, Eagan thinks, to finally see them, here from the Wasteland, with their makeshift weapons from the Old World, with their warpaint tattooing their faces.

Ady lets out a cry of anguish and relief. Eagan lowers his shield and sword as she throws herself into his arms.

"You're back, you're back," she wails into his chest.

Eagan buries his face in her hair for a long moment. She smells of smoke but also of soy soap and something herbal he can't quite place. He wills time to slow. He wants to remember this moment, every detail of her pressed against him, the softness of her hair as it runs through his fingers.

Then he pulls away and squares her shoulders to face him. He knows what must happen next. And there, just feet away, as though apart and unfazed by the tumult, Edgar approaches from the back alleys.

"Ady," he says sternly. "I need you to go with Edgar."

She blinks twice, and her lips part, but there is no sound. She stands in shock. More Raiders approach now, always in pairs, and Ito calls for backup.

"How do you know about him? How do you know his name?" Ady demands.

"Never mind that," says Eagan, looking past her.

Ady turns, following Eagan's eye line. Edgar nears them, emerging from the smoke and shadows with an unsettling calm. Eagan gently places his hand along her face, directing her to look into his eyes. There is no time to explain about the letters, the warning, that someone was coming for her. "Ady, you need to go with him *now*."

"I'm not leaving you!" Ady says, searching into Eagan's eyes with something like desperation. Her eyes then shift to the Brutallion crest on his tunic, and he thinks he catches the slant of a question in her eye. "I'm not leaving you," she says again. "Or Grenn. Or any of you. Please!"

"You must, Ady. We will protect her. You have to go."

One of the Raiders collapses nearby, decapitated. Ito is onto the next, but Eagan can see that his strength is waning. He needs help—now. Shouts arise in the distance, and a cluster of Bluecoats emerges from where the training ground used to be.

Eagan watches emotion flicker across Ady's face, as quick as a shuddering flame. Tears well in her eyes. His pocket watch rests around her neck, and it glimmers in the burnished light.

"It isn't safe here for you," he says, his voice softening. He tightens his shoulders and fights to level his voice. He cannot cry, not now. If he cries, she will never leave him. She will place her hands on his face and determine to stay. And he cannot allow that.

At their feet, Tiri is still shouting for Grenn to wake up, to stay with him. He opens her mouth now and breathes quick, short bursts of air into her lungs. Ady watches on and begins to cry heavier, panic engulfing her.

"Ady, so help me God, you need to listen to me," says Eagan. He takes her hands in his. They are small and delicate, dirty but beautiful, and he kisses her palms, "You must go, *now*. I will find you, I *promise*."

Edgar is upon them, ready.

It happens quickly: Eagan tightens his grip on her hands, speaking softly, "I'm sorry." And he pushes her back. Edgar's arms encircle her waist, and this is when she erupts with alarm. Ady is screaming like he's never heard her scream before. She strains against Edgar's grip, drags her heels in the sooty dust, bucks against his chest, but he is too strong for her—and Eagan imagines, in the shortest of seconds, how Ady must have fought as a girl when loaded on the orphan transport, when brought here to this Citadel, to him, a new and foreign home, so far away from everything she'd known and loved, from where she'd buried her parents. She will find her way again. She is destined to—and he? He *will* find her. He will fulfill his promise. His eyes meet hers one final time, as she desperately reaches out for him before she is pulled deeper into the smoke. He couldn't reach back, and this thought shatters his heart into a million fragments. Edgar does not falter when they reach the rampart steps, but Ady is still screaming, a higher pitch now, and he can almost make out the sound and shape of his name through the haze.

Her silhouette disappears. And then she is gone.

Eagan turns away, dazed and numb, and tries to re-focus on the havoc around him. More Raiders are approaching, a massive untamed horde. Ito poises with his gladius, Tiri gently releases Grenn's unresponsive body and finally stands hurling a scream from somewhere deep and dark inside him. He hooks his mace behind his shoulder, and Eagan lifts his shield high. They brace for the hit.

THE CLIFF'S EDGE

Outside the Citadel, the air is thick and charged with heat. Smoke billows into the night sky and blocks the stars in a chalky haze. The desert wind is strong tonight, gusting through the stark and serrated trees. Ash floats on the wind like tiny speckles of light. A few graze Ady's skin and sizzle away to dust. Still, they run.

She is too stunned to keep crying, too focused on not tripping in the darkness, first over the uneven stone steps, now over the dim and rugged terrain. The satchel bounces with every step, and she feels a bruise bloom on her hip from the metal-bound book. Her skin is scraped and singed already from the escape through the Citadel, but the pain seems to lessen with every step. She is all numbness. She has never run through the desert, let alone at night. Dry dust rises in hillocks around her ankles, and she can feel the dirt cling to her skin. Specks prick her eyes, making it hard to see. There is only Edgar leading the way, a darker shadow in the dark world. Their pace begins to slow.

Could she run back to the Citadel? Could she try to find Eagan? Even as she thinks this, she knows she would be cut down like a tiny tree switch.

Every step up the rampart walk was a battle. Her ankles caught the loose stones, and her rib cage ached from the weight of Edgar's grasp. At what point had she relented in shocked surrender? Was it when Edgar released her to fight off a Raider on the rampart, his aim sharp and precise? Or when he unhatched the door in the Citadel column and she realized, in a moment of intensifying clarity, that Eagan had known about the escape route all along. *Get to the rampart*, he'd always said—now, there she was, in a hidden shaft, hurrying behind a stranger in the darkness, down seemingly endless steps, her vision fogged by smoke and hot tears.

Eagan. The desert wind whips through her hair, and she remembers how he nuzzled her head and how he looked at her with such tenderness and resolution. Is he still alive? Is Grenn? Eagan had known about Edgar and kept this from her. These thoughts loom in her mind as they continue on. But the fact that Eagan knew about him means Edgar *must* be safe. Right?

They have only traveled a couple miles from the Citadel, she assumes, but how would she know? Her head pounds with a dull ache, and she tries to concentrate on the pang—anything to keep from imagining what savage things the Raiders might be doing to him.

At last, Edgar stops running. He scans the horizon as though looking for a landmark and then passes her a waterskin. The water is warm and metallic, but she drinks greedily and relishes the droplets that spill down her neck.

They have reached the edge of a steep ravine that slopes deep down into the earth. The stone on the far side glows a dull, hot red. Ady stares down the steep drop-off, like a cliff. She wonders if a river once ran through here in the Old World, carving out the strata on either side. It seems impossible that this wild and untamed landscape has been here all along, in the short distance from the Citadel, and yet she has never stepped foot here.

"How are we going to get across?" Ady asks, still panting. She has no inkling of what lies on the other side, perhaps the ruins of decimated towns, still littered with skeletons. Perhaps looted medical wards, military bases, scraps from the Old World. Or maybe an endless desert.

Edgar takes the water back and drinks himself.

"We're not," he says at last, as water droplets stream from the corners of his mouth.

Ever since they left the walls and emerged into the desert night, she has not turned back. But now, she forces herself to look the way they'd come. She gasps for breath and drops to her knees. Small stones press into her kneecaps, but she doesn't care. The smoke is a thick, black cloud over the Citadel. Flames cast an eerie, purple glow against the dark sky, but the Citadel itself still pulses red. The walls seem so small from here—so strange that they had contained her entire life. Ady bites her lip as the tears sting her eyes, then stream down her cheeks. Ady can still hear the agonizing screams of women and children, their skin torched, their limbs torn, the Raiders more cruel and barbaric than she'd ever imagined. She envisions the fire in every corner of the courtyard, sweeping from the lecture hall, the library, to her dormitory, turning the pages of her precious poetry book to black ash. She remembers, too, the explosion in the mess hall, how glass shards embedded in her skin and pounded the Citadel in a million tiny pieces. She feels like that—like her whole world has erupted, and she's left with only sharp fragments.

How is it possible that she'd escaped, that Eagan and others could not come with her? She never even got to say goodbye.

"It isn't safe here for you," Eagan said. But the way he said "*you*" was charged with something she'd never heard in his voice before. The Citadel wasn't safe for anyone, but he was saying something else. He seemed to be saying, *you are the one we must save.*

The wind picks up around her, rustling the hair off her shoulder. There is the smell of coal burning, and she figures the fumes must be carrying from the Citadel. If possible, the night seems to shift slightly darker, as if a large cloud mass has covered whatever starlight there's been.

Suddenly, Edgar shakes her shoulders and tells her to look up. The wind gusts are stronger now, but she can hardly focus, can hardly move her gaze away from the still-burning Citadel.

"It's time, Miss Adylyn!" Edgar yells now.

He helps her stand as something tumbles in the breeze next to them. It's a ladder. Edgar wraps a large rope around his waist and grabs hold of a ladder rung with the other hand.

The world is blurring with shapes and sounds and colors she cannot distinguish. Ady strains to see the mass above them and almost laughs. Is she dreaming? Above the sandstone and desert crags, there is no cloud. Instead, there is wood grain on the hull of a ship. A great canvas sailcloth attached to its mast.

"Let's go," Edgar yells over the wind, still holding tight to the ladder. He slips the rope around her, and the ladder lifts, as smooth as rising well water. Ady clings to him, blinking out the world. She does not want to watch the ground disappear beneath her feet. She buries her face in Edgar's shoulder and smells the smoke and salt.

They rise higher and higher until they graze against the ship's edge. Edgar clambers lithely aboard and pulls Ady along beside him. She kneels to the deck, afraid she might vomit, and sits there, rocking her knees, unable to process the gravity of what has happened. Shapes mill around her, but she cannot focus on them. Something fire red pulls Ady's vision back: there is the deep red hair of a young girl, her curls blowing in the wind. She is young, her skin like moonlight. Ady sees her hand a large overcoat and tri-fold hat to Edgar as she says, "Welcome back, Captain."

Edgar straightens his hat and coat. A hush falls, and she can feel the weight of their gaze fall on her. She knows that skin-tingling feeling. Edgar stares down, beaming.

"Miss Adylyn, welcome aboard the Aurora."

Meeting his gaze, it's as if time stands still. He only holds out his hand now, waiting for her palm.

You are the one we must save.

Ady feels her hand meet his. She rises to her feet as the Aurora rises, too, sailing higher into the night.

THE REBELLION

The midday sun scorches the dry earth. The sand burns like coals. The scout runs heavy-footed and sweating, his body dark and ruddy. His feet know the way through the dunes. He knows this terrain like the lines on his own palm. The Wasteland is desolate and gray, with its rain-shadow valleys and flat, expansive salt pans. He avoids the spiny plants and even, once, leaps over a snake he disrupts from sunbathing.

Basecamp is not far now. He can almost see the smoke in the distance.

The rest of the retreating Raiders are still miles behind him, smug with their victory and spoils. Some have likely brought back brides, tiny, frightened things.

His own mother had been a war bride.

All through the battle, he'd been waiting in the dunes, watching for the Citadel to burn gold in the night. And burn it did. But there was something else, too. Something he must tell Doköran and his mage Orius—some dark, hulking thing that rose above the city and swept into the night.

The boy's chest tightens, and he fears he might vomit bile. He needs water and soon. He drained his last pack about ten miles ago. He is tall but young, not yet thirteen, and he has been raised for this, been trained to run.

The camp takes shape at last. Beached boats and tarp tents encircle what was once a small reservoir. He's told these boats used to coast on bodies of water, but he has never understood that term. He has only imagined human bodies covered in rainwater. But even the rain is scarce. The Raiders keep buckets out all times to catch any dew or rain. There is a wooden dock, rotted and uneven, where hunters slaughter and skin their kill. There is a pile of scrap metal, torn from Old World angler shacks, where their blacksmiths now carve weapons from waste. To the south, among the crags, are some of the Rebellions' docked airships, scavenged from the Republic, or rebuilt from crashes. The sails whip black in the wind. There, too, at the center of the tents, wearing his longhorn skull dipped in blood, is Doköran, the Rebellion leader. Even from yards away, the boy can see the raven eye branded on Doköran's chest. The eye watches him as he approaches, as the men part, some clanging their weapons, some chanting *"Huh!"* in welcome.

He collapses at Doköran's boots, dark with years of stained blood.

"What did you see, boy?"

Doköran's voice is deep like a crater in the earth. He towers like the rare desert tree.

A woman kneels beside him and offers a clay carafe of water, but he can barely move to take it. His mouth foams, and his eyes blur.

He can only manage to say: "It's done. Fire." He begins to cough. Doköran runs his war ax along the side of the boy's face to redirect his eyeline back to him. Through ragged breaths, the boy musters, "So much fire...And there's something else..."

CAYHILL'S REBUKE

Ellington stands in Commander Cayhill's barracks. The air lingers with the wake of smoke. There is a stillness throughout the Citadel akin to shock. Ellington keeps his hands clasped before him, his eyes modestly on the desk that separates him like a barrier shield from Cayhill, who drums his fingers in a steady rhythm.

And what he feels is not exactly anger, not exactly fear. Mostly, there is confusion.

He'd known something was amiss when he sent a page to collect all the cohort lieutenants.

He was in his makeshift camp tent, maps of the Old World spread around him. It had been years since he'd last ventured into the Wasteland, and up-close all the dunes looked the same. The landscape was one rugged line of rock walls. But Commander Cayhill had received intel about the Raiders of the Rebellion's garrison—and, according to Ellington's calculations, they were a mere five miles northwest, through a gully of singing sand. Night was upon them, and in the darkness, they could ambush the Raiders, win with a preventative attack. Yes, it would work, Ellington told himself.

But then the page returned with only a trickle of men. The boy was pale and shaking, and when Ellington asked what was wrong, he croaked that he couldn't find some of them.

Ellington did a quick headcount over the gruff and grizzled faces in his tent. But he already knew who would be missing.

A quick search party turned up the body of a young recruit, pierced in the back with an arrow. A Redcoats arrow.

Insurrection! Treason! Ellington fumed as his men delivered the news. A new sweeping count through the camp had determined that nearly sixty men were missing. Eagan, Tiri, and Ito were among them. Ellington's first thought was to continue with his plan of attack—he could deal with the insubordination later. The Republic's fury would be swift and sharp. They could not miss the window of opportunity to take down the Raiders before they launched a full siege against the Citadel walls. Commander Cayhill had sent him here with a job to do, and he would finish that task.

How to describe his surprise, then, at seeing the night sky reverse its darkening? How it warmed from black to blue to orange, like time was going backward, like the sun was setting again? But it was not the sun, and it was the direction of the Citadel, and he knew before his own men came shouting for him. Shouting that some of the men were gone and the falcons were missing. Camp was packed in a frenzy: tools abandoned, food left to rot, tarps forgotten, hanging on posts and tied to skeletal trees. There was no time, either, to form ranks. He led the charge, led them running the way they'd come. As the Citadel came into view and the flames became visible, he could not help but wonder: had his men done this? An act of terrorism against the Republic? Was it his fault the city was on fire? Or, heaven forbid, had the attack come too soon?

Ellington braces himself for Cayhill's reprimand. By the time he and his men entered through the West Gate, the Raiders had all but left. Officials doused the flames with well water, and survivors nursed their wounds. Tiri, Eagan, and Ito were in a cluster together, hovering over some girl. He felt a twinge of regret, seeing them bloodied and bruised. The rest of the Redcoats instantly went in search of their wives, their children. But Ellington just stood numb in the courtyard, shocked by the destruction. Shocked, too, that he'd missed it.

Now, Commander Cayhill stares at him with his steely eyes, and ice seems to settle in his gut.

"Do you realize, Captain"—and the word sounds dragged out, like *Cap-tin*. "That there was a secret society hiding in the ranks of your military?"

Ellington starts. This was not the rebuke he'd expected.

"Sir, I—"

But Cayhill raises his large and calloused hand, silencing him. He reclines deeper into his desk chair. He is flanked on either side by two Bluecoats who stand at attention, their eyes on the back wall like statues. Ellington notices that neither has a scratch or scrape. Their rich blue tunics, too, have no tears.

"My disappointment is a difficult thing to undo," Cayhill sighs, as though he's deeply saddened by the situation. "But I am indeed disappointed. I thought we'd been clear about our parameters when I appointed you to this position. I thought we'd taken care of the problem."

James Alexander, he means. Ellington was there when the man swung in the courtyard. Is this a threat, he wonders?

"I have taken every precaution," he says carefully.

"Evidently not." Cayhill pounds his hand on the desk now. Even the Bluecoats flinch, but slightly. "A great number of your men snuck into this Citadel somehow. They detached from you and your troops. They disobeyed orders."

"I understand," says Ellington, anger flaring now.

But he didn't understand. Because, given the circumstances, wasn't it actually a good thing that the men had returned? As he'd learned in scouting the ruins last night and this morning, they'd helped defend the Citadel from attack. They'd killed many Raiders. Yes, their decision to go rogue was reprehensible. But how many more would have died if they hadn't? And why, too, were there not more wounded Bluecoats? The medical ward—one of the few buildings not to go up in smoke—housed only ten wounded Bluecoats this morning, a staggering few.

"Good," says Cayhill. "Because we have taken the sad but necessary next steps."

"Meaning?"

"Meaning the men in question are under custody of the Republic and will remain so until we decide what to do next."

This is when the doubt begins. Commander Cayhill was the one who sent Ellington out with all his men. Cayhill insisted they *all* must go, leaving the Citadel vulnerable as a bare chest.

Ellington studies the face before him. He has always feared Cayhill, feared being on the wrong side of his wrath. But now as he studies the broad forehead and the wrinkles that fan from the eyes, the short white hair—as he realizes that this man must not have fought last night, while the walls burned around him, while his own citizens died, he was probably here. Guarded by these two sentries. Safe here while his people screamed below—and Ellington does not feel fear. Instead, there is the softest flame of rage.

THE AURORA

There is the slow creak and groan of old wood. Ady stirs, sleep still heavy in her eyes. Something soft grazes her skin. And for a moment, she dreams she is in her dormitory, that the warmth around her is Eagan, his arm on her waist, his breath in her hair. But when she opens her eyes, there is no dorm, no desk, no Citadel wall out the window. Instead, there is a porthole window. There is a large sliver of moon, pearly and white, seemingly close enough to touch.

Ady sits up, heart pounding. The events tumble back to her memory: the fire, Grenn's collapse, Eagan pushing her away, telling her to *go*. Her head pounds, as though hundreds of tiny needles pierce into her skull. She rubs at her temples and attempts to stand, but the floor sways beneath her.

The room is small and orderly with pine walls. The bed is made of stout wood and covered with, she presumes, rabbit skins sewed together in one white quilt. Her satchel lies abandoned on the ground, still carrying her journal and the mysterious book. A faded map is tacked to the far wall, but she does not recognize any of the hills or valleys surrounding the Citadel. Perhaps it's of the Eastern Alliance.

Ady stands again, keeping one hand on the bedpost for balance. She moves to the porthole. The open air is ice cold, but the stars look hot and close. Beside the window, she notices a shelf adorned with miscellaneous tools: a compass, a magnifying glass, open books, and scrolls. There, too, is a small photograph in a gilded frame. Ady picks up the image and remembers, fleetingly, how she once discovered a camera contraption in a found room. It was broken, the bulb smashed, the film gone—but she'd gleaned through other discoveries that this machine could once capture life using light. The picture is of Edgar. She recognizes him immediately, the slop of dark hair, the threat of a beard visible in the chin shadow. His arm is around a woman and a small red-haired child.

Footsteps sound from the doorway and Ady drops the picture back on the shelf. She turns to see Edgar in the open frame.

"Good morning," he says with a sardonic smile. "Or perhaps I should say good evening."

"Where am I?" Ady manages. Her throat is dry and parched, and the words scratch. The headache flares again, and she groans at the throbbing.

"The Aurora," says Edgar. "I'm sure it's all a great shock, what's happened to you. And don't worry about the headaches, you'll get over them."

She arches her eyebrows, surprised.

"The altitude," he says with a shrug. "You'll adjust. That, and you'll get your air legs."

And suddenly she remembers more: the cliff, the ladder, the slow rise onto the ship's deck.

"I need to sit down," she says and sinks to the ground.

Edgar does not move from the doorway, only crosses his arms across his chest. "You've been asleep for two days now, Miss Adylyn. I was beginning to get concerned. We also need to make sure you get something to eat and drink. It will help with the nausea."

Ady presses her palms to her eyes, but she does not cry. It's as if her tears have dried up.

"My friends—my home—Eagan," she whispers. "We left them. We left them there to die."

Surely Eagan could have come. Tiri could have carried Grenn, and they could all have escaped down the hatch. They could all have taken the spiral stairs out into the night. There's room for more on a ship like this! She thinks she might vomit at the thought of what could be happening to them now, if they were even still alive. Was Eagan a prisoner of war—or worse, thrown in a ditch to rot somewhere? Edgar says nothing, and this only makes her anger sharpen. Through clenched teeth, she says: "Why didn't we bring them?"

"They weren't my mission," he says at last. "You were. Some people are destined to do more than survive."

"So what, you're saying some are destined just to die? And die like that?"

He watches her for a moment, his expression pale and placid. Then he says, "I have a lot to show you. Come with me."

Edgar turns and leaves down the amber-lit corridor. Ady struggles to her feet, bracing her arms in front of her, and reluctantly follows. The hallway is lined with star charts and maps of constellations, shimmering figures in the sky. Most of the doors she passes are closed, but a few are ajar. Edgar strides ahead, but she stops—both indignant and curious—and peers through the open ones. One appears to be a workshop, filled with slanted desks and papers, ink pots and pens. Another is collaged with round mirrors and water basins, a communal latrine. The last door glows blue, brighter than the fabric of the sky. She peers through the open cracks and can make out only glass bottles and tubes, an intricate array of instruments. A man sits on a low bench, wearing goggles strapped to his head, and a brown leather vest. He must have sensed her staring, because he looks up and over his shoulder, catching her eye.

"Miss Adylyn?"

Edgar's voice calls from further down the hall. She tears away from the blue room and hurries toward a wide set of stairs. She takes the steps slowly, the wood creaking beneath her, and holds the rail tight until she emerges onto the deck. The sky is thick with darkness, but the ship is bathed in soft gray light from the moon and from lanterns hung at every post. Above her floats a large canvas balloon, tethered to the deck by dozens of coarse ropes.

That first night, the ship felt like a dream, like her exhausted brain was projecting a vision into real life. But here they are, clouds flowing through and around them, silky soft. Edgar stands waiting for her by the helm.

Ady gasps and takes in the crisp cold. The wind lifts her hair as she marvels at the black nothingness bejeweled with stars.

"Surprised?" he says.

"Yes, I mean—we're flying." Her anger is eclipsed momentarily by wonder.

"You didn't know about airships?"

"I knew the Republic had their own fleet," she says, taking in the crew's faces around her. One man cleans the deck with a mop and bucket; another stands starboard, holding what Ady deduces to be a wind gauge. "They're usually docked by the training grounds. But I've never been on one."

Edgar nods with a deep sigh and places a hand on the ship's wheel.

"After the Great War," he says, "most weapons were banned and destroyed. There used to be weapons that could destroy whole cities at once, one giant, unthinkable bomb. And airships much grander than these, all made of steel, that could drop bombs from their bellies." Ady stares wide-eyed as he continues. "All of that was no more. No more guns, no more bombs." He laughs, studying Ady's confused expression. "I consider myself a historian of the Old World. A lot of the Trinity Convention made sense, right? Weapons caused war, so ban the weapons, return to 'simpler' times. Start over. Of course," he smirks, "it's not that simple. Take away the weapons, and man will still find a way for war."

Ady shivers at the tone in Edgar's voice.

From the corner of her eye, she sees a crew member approach. The man is small and sturdy. His hair is a dishwater blonde, and he holds out a black fur blanket.

"I thought you could use this, Miss Adylyn," he says. "It's awful cold up here if you aren't used to it. I'm Calvin, by the way. I navigate this here ship."

"Thank you," Ady says and pulls the fur around her shoulders, noticing his unfamiliar accent. She is about to say more when someone else joins them, the short and fiery girl with red hair.

"She looks ordinary," says the girl. Her voice is loud and sharp.

"Ady, this is my daughter, Ella," Edgar sighs. "Forgive her outspoken tendencies."

"What, it's true?" Ella says, hands on her hips. "Besides, Theodore wanted me to tell you dinner's ready. Shall we wait for..." Her gaze flickers back to Ady.

"Yes," says Edgar, his voice stern now. "We will be right down."

Ella wrinkles her nose. Then she and Calvin hurry off to join other crew members, who descend below deck to the dining quarters. But Edgar does not join them. He only stares out into the sky, his eyes trained on the clouds and stars ahead. To the east, light appears, the faintest pink.

"Sorry about that," he says as she follows his gaze.

"It's okay."

He waits a beat before adding: "Miss Adylyn, I never answered your question. About if some people are destined to die."

"Oh?" Again, thoughts of Eagan and Grenn consume her.

"Sadly, yes," Edgar says. "Just, not you. At least, not yet."

CAPTIVES

The prison is dark and dank. It reeks of rotting fruit and tinny water.
Eagan sits on the cold stone and concentrates on the pounding in his head, keeping time with the rhythm. Across the cell, Ito crouches on an empty barrel, picking absentmindedly at a scab. Tiri fingers the empty sheath on his belt, cursing under his breath every few minutes. Between them sits a moldy hunk of bread and one untouched can of water. Flies swarm over the filmy surface.

None of them have ever been down here before. The dungeon is a series of cordoned cinderblock rooms. These used to be bomb shelters, Eagan knows, hand-hewn and lined with survival materials. A hatch and ladder outside the barred gate lead to the officials' barracks. Had his father been held in this same cell? Were these four walls the last he saw of this earth, before being led to swing on the scaffold?

Eagan brushes these thoughts away and wills himself not to cry. He cannot give up—not yet. Not now. Too much depends on him. All sixty-four members of the Brutallion have been captured along with him.

"I'm sure she's okay," Ito is saying, and Eagan snaps to attention. He thinks of Ady, how her screams tore through him worse than any brutal strike. Her face is lit by the surrounding flames. Her mouth contorts in anguish as Edgar whisks her up the steps. Is she okay? Did she make it out alive?

But no, Ito is looking at Tiri, who scowls at the far wall.

"You don't know that," Tiri snaps and sends the cup of water skidding across the floor. "You don't know anything."

Ito grimaces. He works at his scab until a clean layer of skin appears, soft and pink.

"I know the Republic won't leave Grenn to die," he says. His voice is calm, focused. "I know she didn't do anything wrong."

"She's probably already dead." Tiri rubs at his temples. "Don't you get it? I should never have left her here."

"You couldn't have prevented this," Eagan says at last.

He sounds like his father. He hears that cadence in his own voice as it fills the cell. Hadn't James said these exact words to Eagan years ago? When he and Ady were caught in the forgotten rooms, when they discovered music and received the lashes in punishment? Eagan had felt such guilt then: he should have known better. He should have kept Ady from danger, kept her safe from harm. His back still burning from the whip, Eagan winced as his father applied poultices in their dormitory. He winced even more as his father said, "You couldn't have prevented this. She must find her own way." At the time, Eagan thought this was foolish. Fate did not seem like this fluid, immovable current. It seemed like something he could shift and shape, like clay or stone. Strong, but workable. Preventable.

Tiri blinks at him, and his eyes are alight with every hurt.

"You couldn't," Eagan says again. "If you'd stayed, they'd still have attacked. She would still have been burned, inhaled smoke, all of it."

"Stop—I don't want to hear it—" Tiri pounds his fist into the hard ground.

"And she would still have been in danger."

"Then maybe I shouldn't have left to come back here with you," Tiri says now, and this is when Eagan stands in defense. "You don't see the other Redcoats around here, right? I could be with her right now, wherever the hell they've taken her. I could be doing my job."

"This *is* your job." Eagan's voice is uneven, but he struggles to stay calm. He looks to Ito for confirmation, but there is only a placid expression. "Don't you get it? They wanted us to leave. They must have known about the attack. I don't know why. But didn't you notice that the Bluecoats weren't fighting back until we were there? Or how they attacked us upon our arrival?" Tiri nods somberly, remembering. "Our job is to fight for the people, not just the ones we love. Isn't it?"

Tiri's face is all pain, all hardness, and Eagan forces himself to look away. He sees himself in that wrath—that cold, dry fury—and he cannot break down in front of his men. He leans against the wrought iron gate, relishing in the cool bars against his skin. His stomach aches for food and clean water, but more than anything, he aches for Ady.

Where are you? He thinks, wishing the thought to leave the cell, to fly up the hatch and into the stars, to wherever she is. *I will come for you.*

QUESTIONING

Grenn awakes to the pain of her own burns. She coughs as she sits up, then winces and collapses back on the cot. Her skin is singed. But worse, her stomach throbs from the gash on her waist. Someone has bandaged the wound with clean white gauze. Who has tended to her?

She is in the Citadel, she knows this. There are the telltale block walls and slab floors. There are the sounds through the open window, footsteps on the rampart, and carts rolling through the square. But she is not in her dormitory. The room is small and spartan, but she notices a simple bookcase by the door, lined with the Republic's blue tomes. This must be an officer's barracks. Civilians are not permitted to keep books in their private quarters unless they are the occasional library loan.

Someone raps softly at the door. Grenn freezes on the cot.

The last thing she can remember is finding Ady in the courtyard. Then, nothing. Did the men make it back to the Citadel walls? Did the Raiders win the siege?

But the door swings open to reveal Commander Cayhill. She has never seen him this close. His tall stature fills the doorway with a daunting presence.

"My dear Grenn," says Commander Cayhill. He steps into the room, followed by two Bluecoats. "You must be exhausted. You've been unconscious for quite some time now."

Grenn blinks. How does the Commander know her by name? And why is she here, not with the others? But the Commander is smiling at her, almost tenderly, and the pain in her stomach is enough to cloud her vision. Grenn struggles to sit up again, and she combs her fingers through her matted hair.

"I'm okay," she says, but her throat is so parched that it comes out like a croak.

Commander Cayhill snaps his fingers, and one of the Bluecoats unhooks a canteen from his belt.

"Here." He approaches and offers her water. "Drink. You must be thirsty."

She takes the water and drains it thirstily.

The Commander watches her with a silence and focus that unnerves her. She's seen stillness like this in the falcons when she cleans their cages. The birds are so calm before they attack. They watch, they glide. She's stroked their soft feathers and felt the powerful muscles that can claw a weasel or mouse to shreds. Grenn inches back on the cot, biting her lip at the sharp pain in her stomach. When she moves, the pain shoots up her leg as well.

"Now, Grenn," says Commander Cayhill. He clasps his hands in front of him. "You're one of the good ones around here. An ideal citizen. I see from your lecture record that you've never received a demerit. Never missed an assignment. Is that true?"

"It is."

"I also see that you've been concerned about your friend Ady's behavior recently."

Alarm flares like sparks.

"I wouldn't say concerned, exactly," she stammers.

"Our librarian Ms. Iris tells me you noticed something—" He gestures as if searching for the right word, like plucking a wildflower. "—disconcerting, shall we say? A book that Ady stole from the library? Is this true?"

"I may have seen something."

In this moment, Grenn wishes that she could lie. But the truth has always been natural to her, as necessary and compulsory as breath. She broke under the weight of the librarian's questioning, too. But something in Commander Cayhill's voice gives her more pause. It's the sweetness of his tone, this man with better things to do than talk with a recovering invalid.

She can feel the tiny beads of sweat break out on her upper lip. Commander Cayhill only leans closer.

"Tell me," he says. "You know where she went, don't you."

He does not say this like a question.

"Where who went?" Grenn says. Her eyes drop to her hands, still smudged with soot.

Commander Cayhill laughs at that. He slaps his thigh, and the Bluecoats chuckle, too, in their own quiet way. But Grenn blinks in confusion. Could he possibly mean Ady? Ady left? Is it true that she somehow made it outside the Citadel walls? Grenn coughs again, from shock or from joy, she cannot tell which! And even if Ady did, why would Commander Cayhill care when there were more important concerns, like barricading the Citadel, recovering from the fires, preventing another attack?

"I don't know where she is, honest," says Grenn.

But thoughts of Ady's odd behavior roll through her mind now. Not only the book and the way she left abruptly from the library but the man she claimed to see when no one else saw him. Grenn assumed Ady was daydreaming, caught up in her active imagination, or perhaps that it was some elaborate prank. But what if Ady had been telling the truth? The moment Grenn thinks this, she can feel the tightening in her own jaw, the crease in her brow. Commander Cayhill sees it, too.

"You do know something," he says. When she doesn't respond, he straightens and begins to pace the small room. "We've had a rough few days here at the Citadel, Grenn. Many lives lost. So many. But a lot of the suffering could have been prevented. That's what angers me the most. Yes, it could have been prevented. So now, I'm truly sad to be the one to inform you that there's a group of rebellious traitors under heavy guard right now. They are guilty of treason, every last one of them. They have turned against the Republic, against their own people. Isn't that terrible, Grenn?"

She nods slowly.

"It *is* terrible. You're right." He pauses. "It's a shame that some of our best Redcoats are among them. Eagan...Tiri. I hate to lose good men."

He stops pacing and looks at her again now, but all sweetness is gone from his gaze.

The pain that had concentrated in her stomach now spreads through her whole body, like cactus needles in her skin. She feels her mouth open then shut again. Grenn clenches at the bedsheets, wills herself to stand, but the blood has begun to seep through the gauze again, and she's nauseous with pain. They have Tiri. Tiri is under arrest, and Ady is gone. The only family she has ever known and loved is gone, and the thought is like fire through her body. Bile rises to her throat.

"I hate to lose ideal citizens, too," he says.

Grenn can only stare, too shocked to move, as Commander Cayhill strides from the room, trailed by his men. There is the distinct sound of a clicking latch as the door is barred shut.

UNOFFICIAL MEETINGS

Doköran sits outside the firepit, watching as the women slowly turn the spit and roast a jackrabbit. The women whisper quietly to each other—they are sisters, both his slaves, both beautiful—but their voices are too soft for him to hear. He doesn't care. In his hands is a piece of wood, and he rotates his knife gently in a paring cut. He hates sitting still. He must always be doing something.

The sun sets to the west, and still the officials have not come.

Around him, the camp prepares for the evening meal: children carry buckets of water from the well, scavengers boil quail eggs in an iron pot, watchmen return from the outer posts. His warriors arrived last night from the Citadel, and most spent the day asleep or with their women. They emerge now from the tents, stretch, and take their place around the fire pit.

This is when the wind changes. The air lifts, and Doköran looks up from the shapeless hunk of wood. He knows that smell, sulfur and coal, and he knows that distant purring of the engine. Airships appear in the distance, waving the red crest of the Republic.

Orius' words ring in his ears.

"What has been foretold has begun," he said after the scout returned and claimed he saw a foreign ship. Orius always speaks slowly. He draws the words from his mouth like threads of twine. The mage gripped his staff and struck the sand with every word: "It has begun."

"Tell me what you see," Doköran said, trying to keep the desperation from his voice.

"I see a girl. She is more powerful than we knew. She rises like smoke, she escapes the fires."

Something about Orius has always unsettled Doköran: it's more than the silky slithering of his voice. It's more, too, than the dark shroud he never sloughs off or the knucklebones that adorn his neck like talismans. It's the way his skin is more gray than warm, the way his touch is always colder than human. But Orius has been a long-standing figure in the Rebellion camps, a shade Doköran cannot lose. Where Doköran is, his shadow follows. He first found Orius when he was but a young scout and clambering after a big horn in the hills, learning to hunt and hungry for blood. He saw light from one of the dune caves and heard that voice he'd come to fear and know. Orius was a hermit then, expelled from the Citadels for practicing witchcraft. He is the one who foretells the days in the stars, who knows when the rare rain will fall. It was he who foretold Doköran's rise to power, the monstrous ships in the sky, the siege against the Citadels.

Now, this. A girl.

The camp hushes as the fleet lands just a spear throw from the first tents. Doköran feels the heat of his men's eyes on him. Some clutch their clubs and hatchets: others usher the women to retreat further into the camp. Water in the pots boil over and sizzle onto the open flames. The jackrabbit is overcooked until the camp smells of charred meat. Still, Doköran whittles, one end of the wood sharpening to a rounded tip.

"Doköran!"

The gruff voice calls for him, but Doköran does not look up. The wood softens to his strength, and the shape begins to form. It looks like a hawk's talon, he thinks. He can hear the Republic officials stride through the camp, calling for him.

The knife slips over the wood grain and slices his thumb, but he sucks the blood until it abates. He only stands when Commander Cayhill is in view.

"You're late," Doköran says, dropping the wood to the ground.

The Commander is always so neatly groomed, Doköran thinks. Not a hair is out of place, and someone must clean his uniform daily. This strikes him as funny for a military officer, and he can't help but smile at the sight of the Commander in his gaudy costume, flanked by two soldiers in blue.

"We never set an exact time. We're here now, aren't we?"

"Indeed."

"We need to talk in private," the Commander says.

A murmur ripples through the Raiders. Some of the men scoff. One, a young soul named Alrik, calls out: "Butcher them!"

Doköran straightens his shoulders. Languidly, he draws the battle-ax from his back holster and hurls it in one straight line for the boy's open throat. The blade connects, and blood spurts onto the dusty ground. All whispers cease. His men don't move as Doköran walks to collect his ax. He re-sheathes it without cleaning, and droplets of blood trail him back to Commander Cayhill. "I don't like being told what to do," he says and swallows the urge to hack the officer down. He calmly says, "Follow me."

He strides past the fire pit, past the cluster of men who part for him, and into the canvas tent where Orius sits at the table, staff in hand. Commander Cayhill eyes him with hesitance but says nothing.

"So," says Doköran, turning to face his guest. "I believe you have something for us. We upheld our end of the deal."

There is the slightest hesitation from Commander Cayhill, but Doköran sees right through it: he has known enough Republic scum in his lifetime to know what they are capable of. They lie and cheat; they go back on deals; they have deigned to rule others with their oppressive ways. Well, not him. Doköran's great-grandfather was an early dissenter, a rebel who left. That rage flows through his blood.

The Commander swallows slowly and says, "The situation has changed."

They have met in person only a few times, but Doköran hates him more with every meeting. There is something smug and certain about the man that rankles

Doköran to his bones. The way he refuses to touch anything, accept even a mug of water or prickly pear from the women.

"The situation *has* changed, you're right," Doköran nods. He glances at Orius, who watches with snake-like patience. "We upheld our end of the bargain. The Citadel is on fire. My men found the tunnels, as you said. And now, you owe us a grand sum of—oh, what did we say again, Orius? Thirty thousand pounds and two shipments of gunpowder? Yes, that's right. And that's what we want."

Commander Cayhill wets his lips but stands firm.

"We own every sand-dweller in these parts," he practically spits on Doköran. "You abide by what *we* say. Surely you don't want to risk war with the mighty Republic, now do you?"

"Surely you don't want to die where you stand and have my men disembowel you," says Doköran.

The Commander straightens to his full height. He knows Doköran means it.

"We'll pay double if you do one more thing." His voice is still firm, but tentative, as though backtracking with little steps from a rattlesnake's nest.

"And what is that?"

"The girl," says Orius. His voice fills the room like smoke. "They want the girl."

Commander Cayhill stares at Orius for a long minute, and Doköran thinks he detects the slightest shudder. *Yes,* he thinks. *Be afraid, Republic.* He has seers on his side: he has fate. If the Republic wants the girl, then this has been foretold—Orius has seen this.

"Her name is Ady," the Commander says at last, returning his gaze to Doköran. "She has boarded an airship, not one of ours, and was last seen flying west over these parts. Find her, and we'll pay double."

"We need triple."

The Commander nods. He then snaps his finger as a Republic Official swiftly comes through the canvas sails, handing him a large bag. Commander Cayhill drops it before Doköran. "This ought to hold you over."

Doköran's thoughts are already leaps and bounds away from this conversation. He will ready his men. He will find this girl. He will learn what makes her special, so important to the unfolding of these destined things Orius foretold. With these events in motion, will the Rebellion finally overthrow the tyrants, rise up from the Wasteland? Will he, Doköran, at last show Commander Cayhill his true place? The time of waiting is over. With the gold and the gunpowder, they'll be that much closer to the overthrow. There is change in the air. He can feel it at last.

ANOTHER NIGHT SKY

Ady sits at the desk in the cabin. She's hardly left the quarters. She cannot bear to be around people, to overhear the snippets and stories, laughter and games. She cannot bear the sounds of life continuing on as though untouched and normal. She joins the crew only for meals, and even then usually sits apart in silence.

The stars glisten out the porthole window, and the shaft of moonlight catches the gold of Eagan's pocket watch around her neck. It casts a shimmering reflection on the wood-paneled wall.

Her entire rhythm has been thrown off-kilter. Most days, she sleeps until the sun sets warm and bronze-hued in the west. She likes the quiet of the night and the stillness of the stars. She likes roaming the deck, too, while the crew sleeps in their barracks. It feels then like the ship is hers alone. She stands on the deck and lets the wind roil her hair, tries to imagine what mountains and valleys are hidden below the clouds.

Now, open on her desk, is her journal, one of the few items that escaped with her in the satchel. (Along with the strange book from Edgar with its emanating light. She has refused to touch it.) The cover of her journal is worn and bruised, but the parchment is clean. She opens to a blank page now and takes one of the ink pens from the desk drawer.

Dear Eagan, she writes. Even the letters and shape of his name make her want to cry.

I hope you are well. I hope you're alive at least. I feel in my heart that you must be. It's impossible to imagine this world, my world, without you in it. There are so many questions I want to ask you. There are so many things I don't understand. How did you know about Edgar? Why did you want me to go with him? You said you must go, as if—but all that pales to the ache I feel. The pain is everywhere, living inside my core. I just want to see you. I want to know that you are okay, that I didn't just abandon you or Grenn to die.

She pauses, pen in hand, and looks out the window. She wonders if they're passing one of the few constellations she knows, the large bear, but the ship is too high for her to make out the full shape.

Ady writes again.

Everyone has been nice here so far, except for one girl, but it's nothing to worry about. How I wish we had Swifts, so I could send this to you, have some way of letting you know that I'm well, that we made it out. I am aboard an airship. Where we are going, I have no idea. I am losing track of days and time, constantly praying that you are safe. Please be safe. I need you to be. I love you.

Ady feels for the pocket watch and runs her fingers along every notch in the gold chain. Eagan had known something. He'd sent her here, and as much as she didn't understand, she needs to trust him. He wouldn't want her to sit and wallow, to spend hours staring into a pillow until the tears no longer stream. He would want her to be herself, explore, and ultimately find a way back to him.

The dinner bell rings down the hall, but Ady is not hungry tonight. The first night was uncomfortable enough as the whole crew stared at her. Perhaps they, like Ella, thought she looked ordinary, and how Ady longed to tell them that she was, really. Just a girl from the Lower West Citadel who'd escaped somehow, who'd been singled out.

She hears the pounding footsteps as the crew gathers in the dining hall. She imagines Edgar taking his place at the end, Ella beside him. Then the others, some she hardly knows, some who've been kind, some who've told her stories of the skies. There are Dec and Dax, the Boatswain twins, who have that same unfamiliar accent as Calvin, the navigator. Then there is Ella, the first mate; Theodore, the cook, and Cooper, the gun master. The only one Ady has not seen in the dining hall is the man in the blue room, bent over his equipment. Does he ever leave his work station?

Ady closes the journal and ventures into the ship's hallway. Voices rise in a cacophony from the dining hall. There is laughter and the clatter of tin spoons and plates, the smell of something meaty and broth-boiled. She moves quietly down the corridor and, for a moment, feels she is back in the Citadel, awake at night while the city slept, roaming through forgotten rooms, adept at not getting caught. She has explored some of the ship's quarters when she's had the energy, but most are empty sleeping lodges or engine rooms to keep the large canvas balloon pumped and heated through all hours of the day and night. Ady passes the dining hall, keeping to the far wall, and makes out only snippets of conversation, some old story from the Boatswain twins—"That's not how it happened." "Is too!" When she passes the blue room, she tries the handle but finds it bolted shut this time.

Out in the open air, the deck is hers, empty, quiet, and moonlit. The sight of the open expanse of night still catches her breath. It feels as languid and magical as her dream with the mystifying pool of water, black yet promising. Ady walks to the bow and watches the clouds part for the ship like lavender mist. She leans over the deck to see the propellers beneath the ship that churn the aircraft forward.

The air is cold, but Ady relishes the night wind on her face. It's like a cleansing, whipping away the smoke, sandy grit, and pain from the days past. She can only hope that Edgar has a plan, that there is a purpose behind her place on this ship—wherever they're going.

An orange light to the far east catches her eye. She turns and stares at the horizon. It's much too early for sunrise. And yet, there it is again, a sudden flare, as bright as sparks. Something catches in her throat. She's seen that kind of light before: the rich heat of fire, the amber that burns. She squints into the night sky as another flare appears, streaking like a comet.

Someone is following them.

PRISON BREAK

Ito is the one who thinks up the plan. Eagan stands by the gate as Ito removes the belt from his tunic. The leather is thin, too worn to really do the deed, but it's enough to trick the guard, who sleeps with loud snores outside the door.

Ito stands on the barrel he'd been using as a seat and quickly knots the belt to one of the ceiling beams. Tiri jumps to his feet, prepared to catch him if he slipped. Eagan waits for the makeshift noose to slip around Ito's neck before he bangs his fist on the gate and shouts, "Guard! He's trying to hang himself—help—guard!"

News arrived the night before that Commander Cayhill planned for them all to hang the next morning publicly. "We must strike down treason by cutting off the snake's head," said the messenger, a young recruit reciting the Commander's orders.

The Commander would settle for nothing less than public humiliation. A private death in the cell would mean defeat for the Republic. Sure enough, the guard is on his feet in seconds, sleep still crusted in his eyes. He fumbles for his keys and throws the door open. Ito hangs from the ceiling while Tiri holds his legs. There is the quick and claustrophobic confusion of assault as Ito jumps down, and Eagan hooks his arm around the guard's neck. The man writhes, turning blue until Tiri takes the guard's dagger from his belt and plunges it through his chest.

Eagan releases the man and stands, weary from hunger and exhaustion. He needs cool water to clean his face and wash the darkness of these days off him. He takes the keys from the man's belt and passes them to Ito. "Free the others," he says.

It's early morning. The birds have not yet sung to announce the day. Above ground, it should be dark enough for Tiri to leave first and find Grenn. Most of the dormitories have been damaged by the fires, so she'll be held in the infirmary or the officials' quarters if they were questioning her. If she's still alive. Eagan would follow with what's left of his fighters. They should still have time to reach the airship docks and commandeer enough ships to carry his men. Edgar made him memorize the coordinates: he knows where to go.

The first letter arrived almost two years ago from one of the Swifts, the Republic's carrier birds. Eagan was returning to his dorm from the training grounds, hot and sweaty, ready to rinse with a bucket of water. The bird was outside his window, with a small scroll clipped to its foot. The note was simple but unsigned. It said that Eagan needed to keep Ady alive at all costs—that she was important, that the Republic was not safe for her—and that someone would soon come to bring her to refuge.

Be vigilant, the note ended. *Things are not yet in motion.*

At first, exhausted and stunned, Eagan considered approaching one of the Republic officials with this note or showing it to Ady herself. But something in the writer's tone gave him pause. Ady was important and not just to him. How had this person found him? Why did anyone else care about a single civilian's survival? And worse, why would the Republic not be safe for her in particular?

Eagan quickly scrawled a reply back with a list of sharp, short questions. Weeks passed before another Swift appeared, a small swallow in the window. He fed the bird seeds he swept from the mess hall, and the exchange became a regular rhythm. The mysterious writer was always vague, never betraying his identity, but always providing just enough information that Eagan trusted the letters. The writer knew that Ady had been sent on a transport from the North East Citadel, that she believed her parents and brother to be dead, that her hair was a wild snarl of dark waves, untamed and beautiful. Eagan never told Ady about the letters; that seemed a betrayal of the writer's intent. He also didn't want her to worry—he worried enough for the both of them, always putting herself needlessly in danger, taunting the Republic when she was late to lecture or lingering in the garden after hours. He looked out for her as his father had done.

After the winter months of this year, there was a long stalemate with no letters. After training, Eagan would sometimes stand on the rampart walls and search the sky for any sign of the tiny bird.

The last letter came only two weeks ago. The instructions were short and clipped like military orders. A man by the name of Edgar would reach the Citadel walls on the South side at twilight, just before dawn. Eagan was to smuggle him into the walls. The time had come to get Ady out of the Citadel.

The rest of the Brutallion are as bloodied and bedraggled as Eagan. He does a quick count in the dimly lit shaft, and estimates about forty of his men remain. Felix and Magnus, Thomas, and Howe. Even young Ivan, looking bewildered to still be alive, stands among them. Eagan feels them watch and wait for a rousing speech, but there is no time. The dead guard will soon be missed, and Eagan hasn't the energy. Besides, there are surely more guards outside the door, waiting. Instead, he places his hand on Ivan's shoulder and says to the crowd, "You are all good men. And we're going to get out of here, I promise you. But we need to be fast. I'm going to need my best pilots."

THE RESCUE

Ellington paces in his quarters, back and forth over the worn wooden floor. It's not yet dawn, and the periwinkle light fills the room with a softness. He craves this quiet: he needs to think.

The Brutallion are sentenced to die. A young woman is imprisoned here in this very building for aiding and abetting. And on one level, Ellington understands this. The men denied his orders, they had been meeting in secret, a clear violation of the Republic's rules and curfew, *treason*. And yet, they'd defended the people. Wouldn't more civilians have perished in the siege had they not returned? They must have sensed that something was wrong. It is that intuition which makes Ellington feel acute shame. He should have seen the signals. He should have known that leaving the Citadel unguarded was like inviting invaders. The Raiders wanted them to attempt an ambush.

So, it seems now, did Commander Cayhill.

Ellington steps to the window and surveys the courtyard below. Sooty ash covers much of the ground. The usual patchwork of stones is slathered still with blood and glass, abandoned carts and broken weapons, children's shoes. The death toll still rises, but Ellington knows it to be in the hundreds. Last night, a smoke column rose to the clouds as infirmary workers carted bodies outside the Citadel walls and incinerated them before conducting a mass burial of the remains.

Did the Republic care about its own people at all? Why didn't Commander Cayhill send his own men to fight against the Raiders? Why, too, Ellington now wonders as he runs his hand against the wooden beam, did the Raiders not attack the officials' quarters? This structure, which houses all leaders, the high-ranking Bluecoats, even Commander Cayhill, still stands. Completely untouched.

Ellington presses his hands to his temples. Is *he* treasonous for even thinking this way? He has lived in the Lower West Citadel his whole life. He was a boy soldier at age twelve when his sword was nearly as tall as he was. Early, he learned to be focused, unwavering, to report on his friends who slept through training, to revel in their punishments as he received extra rations in reward. Before he knew the letters of the alphabet, he had memorized the words to the Chancellor's pledge:

To our great and mighty Republic

We pledge allegiance to Thee

Mother of the land

Father to the lost

Home where we are free...

He grew from sharpening swords and training falcons to leading an entire militia. He was unmarried. His life was hitched only to this: the Republic and its mission, the Redcoats and his work.

There is a creak outside his door, and Ellington turns, startled. The men are not usually awake this early. The sun has not yet crested over the far hills, and the night sentries are still at their posts on the rampart walls. Ellington strides across the room and presses an ear to the door. But he hears only silence. Slowly, cautiously, he steps into the hall. The corridor is empty, but there is the distinct heaviness of boots on the far stairwell.

Tiri's broad shoulders fill the narrow shaft. He tries to keep each step light, but the stairs groan under his weight, like water-logged wood about to break. He moves as quickly as his body can carry him, though his stomach roars with hunger, and he aches for clean water. If Grenn is still alive—and she must be! If she is dead, he fears he might rampage through every room and slit the sleeping throats!—she should be here. He knows it. He can almost feel her presence through the walls. The dormitories are severely damaged, and the Commander will surely have grilled her with questions. Hopefully, questioning is all they've done. As Tiri steps onto the next level, he shudders at the thought of what terrors might have befallen Grenn.

He has passed most of the high-level officials' private quarters: Commander Cayhill and Captain Ellington, their second-in-commands, and the top-ranking Bluecoats. Here, there are rows of empty offices and a few dormitories where guards snore from their cots. The dormitory doors are left open a crack. Any sound will wake them. Any wrong door could cause someone to sound the alarm.

Tiri jolts at a sound behind him. He turns and reaches on instinct for his mace. But it's not there—all weapons were confiscated. He has only his fists, which he holds out, bracing himself.

"Show yourself," he whispers, his voice low.

The figure steps closer, out of the stairwell shadow. It's Captain Ellington.

He's still wearing his Redcoats uniform, but he looks haggard, as though he hasn't slept in days. Instead of his usual stature, that self-assured arched back and high brows, Captain Ellington looks genuinely shocked to see him. His arms are raised as if in surrender.

"Captain," Tiri says. Should he nod in reverence or step away? The Captain is alone, and Tiri easily has weight on him, could leave him knocked out in the hallway for someone to find.

"You..." Captain Ellington lowers his arms and looks around. "How did you? Never mind. Where are the others?"

Tiri narrows his eyes. "It doesn't matter."

"I mean you no harm." Captain Ellington softens his eyes and his voice. His shoulders are stooped with the exhaustion of a man who's lost many men. There must be great sorrow in that kind of responsibility. Tiri surprises himself by even thinking this. "I want to help."

"I'm looking for Grenn. Is she here? Is she—" He cannot stomach to say the word *dead*. But he needs to know. By his mental calculation, Eagan and the others will have left the prison already, have made their way past the training ground, and ascended the airship dock. He needs to find her *now*, lest they leave without him.

"She is your girl?"

Tiri studies his face. This could easily be a trap. Why would the Captain help him, a traitor? And why should he trust the Captain, when the Republic had sentenced all of the Brutallion to death?

But he is weak from fatigue, from fighting, from hours in the musty underground cell. And if he attacks Ellington now, the sound will rouse the sleeping guards.

"Yes," he says.

Ellington nods: "This way."

He turns and hurries back to the stairwell and up two more flights. Ellington walks quickly but with assurance. He leads Tiri along the top floor and into a back room. He removes a set of keys from his hip pouch. "Only officials can get in," he murmurs as the latch unlocks and the door swings open.

Tiri bursts blindly into the room. His mind throbs with one motive.

Grenn is the only one who can calm him. A single touch of her soft hand on his arm can make the heat of his anger subside like cool water trickling down his neck. She is the sun he revolves around—and not in any glorified way. He sees her own flaws. Sees her penchant for order. But there is a gentleness that she wears like a cloak. No one has ever touched him with kindness, not since his father died, fighting alongside Ellington in an early attack on the Raiders. His mother died in childbirth. He'd never known the feel of a woman's lips on his skin, never been told it was alright to cry when his rage flared higher than the Citadel walls. Grenn had been in his lecture classes before he and Eagan were recruits. She'd helped him learn letters and numbers, spending long hours in the library as his tutor and friend—before she was more.

Now, she lies on a cot, bloodied and broken. Bandages encircle her waist and leg. One arm dangles off the edge of the mattress. His first thought is that she is dead. Her skin is pale as clouds, and her tunic soaked in blood. A moan escapes his mouth as he rushes to her side.

But she opens her eyes and gasps, too. Her eyes are that bright and perfect blue. He thinks he has never seen anything so beautiful.

"Grenn, Grenn," he says, brushing the sweaty hair from her forehead. "We have to get you out of here."

Her lips are parched and cracking, so she only nods. Tiri lifts her gently in his arms—she is lighter than a sack of grain. The light warms in the window, and he knows that soon, the sun will rise, and the Citadel will be alive with activity. He must reach Eagan and the others at the airship docks.

But first, he stops in the still-open doorway, where Captain Ellington hangs in the shadows.

"Thank you," he whispers sincerely.

SKYRAIDERS

The water is cold and soft on her skin. Ady steps forward, heel to toe, each step meticulous. That white light still pours behind and around her, she can finally see her own shadow on the water's edge. She breathes in and out. A soft cloud forms in the cool air, like a ghost from her lips. The white hem of her tunic brushes the water as she steps in up to her ankles. There is only more darkness around her, water-smoothed stones under her feet that also rise cavernously from the depths. She knows this place, knows its heavy wet smells.

The cavern quakes. The water ripples, as though tiny raindrops have erupted on the surface. Again, there's a shake, and small rocks from above fall into the water. Still Ady steps forward as the pool laps her legs. With each quake, there is the distant and muffled sound of an explosion.

A tremor shakes the ship.

Ady sits up in bed, coated in sweat. It is night—she knows by the silver frosted light from the porthole. But she felt a shiver through her body and the very walls of the cabin as something rocked the hull.

It strikes again, an explosion outside the Aurora. This time, a fiery orange pierces the night sky like a flaming arrow. Ady throws herself from the bed. Have they been followed by the Republic? Has Commander Cayhill's fleet discovered them so quickly? Still in her under-smock, Ady laces her boots and hurries down the passage. Above deck, there is the clamor of competing voices. The ground pitches beneath her feet as Ady races to the steps and ascends into the open air.

The deck is awash with chaos. The Boatswain twins swing from the ropes as they adjust the balloon; Ella and Cooper, the gunner, roll out cannons to the open ports. Ady squints as the wind whips her hair and carries the scent of smoke and pewter.

"Miss Adylyn," Calvin calls from behind her. "Best get below deck, ma'am!" He scurries past her toward the bridge with a scrolled map in hand.

Ady ignores him. She sees that he is heading for Edgar up ahead, manning the wheel at the bridge. She follows, stumbling under the heavy wind. The Aurora is going faster than she's felt before, and the deck seems to swim beneath her.

"Edgar!" she cries, gripping onto the bridge railing.

Edgar does not turn. His stony gaze stays transfixed on the sky before him. "Miss Adylyn, you need to get below deck *now*."

"What's going on? I can help."

She feels silly about saying this, but she means it. She wants to help, really, but everyone seems to have their place and role on the ship around her. And she's supposed to simply hide below deck?

The clouds around them part, and an explosion sounds off illuminating the night sky, and for a brief moment, Ady can see the shapes of multiple ships. She quickly counts five. They are not the same honey brown as the Aurora, with its milky-cream balloon. Instead, set against the midnight blue sky, they are a black wood. The very ships seem armored in scrap metal along the hull, rough and ragged. This ship has side propellers and sails in black.

"Stay low," Edgar directs over the fiery blasts. His tone is so firm that Ady blinks at him in confusion. "These are not just Skyraiders. They're the Ravens."

"The Ravens?" Ady asks nervously.

"Miss Adylyn, they must not see you."

Ady crouches behind the bridge railing and rests her head against the wood grain. Even when she closes her eyes, the orange glow is there, with every blast that streaks the sky. It returns. The fire, Grenn, the Raiders, Eagan, that smell of death that clung to her skin for days. Ady presses her palms into her eyes, willing the smoke to vanish. Another explosion shakes the Aurora, this time from the onboard cannons. When she looks up again, the two nearest ships are closing in, but the one port-side is now aglow with flames.

"Captain, we must adjust direction and get her to turn 80 degrees, Sir!" Calvin anxiously directs while looking over his map, holding it tightly along the wooden compass platform.

"We've got one shot," says Edgar, nodding to the open clearing. He then shouts over his shoulder to the Boatswain twins: "Dax, get those lines to the starboard side. Dec, turn her 80 degrees!"

Ella joins them on the deck, her wild red hair a flowing red wave. "Cannons are active, Captain, gunner's on it!" she shouts over the wind's roar.

"And Bartholomew?" Edgar says back.

"Not yet."

"He won't let us down."

Edgar winces as he turns the ship sharply, an adjusted path northwest. The Aurora's balloon catches an air current, and the ship picks up speed. Ady can feel the weight of the wind on her skin, feel the way she's pushed back against the bridge. But the Ravens must have better fuel, Ady thinks, or more coal, more man-power, because their ships are still gaining on them. How will they ever be able to outrun the Skyraiders' fleet?

Another explosion strikes, this one closer, as a cannon hits below deck. The ship tilts violently to the left and screams rise from above as the twins clasp to the web of ropes.

"Steady—" Edgar speaks as if to himself and his crew. His grip on the wheel only tightens.

The ships are so close now that Ady can make out the crew members' individual faces on board. The burning ship draws her eye. She remembers the heat of flames that close, the way the very air seems to bend. She shivers next to Edgar. He said she could not be seen, but who would recognize her? Who would know? These are not of the Republic's fleet. These are Raiders of the Rebellion, their fleet in the skies. She knows, too, by the telltale paint on their faces, streaked like blood. One man catches her eye. They're close enough to see the features on his face, the black and crimson lines of warpaint. His head is mostly shaved, but matted strands of hair string out like feathers pulled back to the top of his head. He looks at her— worse, he *sees* her, and his mouth twists into a horrid smile, all while his men hurry to extinguish the flames around him, dowsing water, raising the black sails. He stands by the bow. His gaze pierces her, and she can't look away.

"There he is," Edgar shouts, and Ady finally tears away. "Bartholomew, you've done it again!"

A man has emerged onto the bridge. She knows him at once: the man in the blue room. He wears the same leather vest and the goggles now over his eyes. He carries three large precarious glass vials. Inside the tubes: a bright and luminous blue liquid, which moves like stardust in the ocean.

It happens so swiftly that Ady almost doesn't believe her eyes: Bartholomew kneels behind the helm, where a small black box is bolted to the deck. He tilts each vial and empties the liquid into the case like he's adding shimmering soap to a tepid bath.

"Barth?" Edgar yells back to him.

"Not yet!"

"Bartholomew!" Edgar yells once again.

"Now!"

Edgar turns the wheel hard to the right and heaves on a lever Ady hadn't even noticed, blending into the wood.

"Hang on, Miss Adylyn. It's going to be a bumpy ride." Edgar smiles at her cryptically and grabs hold of his Captain's hat.

Blue light emanates behind the Aurora. It seems to pulse from within the ship's very hull, then moves over and around them, a protective guard of light. Ady shields her eyes and sees that even the Skyraiders look stunned. There is a soft clicking sound, like a bird about to sing. The sound revs to a high pitch just as the ship bolts forward into the night. Ady cannot move; every part of her is held firmly in place by the strength of the ship's speed. Ella holds tight to the side deck, Bartholomew to the helm, the twins to the ropes, and Ady has the surreal sense that she is floating, as if in water. Peering over the railings, she sees that they have left the enemies behind in the night sky.

Edgar begins to laugh as though he enjoys this. The Aurora finally slows after leaving harm's way.

Bartholomew reseals the now empty vials and meets Ady's eyes. Finally, she sees his face, which is lined and weathered. She can't offer even a smile as she is still shaken.

High above them, beyond the clouds, a hawk flies over the Aurora. His feathers catch the moonlight, his underbelly glows white. Soaring, he screeches and continues to fly due northwest.

THE HAWK FLIES

The moon is as wide and bright as a silver coin. The sky, still that dark and misted night. Through the darkest blue, the hawk flies.

Below, the terrain is rugged and coarse, the dunes eroded by wind and blowing sand. He flies west, the ship a speck behind him now. He flies over the cliffs that jut from open ground, where water once lapped at the shore, where children once bathed in the sun while their parents looked on from the beach. Now, there is only dry and caked ground, black as pitch.

Still, he soars.

West, into the night, on toward the sun that is setting on faraway places, out to where the water still flows and tides still ebb, tugged gently by the moon. He knows his way, knows the wind pattern to catch under his wings, knows how to glide softly and catch the thermals. The expansive seafloor glints beneath him: sunken ships, half-buried in dust, bones, and seashells, capsized lifeboats as evacuees escaped the bombs. He flies on, northwest until it appears in the distance. A shelf cloud blankets the horizon. He approaches, eager now, and flies into the cloud, which is thick and viscous as smoke. Into crystals of snowflakes. To rain. But then, the clear shimmering sky! The curved hills afloat against the horizon, lined with towering trees of green, the gently falling water reflects the light of the stars—

THE CHANCELLOR

Commander Cayhill stands at the airship dock. The wooden scaffold extends from the rampart and overlooks the dusty brown earth below. Around him, ships are tethered by ropes to the holding bars, and the hulls bob like floating bodies. Three ships from his fleet are missing—the affront! the treason!—and someone will surely swing for this.

A chill has settled over the Citadel, and he could go for a mug of warm broth. But the Chancellor's airship is already a speck on the horizon, small as a bird's wingspan from here.

How had he failed so miserably? How had the girl (practically a child!) escaped from his grasp, that blasted book surely with her? All this time, she'd been living here, sly and unassuming, and just when she'd been revealed, he missed the mark. They'd been waiting for the signs for so long. About a week ago, word arrived by Swift, tipping him off that the dark powers were on the alert: the wanted one would soon reveal herself. All Republic officials in the Citadel were notified. He personally oversaw the deal with Doköran—and then the wait. He'd had his suspicions about other girls in the past, even Grenn, with her refined air, but it was the librarian of all people who apprised them of her identity. Ady the orphan had been seen with *the* book. The Rebellion's siege was to be the perfect distraction, allowing them to find the book at last—and the girl.

The Chancellor's ship nears now, glinting in the early sun, and Cayhill braces himself for the rebuke he knows will come. His task was simple, really. And it should have worked. Ellington had taken his orders without question, he'd led his men, every last one of them, outside the Citadel walls and on toward nothing. The Bluecoats did their part: they searched Ady's room. And despite finding quite a collection of illegal items—books, as if women should read for pleasure, various items from the Old World—she was not there. The Raiders arrived as planned. His men stood back. It was a pity, really, how many innocents had to die. But it would have been worth it had the plan succeeded. Had *she* not escaped.

And just how had she escaped? He fumes as the Chancellor's ship lowers now to the dock. The Bluecoats beside him step forward as bondsmen leap to the scaffold and hastily secure his ship. It's those traitors, led by that bastard son of James Alexander. The Citadel's best soldiers have turned against him and the Republic. They broke from their orders and returned to the Citadel without permission, they helped the girl and escaped from prison and now—anger surges through Commander Cayhill—now they have taken it one step further. They have stolen Republic airships and taken to the skies.

Oh yes. Someone will swing for this. And that someone will not be him.

Now, the Chancellor descends the gangway.

Commander Cayhill stiffens. He is not a man accustomed to feeling fear. Even around Doköran, who he despises with every fiber of his being, what he feels is more akin to disgust and unease. But around the Chancellor, Cayhill remembers what it was like to be a small child, afraid of his own father's shadow. The Chancellor is tall and thin. His hair is shaved short, and wrinkles crease his face. His crimson robes flow behind him in the whipping wind.

"Chancellor," Cayhill says with a nod. "It's good to see you, sir."

"I wish I could say the same." The Chancellor stops a few feet away. Four soldiers have followed him off the ship, and they stand in neat rows behind him. "I see you're missing some ships, Commander. Cost of battle?"

"In a manner of speaking."

Cayhill clasps his hands behind his back and wills himself to look stronger and sturdier. The wind is strong today, and it cuts over the scaffold. The Chancellor's ship sails beat like drums against each other.

"Where is she?" The Chancellor demands.

Cayhill swallows hard. "We don't know."

"Unacceptable."

"We had some unforeseen circumstances arise, my lord. The Brutallion. Apparently, they still exist."

The Chancellor says nothing. His silence is even worse than the pebbly pitch of his voice, low and grinding.

"But we're working on it," Cayhill quickly adds. "We have recruited Doköran and his men to help us track down the girl, and perhaps they will be of use in finding the traitors, too."

"Why would I want to rely so much on the Rebellion? You make Doköran sound like a more worthy Commander than you, Cayhill."

"He is Wasteland scum, my lord."

"So I suppose you are lower even than that."

Cayhill drops his gaze. There is no use arguing with the Chancellor. One snap of his fingers and his men would throw Cayhill over the scaffolding and down to the rocky ground.

"We have had traitors rise up against us, my lord," he says carefully. He should have killed the Brutallion when he had a chance. He should have sent in his men to slit their throats in the night. "We could not have foreseen that."

The Chancellor smiles now and shakes his head. "Let me tell you a story about a traitor. There was once a man who was put in charge of an entire fortress. A beautiful fortress in the desert. He had one job. For years, just one job. Wait for any sign of the foretold events to be set in motion—look for a simple little girl. And just when she reveals herself, when his entire army is gone, when it should have been so simple, he fails. She escapes, the Citadel is nearly destroyed, his fleet is stolen, and he is disgraced. I have to say, Cayhill, this failure is so great that it almost seems... ah, what's the word? Purposeful."

Alarm spikes and Cayhill looks up, startled.

"I assure you, my lord—"

But the Chancellor raises his palm and continues. "No, let *me* assure you. You are very replaceable. Do not forget that. Do you know what happens if we do not find this girl? It will be your head if we don't get hers." The Chancellor looks around for a moment at the rampart walls. The air still smells faintly of smoke from the mass graves.

"I think we'll stay a few days," he says. Then he turns and exits the gangway toward the barracks while his men follow. Cayhill watches them leave. The two Bluecoats with him exchange glances. This is when Cayhill realizes that what burned more than the Chancellor's threat was that his men witnessed his humiliation.

He will set this right. He will find the girl.

PARTING OF THE CLOUDS

After eight days aboard the Aurora, Ady has settled into a restless rhythm. She strolls the deck alone at night, she sleeps fitfully during the day, crying into her pillow in anguish. She tries to find Bartholomew to investigate the blue vials, but he has vanished into his workshop again and locked the door. Mostly, she passes long hours writing to Eagan in her journal. Perhaps wherever they're going, she will be able to find a Swift and send a message, simply to know if he's still alive. For now, the letters are enough and provide a continuous one-sided conversation.

There has been a change in the air since they left the Skyraiders behind. She can smell it, the salt and the softest floral scent.

At noon on the eighth day, she sits at the desk, unable to sleep and slip into dreams. The journal is open before her when there's a rap on the door. Edgar enters.

"Miss Adylyn, it's time," he says quietly.

"For what?" She can't even turn to face him.

"We're nearing our destination. I thought you might want to come and join us on deck."

The words from yesterday's entry bleed through the page, and she can make out the curved letters—*Are you alive?*

"I don't feel like it," she says. There is only one place she wants to see right now: the familiar sandstone and cinderblock of the Citadel, a place she never imagined she'd miss. And with every hour and day, the Aurora flies further and further away from home.

"I can imagine how you feel, you know." Edgar steps closer until she can see him in her periphery. His thick hair is wind-blown and lays in a tuft of curls.

"How could you possibly?" she snaps.

Immediately, she regrets this as Edgar's features soften. He nods at her, thinking.

"My wife died." He says this so casually, like referencing a bird outside the window, but she can see a soft grimace in his face and knows that it pains him to mention. "We'd been married only five years. We were traveling in the Eastern Alliance." Ady says nothing but listens intently.

"What I mean by this, Miss Adylyn, is that...just because we've lost our love, it doesn't mean we lose our life. That didn't come out as eloquently as I'd hoped, but hopefully, you get what I mean. There is more to do and live for. And you, Miss Adylyn, *you* are someone very important. Maybe you've gathered that by now. You are not just another citizen of the Republic. You have much more to give this world. Love still fuels your heart. It fuels mine every day." He pauses, searching her eyes. "Now, will you come join us on deck? You won't want to miss this."

He extends his hand. She stares back in silence and takes it.

Above deck, Ady meets Edgar on the bridge. She wears fresh clothes borrowed from Ella—black pants, a white button-down shirt, and a cape over her shoulders buttoned at her neck. Apparel in the skies are much different than the Citadel. She carries the book and journal in her satchel, and feels the burnished bronze of the pocket watch around her neck. Her hair whips and stings her face, but she breathes deeply as the ship coasts through the clear sky. Because Edgar was right. Love does still fuel her heart, and Eagan would want that for her.

The sun is a blistering white as Ady squints to view the horizon. Far below, she sees waves lapping under the Aurora. She runs to the edge of the ship, leaning over. She can't help but smile for the first time in what feels like ages.

"Water!" she exclaims to Edgar. "There's really water!"

"The Forgotten Sea, Miss Adylyn."

Ady proclaims to herself in disbelief, "The sea really does exist."

She watches the water ripple underneath them, creating patterns and repetition. Each wave deems different. They flow together, yet apart. *Something so powerful to be a part of,* she thinks to herself. Time almost stands still as she gets lost in the gaze of watching the waves. An hour, maybe more, easily passes. Although she still feels like no time has passed at all since the night they escaped the burning Citadel.

Ahead now, she sees a cloud barrier. The clouds are white as flower petals. Beyond and above them, the sky seems a rich gemstone blue.

"What is that?" Ady asks over the wind.

"A welcoming," Edgar replies as he turns the ship's wheel slowly.

Ady walks back to meet Edgar on the bridge. She keeps her eyes on the horizon, captivated by this cloud line.

They are upon the clouds in a matter of minutes. The Aurora glides slowly along.

Fog begins to descend upon the deck as they enter, thick and shimmering like tiny diamonds. The air mists her face. These clouds felt different than the others these past days.

The ship goes quiet. The Boatswain twins hold fast and silent to the ropes; Calvin and Cooper peer over the deck; Ella beams at the bow. They are all silent as the ship glides through the creamy sky. Edgar is at ease, smiling to himself when the clouds turn crystalline and seem to reflect tiny sparkles of light across their skin.

The clouds shift, as though they've entered a second layer of fog. Ady raises her hand as they enter the thickest part and watches, amazed, as water particles glimmer on her fingertips. They pool there, and she could swear the water gleams as though colorful prisms reflected light beneath. As they sail further and deeper, the air becomes lavender and bluish-white. Fringed white flakes fall from the sky and land on Ady's hair and hands. Above them, the balloon groans as ice settles onto the canvas.

"Hang on!" Edgar calls out. He adjusts the lever beside the wheel, and the Aurora creaks and grinds through the sky. Ice has crusted along the wooden hull as the ship begins to rattle.

As they pass through a new layer of clouds, there is the gentle patter of rain as the ice melts. The rain feels soothing as if it is purifying her from the long journey. Ady looks up and closes her eyes, savoring the water on her skin. The rain droplets along the Aurora's deck are gentle as the ship continues on.

"Now for the fun part," Edgar grins to himself.

Pearly white clouds surround the Aurora once again as the shower abates. Ady opens her eyes. These clouds are warm and gentle. A moment of silence remains with them as they sail. Then suddenly, the ship bursts through a final cloud layer and into the welcoming sunlight.

Ady shades her eyes, but then quickly widens them, gasping as she takes in the view. Before her laps a different sea of blue, cascading out from the cloud line. The ocean spray looks close enough to touch. And rising above the sea, islands hover high above the waves. Waterfalls cascade from the floating islands before them, sending a trickle of ripples out across the expanse. Rainbows glisten where water meets water. The highest islands shimmer with waterfalls that seem to evaporate into colorful prisms in the sky.

Ady moves slowly back to the deck railing and stares at the floating islands, the waterfalls, this cerulean blue sea, how it catches the sun in a million glittering flecks. Tears stream down her cheeks.

Edgar smiles knowingly.

"Welcome to Atheria, Miss Adylyn."

She notices now that the wind has subsided. Her hair falls gently down her spine as they fly toward the islands. The sun provides a soft warmth. She looks closer to the islands and has never seen green like this, not even in the garden, one of the few living patches of land in the Citadel. The evergreens loom high here, with budding white flowers that line the grounds. Honey-hued stone cottages dot the islands, some taller stone structures peeking over the trees. And the flowers, the many flowers as they pass another island! They are every color: golden yellow and scarlet red as the Redcoats' uniform, purple and orange as the most vibrant desert sunset. And everywhere, there are waterfalls, some falling from island to island like latticework. As they pass one island, Ady notices a cluster of fawns. They stand near berry bushes and honeysuckles, and they watch unblinking as the ship sails past.

The largest island is ahead of them now. This one floats higher than any other, and the grandest waterfalls plunge from this height. White pillars peek over the treetops like tower spires. As the Aurora ascends, Ady strains for a clear view of the structure on the island. But the bright marble catches the midday light so that she squints as though looking straight into the sun. It's majestic in its presence yet welcoming. Had this place survived from the Old World, evaded the attacks of the Great War? She wonders. The questions collide in her mind—the islands are floating, the ocean water is contained here and here only from an entrance in the sky! How could such a place be possible? She sees a dock high above, awaiting their arrival, a mid-air platform for them to moor the ship. Six people stand on the ledge, clothed in navy robes, watching for their approach. Their hands are all clasped behind them.

As the Boatswain twins and Ella ready the landing gear and bowlines, Ady returns to the bridge and stands beside Edgar. Someone here had wanted her alive, knew about her existence in the Lower West Citadel, and plucked her from her people. But why? She looks at Edgar and tries to hide the growing fear, but he must sense it in her. Because as he cuts the wheel to the starboard side, he says softly, so only she can hear: "It's alright. Welcome home, Miss Adylyn."

ATHERIA

The Aurora docks to the wooden scaffold with a soft and gentle sway. Up close, the floating island is a near-impossible green—greener than any shoots that bloomed in the Citadel, that pressed through the dry and crumbling desert ground, struggling to live.

"It's time, Miss Adylyn," Edgar says behind her. They stand starboard and watch as the twins tie the Aurora to the docking post.

The gangway lowers, and Edgar waves her ahead of him with a solemn nod. Ady steps onto the planks, hovering for a moment over the shimmering ocean below. Then she descends, one foot before the other in mincing steps. The air is at once salty and sweet like someone is brewing a rich tea in the sky above them. Her hair lifts gently off her neck, but it is neither cold nor warm.

When she reaches the dock, she half expects the ground to feel soft, as though the whole island is made of clouds. But it's firm, steady as an anchor, and she steadies herself.

The six Atherians in navy robes, with gold ropes around their waists, look on, stoic and still. They are tall and narrow, with dominant jawlines and chins. Some are pale as the cloud line they just passed through, while others are dark, their blue eyes sharp and crystalline. All of them, she notices, have long white hair.

One of the figures approach now, head lowered to the ground. The Atherian is taller than any man she's ever seen, with skin rich as amber. The figure's face is old but still fruitful.

"Hello, Miss Adylyn," the figure says.

Ady glances at Edgar, who seems unfazed by the fact that this stranger knows her name.

"Hello," Ady replies.

"I am Kyrre of the Nobles. Welcome to Atheria. We've been expecting you for some time." She sees now that the Atherian's eyes are so blue they verge on violet. "And you, good sir!" Kyrre says, reverting attention to Edgar. "We owe you a great debt of gratitude!"

"I'm pleased to have been of service," Edgar says with a laugh. He looks back to the Aurora and signals for the crew to stay aboard. Ella stands at the helm with Calvin. The Boatswain twins continue tying up the lines in silence.

"Now, Miss Adylyn," says Kyrre, whose voice is so honey-sweet it sounds almost insincere. But that smile—it radiates through the tall and glistening body. "Someone is waiting for you."

With a turn, the other Nobles follow suit, as if on cue. They follow Kyrre up a stone path and into the lining of trees. Ady waits for Edgar's nudge, then proceeds behind them. The path is narrow and wide at different turns. Rocks along the grass are moss-covered and dotted with dew. The trees provide a thick canopy that shades them from the luminous light—and Ady thinks they are taller than the tallest buildings in the Citadel. She does not sweat, even as they start up an incline. She feels nothing at all, there's only a cool stasis, like soft standing water.

Overhead, the hawk glides on what wind there is; his feathers catch the sun against the cerulean blue of midday. His familiarity brings a calmness over her.

The Nobles say nothing as they ascend from the dock and through the wooded path. They walk in an ordered pack, silent as monks.

A palace takes shape in the distance, over and between the tree boughs, stone and spire and crystal-white marble. With each step, a chill runs over Ady's skin.

They reach a clearing, which reveals a grand stone staircase built straight into the ground. A white stone balustrade lines the walkway, almost too bright to bear as the shimmering specks reflect off the sun. Here, the Nobles stop, so suddenly that Ady almost gasps in spite of herself. Kyrre turns back and signals for her to take the lead.

She stares at the grand steps that climb upward to an ornate palace entrance. Slowly, she takes her first step and continues at this pace. The palace is finally in clear view. White layers of stone construct the palace, leading to sloped turrets of patina green. Halfway to the top of the grand stairs, the double doors become more visible, and she can barely make out the intricate details carved into the warm chestnut wood. As she keeps her gaze on them, they open. A man appears before her at the very top. He is cloaked and shadowy, dressed in the same rich navy robe as the Nobles.

And she knows before he lowers the hood. She knows by the stoop in his shoulders, by the hands that lift to the cape. She remembers those hands stealing rations from her plate as children, playing games with small sticks and stones they found, helping her bury her mother. She would know him anywhere. And suddenly, it seems inevitable: someone had known of her existence, someone wanted her alive, little Ady in the Lower West Citadel. He'd sent Edgar to find her—

"Athos!" Ady cries.

She runs the rest of the stairs, so fast she almost trips on the marble.

"Athos!" she cries again before throwing herself in his arms. He is tall now like their mother, with the same dark hair. A beard wreaths his face. When they last saw each other, they were so small, so frail and frightened—she was sitting on the back cart of a caravan, drifting out of the North East Citadel, sent away to the desert, away from everything she'd known and loved. The last thing she could see as she was whisked away was tears in his deep brown eyes.

"You're alive, you're alive," she gasps, pulling away from him at last, wanting to look into his eyes. They once again well with tears.

"My sister, I'm so glad you're finally here. And safe," he says. They embrace deeply again. "I knew you would come. Now, let's get you inside. We have much to tell you."

CHAMBERS

Ady follows Athos into the grand palace. Just inside the warm wooden doors, there is a long main hall with milky marble walls, an opulent white. Vast pillars, wider than her arms could encircle, tower like tree trunks, lining the foyer. The arched ceiling leads to gilded gold crowning and is inlaid with glass panels. The sun falls through the skylights in even beams, where the warm glow lands upon the floor and illuminates the green and blue geometric shapes hidden in the marble flecks. Ady blinks, dazzled by the sight. The Citadel was all gray and brown stone, all menace and control—but here, it's as though the palace is built of gold and pearls. Here, the air itself is sweet, and the long hallway seems to invite her in, deeper. Everything is white and clean, so bright it's almost blinding—as though sun rays hide behind the marble to make everything shine.

As they walk, she can tell that Athos has much to say. He glances at her, then looks forward again as they continue down the hall. He is no longer a boy. He has grown into a man who looks so much like their mother that it's like walking beside a ghost. He has that same clipped and gentle smile. The same neatly combed hair, hazelnut brown. The same quiet calm. But he is here, breathing and well, grown and handsome. He has been searching for her.

"I can't believe you're alive," Ady says. She looks over her shoulder to see that Edgar and the other Nobles have stopped by the palace doors and are engrossed in deep conversation. She and Athos continue alone. "I thought you were dead. Or perhaps a recruited soldier by now?"

He gives a half-smile.

"Some soldier I'd be," he says softly.

"I sent many Swifts back to you, with nothing in return for quite some time." She pauses.

Ady thinks of her recurring dreams: the cavern and the water, that blinding light from behind her that seemed to beckon. *Come—turn—see.* How many times had that dream appeared to her, had she stepped with bare feet into the trickle of cold water? Had that been someone or something from Atheria trying to communicate in some way?

"Why haven't I heard from you?" Ady ventures. She means this to sound soft, but it comes out stronger than she intends, fueled by her years in the Citadel alone. Why send a stranger to practically seize her from her home? Why wait until now to find her?

"I've been trying to reach you for some time," Athos says, his tone still gentle. "Getting you here safely has been my sole mission." He must sense her next question because he quickly adds: "I assure you, sister, I will answer everything. But first, there is something I'd like you to see."

They've reached a grand atrium now, with halls that fan out like sun rays. She looks up, and the ceiling here tells the story of angels with great white wings. There are detailed paintings of the beautiful beings flying amongst the clouds within the sun's rays. Ahead in the north archway, steps lead to the back grounds, and Ady can just make out the emerald green grass and trees in the distance. But Athos takes one of the east corridors, and Ady follows, keeping one hand firmly on her satchel. So far, they haven't seen anyone—no other Nobles, though she senses onlooking eyes and almost makes out the faint dance of whispers from closed doors.

This new corridor is narrow and arched, with open-air windows along the left side. That ambrosial sweet air filters into the palace. At the end of the hall, there is a mahogany door. Athos stops just before entering.

"Now this is a surprise. We've been preparing this for you."

The door swings open, and Ady enters. The room is an almost blinding white, and she blinks, taking it all in: there is a bed with white posts and pure cream linens, softer than butter. Beaded pillows lay against the sheets, threaded with tiny iridescent shells that catch the light. There is a chaise with ivory and navy stitchings—a case full of books, not a one covered in the Republic's dusky blue binding—a mirror framed with raw-cut quartz crystals—and a dresser studded along the edges with mother-of-pearl. Never has she seen anything so bright and airy, as though the room captured and contained starlight. And this is all for her?

A deep royal blue and white crystal point sits atop the dresser. Ady gently picks it up, turning it slowly to examine its polished edges.

"It's a crystal that brings forth the wisdom of the universe. It remained hidden from humanity for thousands of years, much like Atheria." Athos says softly. "It may impart clarity to your head and heart."

The crystal feels cool in her grasp, yet warm, calming. *Such wonder here.*

Ady then moves to the bed and runs one hand along the cushioning, softer than fur. All she has ever known is the gray and brown of the Citadel. Desert dust and cinderblock and scratchy wool. This is like cloth cut from the clouds.

Beyond the canopy, she now sees a balcony with folding doors that open wide. Sheer curtains flutter like butterfly wings in the breeze. In just a few steps, Ady stands on the balcony and overlooks the island that slopes around her in rolling knolls of green.

"Beautiful, isn't it?" says Athos, coming to stand next to her.

"The most beautiful place I've ever seen."

"There's so much I want to show you." Athos leans over the balustrade and surveys the land below.

The sun hangs high above them, though Ady could have sworn it was midday hours ago now. The light falls evenly over Atheria, from the cliffs along the island's perimeter to the treetops that glisten like jewels, to the brooks that weave through the forest floor.

"This place—" Athos says. "There's nothing like it in this world. Atheria's been hidden for centuries upon centuries, for safekeeping. Until the time was right to forge its place into the New Earth."

"I don't understand," she says in almost a whisper.

Athos straightens now and places one hand on her shoulder. The touch feels so fatherly and foreign that Ady wonders if her own father used to calm Athos like this, one hand on his shoulder.

"Adylyn," he says, his voice all serious now. "We've been sent here for a divine purpose. Something powerful is working with us, something far beyond us or this world. I don't know how best to say all this, forgive me. I know it's a lot." He sighs and strides back into her chambers now, his hands clasped behind his back. But then he turns sharply—suddenly—and says: "The book. Did Edgar give it to you? It's been kept safe?"

Ady fumbles for her satchel and retrieves the metal-bound book. She hasn't opened the pages since that night in the Citadel when the parchment seemed to burn with hidden flecks of light.

"Could you read anything?" Athos asks, and his tone is so urgent, so eager that it almost frightens her.

"I—I only saw some glimmers, like a light coming off the pages. I didn't know what it was, but it was all I could see. No words. No symbols. Nothing more than that."

A smile bursts across Athos' face, and he rubs one hand across his temples. "My God," he says under his breath. "It's true. That's brilliant!"

Ady holds the book to her chest, and warmth seems to spread from the metal bindings and up into her arms.

"This book, Adylyn—" Athos says, joining her on the balcony again. "It is very sacred. Inscribed from the Heavens. Protected by Atherians, who are the guardians of humanity. It is called the Book of Light. Only the chosen may read it."

"What makes you think I can read it?"

"Because," Athos says—and she'd swear later she could see a sheen of tears in his eyes—"you were destined to, my sister."

Doköran

Doköran knows something has happened the moment that Orius enters the tent. The mage is smiling. His smile, as it turns out, is even more unsettling than the usual wrinkled frown. He grips his staff, and his knuckles are bone-white.

Doköran's muscles tighten instinctively. Before him is a tray of untouched meat, clouded by buzzing flies. The wine in his horn-mug is, disappointingly, gone. One of the slave girls has been kneading between his shoulder blades, but her hands are small, and she's beginning to just annoy him. He bats her away, demands a fresh wine flask, and the young girl slips from the canvas tent.

"What is it?" Doköran barks, as he takes a bite from the drying meat. It's salty with brine.

"I felt a change," Orius says, stepping forward. "In the skies. We have them."

"Who? The girl?"

Doköran looks up, interested now. Had they found her so quickly? He'd only recently sent word to Corvis that she was their new goal: that she was last seen flying west over these parts.

"No." Orius shakes his head grimly. "But they will lead us to her."

He describes what he saw: three stolen ships, their sails in the Republic red, refugees searching for the wanted one. Their own fleet, the Ravens, led by Corvis the brave and the bloody—flames in the sky, the sputtering engines, splintering wood and gun smoke. Canon fire among the stars. An affront to the Republic, ships from their imperial force overtaken so easily by the Skyraiders.

"Their ships went down in Death Valley." Orius tilts his face back as though smelling something distant in the air. "Not long ago. We'll have found them by morning."

THE ATHERIANS

Night in Atheria brings a fluid coolness. The stars here glimmer like diamonds over the island. Ady stands on her balcony for what seems like hours and watches the color drain from the sky as constellations appear.

Athos left her hours ago, telling her to rest. She was to meet him after dark. He had something to show her. Ady passed the afternoon in dreamless naps on her canopy bed and exploring every drawer and chest in her new room. Mostly she found arrays of silks and embroidered dresses in every color imaginable.

Just before sunset, as the sky warms to pink and crimson, there is a knock on her door. Two Atherians enter, both taller than any human that Ady has ever met or seen.

"Hello," Ady says, perched on the chaise. She is surprised to have visitors—and also surprised by their stature and beauty.

The figures, like the Nobles, look like humans—but not. They are divinely feminine. Radiant and beautiful. In addition to their height, taller than any door frame in the Citadel, their skin seems almost effervescent, letting off the slightest glimmer of light. One is darker than Tiri, with skin like the night, contrasting beautifully with her eyes, as it seems all Atherians have the sharpest blue eyes. The other is peach-pale. They carry steaming silver platters. Both have hair whiter than the clouds, cascading down the middle of their back. Two small braids pull from the sides of their hair. Their smiles are welcoming and gentle.

"My name is Gaia," says the peach-pale one.

"And I am Echo."

Their voices are resonant and warm.

"We've brought you some of the best food Atheria has to offer," says Gaia, who places the platter beside Ady on the lounge. "Everything you eat here is grown and tended to in Atherian soil. We have beet salad, bean soup—"

"And the best rhubarb wine you've ever tasted." Echo sets down the platter and pours a goblet of the blush wine for Ady.

"Well, I've never had rhubarb wine, so I'm certain this will be the best," says Ady. When she brings the glass to her lips, she's surprised by its tart flavor—the wine bubbles on her tongue.

"We also have a blend of herbs that we call Enchanted Tea. I picked each of these leaves myself for you. This tea has many healing properties. It calms the mind and heart," Gaia says.

"I would love to try it," Ady adds as the rhubarb wine settles down in her mouth.

Gaia pours from a white tea kettle, embossed with gold. The steeping tea streams out mystical hues of magenta, then violet, cyan, emerald green, and finally hues of gold. Ady's eyes widen at the cascading rainbow of colors.

"Rose, lavender, butterfly pea, mint, and lemongrass," Gaia explains.

They stand back as Ady samples from the platter. She's never seen so much food all for one person! The soup broth fills her nostrils, and the beet juice speckles her cheek when she cuts into the vegetable's raw middle. But she's never tasted such food, such flavor, or seen this variety of color on a plate.

"In the Citadel, we never ate like this," she says between swallows of food and tea. "We'd have alfalfa and potatoes, maybe the occasional squirrel."

Gaia and Echo smile softly.

"You'll find that we do things very differently in Atheria," Gaia says. "We choose not to take any living creature's life for any reason, not even for sustenance. Earth gives us what we need, and that is more than enough."

"And I think you'll agree that this is much better than squirrel," adds Echo.

Ady moves onto dessert, a cold bowl of sherbert topped with fruit. As she spoons the dish, she feels the watching eyes of Gaia and Echo standing over her.

"You can join me," Ady says, gesturing at her table's empty chairs.

Gaia and Echo nod in thanks perfectly in sync, and they both sit.

They tell their stories: both are Atherian natives. Echo was born four hundred years ago and raised by a family of merchants. Many years were spent devoted to the study of Atherian silks, harvesting the silk pods, and sewing the most beautiful mantles and vestments to sell. Gaia is over five hundred years old and was raised by tea-makers, the finest herbalists on the islands. With one touch, Gaia can restore life to a plant or coax a tree to bloom before its time. Athos recruited them both for the palace when he arrived in Atheria. He said they would be needed when the anointed ones arrived and that they would be guides and friends. Now, Gaia grows and maintains the palace's flower and tea gardens. Echo created and crafted all of Ady's Atherian dresses in her wardrobe, she's the best designer in all of Atheria.

"Each piece takes a good month," Echo says, clearly proud.

"So..." Ady looks back and forth between Echo and Gaia, Gaia and Echo. Neither looks a day older than thirty. Their skin is taut and unlined. "You're both...hundreds of years old?"

They smile in tandem.

"Athos hasn't told you much about this place yet, has he?" laughs Echo.

Ady shakes her head.

Gaia extends a hand, and Ady takes it, marveling at the Atherian's soft skin.

"Then let's show you some of Atheria," says Gaia.

"Athos did say to meet him in the Crystal Hall," Ady says, standing.

The Atherians are both already moving toward the door. She follows.

Night has fallen over the palace. The moon shines pearly and clean through the glass shafts outside her door.

"This way," says Gaia, who leads them through the round central atrium, lit by sconces, and toward a western corridor. Gaia's tall physique towers over Ady, but she can still make out the shimmering marble on the floor before her. Flecks of mica catch the moonlight and send tiny shimmers along the far wall.

"The grounds are to your right," Echo nods to the arched windows that line the corridor. "You can find Gaia there almost *always*."

Ady looks right. Shafts of moonlight illume the soft rolling lawn of the grounds.

The sound of metal hitting metal catches her attention, and she pauses in the hallway as the Atherians continue. Ady moves to the nearest opening and places her hand on the stone. Steps below, on the grounds, she sees two figures fighting. One is as tall as Gaia and Echo, but more muscular, an Atherian. His long white hair is not braided but flows as the figure moves. The other is shorter and lithe, human, but just as strong as his opponent. His hair is dark brown, Ady can see this from here. Both hold bo staffs and wield them expertly. She has never seen weapons like this. When she watched Eagan and the others practice on the Redcoats training ground, she marveled at how they collided sword with sword or commanded the falcons with a single move of an arm. These two fight close, they fight nimbly. But there's also no sense of aggression. As Ady watches, she sees the human man halt and, as if sensing her gaze, meet her eye. The Atherian stops, too, letting the staff rest on the ground, and there is a brief exchange between them that she cannot make out. Like a lesson. Just as quickly, the bo staffs are raised again.

Laughter from the down the hall awakens Ady from her trance.

"Come now, Miss Adylyn," says Gaia. "There'll be time for that later."

Ady hurries to catch up, her feet pounding the stone walk. As she nears them, she can just hear the softest tête-à-tête in a language she's never heard before. Gaia and Echo lean close to each other, but they pull apart as she joins them again.

"We're here," says Echo. "This is where we leave you, Miss Adylyn. But we'll see you again."

Echo places a slender hand on Ady's shoulder. Then, they turn and retreat the way they came.

Ady looks ahead now. A few paces away, Athos stands in the passage.

"I like them," she says as she nears Athos.

He smiles in response. "I thought they would help you tremendously along this journey. True Atherians to help you understand this way of life."

Athos then leads her deeper down the passage before he stops at two metal doors.

THE CRYSTAL HALL

Ady runs her hands along the doors. They are closed and forged with bronzed brass, embossed with intricate markings.

"These doors look so familiar," she says. "I feel like I've seen these carvings before."

That familiar feeling, an unknowing knowing. She's encountered this braid, this ornate knot and crest. Sometimes she sees things—or recognizes them from some deep recess of memory. She's encountered these markings in dreams. Hasn't she? Are they stitched in the tunics she's always wearing in the cavern within the water, or are they hidden shadows on the wall? Has she dreamed of being here, walking through this very doorway? It's that still, calm feeling she used to know in the garden when the world changed shapes before her eyes.

As quickly as the feeling tingles the hair on her neck, it vanishes. And Athos opens the door.

Inside, the room is round, encircled by twelve stone pillars like a small temple. The floor is the same symmetric stone, but there is a pattern, too—like ivy plaited in a great garland wreath. Moonlight cuts through arched windows and catches the divots on large, bright, and beautiful stones inset in each of the pillars.

"This is the most sacred space in all of Atheria," Athos says. "This room houses the foundational stones of the New Earth. The Nobles have protected them for centuries."

Ady moves forward and places one hand on the first pillar. The moment she touches it, feels the cold on her fingertips, she knows: these stones are ancient.

"How long have you been here?" Ady asks, almost in a whisper.

"A few years. Two in our time, sixteen in Atherian time," Athos answers.

Ady looks at him, bewildered. "What do you mean?"

"Time here moves at a different pace. The Nobles you met upon the airship dock are some of the oldest in Atheria. Some are 800 years old."

"How...?"

"Atheria is other-worldly. It has always been a hidden place," Athos says, striding into the center of the room. He looks so scholarly in his dark robes, and he commands the space like a Speaker about to lecture. "It was created in the way humans were meant to live. And it has been part of this dimension to look over humanity: preserve the Earth from absolute destruction. Atheria was to remain hidden here until the time came for this place to be revealed. And the time has come. The Old World has nearly destroyed itself, and humanity was almost lost completely."

The Great War, Ady thinks, and she remembers the many hours of lectures she'd endured in the Citadel. They learned how war was like one lit match in a room of dry wood. One bomb, one attack, one well-timed assassination, and suddenly the whole world turned on itself. Brothers killed brothers. Whole cities dissolved like dust. Millions of lives were snuffed out like a blown candle.

"We've been preparing and waiting for you."

He speaks effortlessly, as though he has prepared to speak these words for some time.

She stares at him quietly, waiting for him to go on.

"Mother came to me those years ago. Delivered to me the book, my quest, and the way to Atheria. I escaped the Citadel safely because of her."

"Mother came to you? How? Athos, she is dead." Ady feels the tears well in her eyes; how could he speak like this?

"She is alive, Ady. Within you and me."

"I don't understand. And if so, why wouldn't she have come to me too?"

"You were to bear witness to the corruption of this world firsthand. To the destruction that humanity faces, so that *you* may be the voice of the people," Athos pauses. "I was sent here to prepare in guiding you on this journey. You and others."

"Why haven't you come for me until now?"

"It was so unbearable to know your life has been at risk every minute. You had to personally experience the Republic and their tyranny. Only then would you have the tools to overthrow them." Athos walks up to her. "You, Ady, are part of a divine plan instated before your birth. Since before the Republic or the Great War. Mankind has destroyed itself like never before in history. The Council of Light has deemed it necessary to step in and restore what remains with the help of the chosen. Together, with other anointed ones, you are called to eradicate the dark forces from this world. With you wielding this mission into place, you are chosen to be the spark that ignites this plan."

Ady blinks and opens her mouth to speak. But what is there to say?

She turns slowly about the room, taking in the different stones—jasper and beryl, emerald and sapphire. And for a brief moment, she wants nothing more than her bunk in the dorm, books smuggled beneath her cot, undrunk barley tea, and a milk saucer by the window sill, the sights and smells and familiar cinderblock walls that previously made up her life. Those days feel so foreign now: how she explored forgotten rooms, how Eagan entered silently through her window, how he kissed her beneath the stars. All gone in the fire. Now here is her brother, telling her she is to initiate a divine mission.

Wake up, Ady tells herself, biting her lip so hard she almost bleeds. *Wake up, wake up.*

"Ady," Athos says slowly. He looks at her with such solemnity that she takes an instinctive step back. "I know this is a lot to take in. I'm trying to explain it all clearly. Forgive me if I get ahead of myself. But in this plane, time is not on our side. What may seem like months or even years to us here in Atheria is but days to the outside world. We must prepare you for what is coming."

Ady's head pounds with nauseating exhaustion. She rested all afternoon, but the hours here seem long and languid as shadows. Athos is looking at her with such earnestness that she thinks she might cry.

"What if I don't want to do this?" she says, willing her voice to sound brave. Instead, it comes out like a small croak.

Athos nods. "Then, I pray that you'll change your mind." "I didn't ask for any of this." Her tone sharpens, and his shoulders straighten in shock. "I didn't ask to be brought here. For my loved ones to be left to die."

"That shouldn't have happened—"

The moment she mentions them, her handle on the moment slips, and she slides to the floor beside a stone pillar. The tears burn in her eyes as she imagines the flames on her skin, a sword thrust through Eagan's bones. None of this had to happen! She wanted to die beside Eagan if that was his fate. "But it did happen," she gasps. "Edgar forced me here, against my will, and we left Eagan and my friends to die in the Citadel. I did not ask for this."

Athos is silent for a long moment. When he speaks again, he kneels before her.

"Here, we wouldn't force you to do anything. It's your soul's free will," he says, and it's clear he chooses his words as tenderly as plucking berries. "The Council of Light chose you. The choice to accept *is yours*. But Ady—the Republic would have killed you had Edgar not brought you here. They know about the book, and now they know about you too. They want nothing more than to see you dead and to have that book for themselves. It's too powerful. It holds all the secrets of the universe."

She looks into his eyes now, so close, so familiar.

"How do you know it's me?" she whispers.

"The Book of Light. It provides its reader exactly what they need to know—and you are called out by name. That part I have read. You are prophesied to be able to read it. All of it."

"I can't read anything. There's nothing there," Ady proclaims.

"You will as your power and belief in yourself grows." Athos pauses. "The book is meant to guide you along this path. It outlines innate details directly from the Council of Light. You won't be doing this alone, other anointed ones will join you along the way. If they shall will it too."

Ady can't help but process in silence. A million questions race through her head, but all she can muster is, "And the carvings on the front, what are they? What do they mean?"

"They are the codes of creation."

Athos leads Ady back to her room in silence. He chastises himself with every step down the moonlit hallways: had he approached the conversation too quickly? Should he have waited before telling her about this divine quest, the sacredness of the book, and her hopeful fate in Atheria? Beside him, she looks wan as a ghost, here but not fully. She says nothing as she enters her chambers and shuts the door solidly behind her.

She has been gone but a moment when a shape appears beside Athos. Rylan of the Nobles.

Rylan is older than most of the trees on the island, with skin like bark. The Noble walks beside Athos, back to the central atrium, striding almost too close for comfort.

"The unveiling?" Rylan says. "How did it go?"

"She's handling it." Athos keeps his voice measured, betraying little emotion. He has mastered this Atherian quality over time. "She needs time."

"And that is a commodity we don't have," Rylan insists, and Athos can feel those blue eyes burrowing into him. "Does she know of the unlocking of the gateway?"

"Not yet," Athos says. "But she will."

INTO THE WATER

Back in her chambers, Ady goes immediately to draw a bath. The wide marble tub sits behind a partition off the main room. It's time to wash this day—these eight days—from her skin. She turns the gold handles as steaming water cascades like a tiny waterfall into the basin. A glass vial of steeped tea leaves sits on the ledge of the tub. Gaia informed her that the Enchanted Tea could also be poured into her baths, that it would provide strength, vitality, and healing. Ady now pours some into the tub. The same rainbow hues of colors emanate along the stream of water. She has never bathed like this: at the Citadel, there were coarse cloths for towels. There was well-water heated in great cauldrons, then passed assembly-line style in wooden buckets. They stood in lines outside the mess hall for the weekly cleansing, which offered barely enough to wet her head, let alone rinse her entire body.

Steam beads on her face. She unbuttons her clothes and leaves them in a dark puddle on the floor. Her body is still riddled with bruises, purple and green; the burn marks along her arms are still painful, scabbing over. When the water is el-bow-deep, she slips into the bath and sees other crystal vessels along the rim, oils of rosehip, lavender, and field flowers. The water takes her like an embrace, and she settles against the marble tub that fits the arch of her back like it was made for her.

I didn't ask for any of this.

Her own words come back, and she winces at the memory of Athos' pained expression. But it's true: that night in the Citadel haunts her, the way she dug her heels into the dirt, the way her strength was not great enough. She had never asked to be brought here, no matter how beautiful a room they gave her.

And yet, hadn't she always dreamed of a life beyond the Citadel? Unlike Grenn, Ady had never yearned for a couples' dormitory. She never wanted to rise in the Republic's ranks. Something had always burned in her. It seemed she'd always known there was something beyond the desert fortress. She'd imagined, perhaps, that some faraway city had survived the Great War, that more survivors lived differently, peacefully. But she had not anticipated this. And what was it Athos had said? That Atheria was a hidden place, intended to watch over humanity and preserve it from destruction? Well, if that was true, hadn't they surely failed?

She looks at her arms; the bruises and scrapes fade as trickles of Gaia's tea glide along her skin. She turns her hands and arms slowly, watching the magic properties heal her wounds. Her burns, no longer painful, slowly vanish. Her eyes widen as she feels her body calm for the first time in days.

Ady leans back and lifts one foot from the water, resting her heel on the spigot.

The dream comes swiftly.

The water rises. She is in the cavern again; she knows by the smell. She is wet and cold, deeper in than ever before. The tapering rock walls feel far away. She can hear the distant echo of water meeting stone. She wades forward, and the water-heavy tunic clings to her knees, dragging behind her like a veil. Something is beckoning her forward, drawing her deeper. Her feet venture into a cold patch of water, but she does not slip on the smooth stone. She only walks forward—the light flares behind her, brighter than stars—she keeps walking until the cool surface reaches her hipbone— and she has the distinct feeling of suffocation, that the walls will crush around her, that her bones will break and no one will hear, no one will come—she will drown here alone. Is this what death is like? A slow fading into the darkness—or a Raider's blade among flames? Then a voice whispers through the cavern. It is soft and feminine and familiar. She knows it from somewhere. "I am with you, Adylyn."

And then she sputters awake. The faucet is running again, and the tub almost overflows. Ady gushes from the tub and coughs water from her lungs. She'd been fully underwater, floating and asleep! Had her foot slipped to turn the faucet? She drains the tub, sitting still in the marble until every last ounce has slipped away in its tiny whirlpool. She rocks in the empty basin, naked as the water evaporates from her skin, and she whispers, "Eagan...Eagan..."

DEATH VALLEY

The world is all black and still—and then, a voice. "Eagan...Eagan..."

He awakes to the sound of Ady. He knows every pitch and timbre of her, and this is a plea. Is she hurt? Is she frightened? Is she calling for him, or is he dreaming? Eagan blinks in the dimness and winces as pain shoots through his left eye. There is a trickle of wetness on his temple. Blood? He tries to move his arms but finds that his hands are tied behind his back.

The scene takes shape. They are in a cave of some sort. Sunlight gleams through the opening some yards away. Ahead, two Skyraider ships are grounded, their black sails limp in the dry air. It comes back to him quickly: the way they appeared like birds of prey on the horizon. His men were ground fighters, not airmen. They were swordsmen, runners, archers, trained on the rampart walls. They could not fight like this—though try they did! The fire, the rush to find cannons aboard the Republic's stolen fleet, the terror of watching the earth get closer as they descended. They were downed within minutes. The Ravens attached ropes to their wooden hulls. They commandeered their ships and brought them to the ground.

Eagan looks around, frantic now. Tiri, he sees, is tied to his left, his arms around a wooden stake in the ground. Ito lays to his right. Other survivors of the Brutallion are clustered among them.

"I was starting to get worried," Tiri says, but his voice is no louder than a gruff whisper. He doesn't move. He stares at his boots, still as a stone. "You've been out for hours."

"Where are we?" Eagan whispers.

"One of the Ravens' camps on the outskirts," Tiri says. "It sounds like they'll take us to their main basecamp."

Perhaps it's just the darkness, but he could swear that Tiri seems not fully there. His eyes are glazed over.

Eagan hears the Raiders now: that wild cackling laughter in the distance. And he can smell their smoked meats. But what is there to eat out here in the Wasteland? Rattlesnakes? Vultures? Eagan peers toward the cave entrance and makes out shapes of men milling around. Human bones hang from the entrance, where they dangle like wind chimes. There are tents and stands, piles of scrap metal and parts—like a great desert marketplace hidden in the cliffs. There is also the smell of coal and the distinct chiseling of a blacksmith forge. Somewhere, someone is making weapons.

The closer voices come from the grounded ship. Eagan smiles, noticing a deep gash along the hull of the Ravens' aircraft. His men had done that at least. Some of the Raiders now knelt upon the deck and seemed to be patching it, lowering buckets of tar and scrap wood to workers harnessed below.

"Where's Grenn?" Eagan whispers.

But before Tiri can answer, an inhuman sound pierces the cavern, like a raven cawing. Eagan flinches and instinctively tries to reach for his sword, but the rope burns into his wrists. A man strides toward them from the ship. The light from the cave entrance illuminates one side of his face. He looks scarred and half-bald, with a few thick dreads of hair sprouting like wild plants.

"You're awake," the man says, cocking his head at Eagan.

The captain from the air battle. He recognizes him immediately, the way he stood at the bridge and watched the unfolding fight. Eagan says nothing.

"Little traitorous scum. And foolish! You know the Republic has a bounty out on your heads? All of you. But that's good news for Corvis." He pats his own chest. "Doköran will be pleased."

Eagan can smell him even from feet away, as if he carries the carcass of a dead animal beneath his coat. Corvis straightens and then cocks his head like a bird, toward the cave entrance, as though listening for some faint sound in the wind.

"We've done nothing wrong," Eagan says, but even that sounds flat. He can feel the weight of all his men's eyes on him. He has led them here: away from one prison and into another.

"Stolen ships?" Corvis practically spits at Eagan. "Invading our airspace? You fly over the Wasteland, you meet the strength of the Rebellion. The Ravens." With the heel of his boot, he kicks a billow of dust toward the men. "But you've damaged my ship. Pity. I like that ship. That's why your men will help fix it. But not you. No, you will sit here and watch. You will see them work and sweat and hunger. *Captain.*"

It takes all his strength not to shout a retort—these are *his* men, they are good men, they have done nothing to deserve this. But he knows it will only bring another blow to the skull. He blinks at the dust in his eyes and stares at the ground.

"And you..." Corvis kneels before Tiri and smiles, showing his long and jagged yellow teeth. "You must be Tiri. That little blonde one was yours, wasn't she? She kept calling for you. Over...and over."

"Don't you lay a hand on her!" Tiri strains at the ropes. The veins in his forehead become visible ridges.

"Oh," Corvis laughs that raven's caw again and stands. "I've done much more than that. She's a real find for us out here—we don't usually get fresh ones. I could get a nice bargain for that skinny little thing. Real silver, perhaps. Or a year's supply of meat." He narrows his eyes at Tiri and smiles again. "But I think I'll keep her for myself."

More of the Ravens approach from the ship. Pipes and axes and hacksaws swing from their waist-belts. They have the same warpaint smeared across their cheeks that Eagan saw in the Citadel. Others wear bones strung around their necks. One wears a dried-out tongue. Still another has a shrunken head, shriveled and pinned to his waist pouch. They cut the ropes on several of the men's wrists, nicking some who cry out in pain. Eagan notices Ivan among one of the freed. He stands small and shivering beside the others, pale in the dark.

"Just a few of them," says Corvis, one hand raised. Then to Tiri he says: "They make one wrong move, she's dead."

GRIDLINES

The morning dawns bright and blue. Ady awakens at first light, as the golden sun rays reflect across her chambers.

She rolls from her bed and dresses quickly in a cloud-white robe from the wardrobe. Echo's handiwork shows in the intricate stitching along the hem.

All night, Ady's dreams were fitful. But there was always water. In one, the well in the Citadel had dried up, and the people dug through the dirt, desperate for groundwater—anything. In another, the vast deserts they traversed aboard the Aurora were rollicking with waves. Vessels struggled to stay afloat during a storm surge. Then there was always the cavern, the water rising up to her thigh.

She needs to get out of this room. She needs air. It's time to explore Atheria for herself.

There is no sign of Athos or Edgar in the central atrium or the main hall, not even Gaia or Echo or any of the Nobles. *Do they sleep?* she wonders. Do Atherians even need sleep? She can almost imagine Gaia standing in the grounds all night, like a tree waiting for the sun to return. Or Echo, resting by the stone statues, still and cool and beautiful as one of them. The palace is so still that Ady's footsteps ring with every step on the marble. She reaches the large wooden doors undisturbed and steps onto the grand staircase. She takes a deep breath.

Athos said she was anointed. That there would be others. She'd only seen the word 'anointed' once—in a Citadel forgotten room. This one was smaller than the others, more like a closet than anything else. There were small wooden benches, mostly rotted, and she stepped over kneeling pads and strewn books, their pages thinner than any book she'd ever seen. She knew this room was more forbidden than the rest because it was one of the few that had not been ransacked by the Republic, only boarded up—not even used for storage. The faded nameplate by the door said Chapel. It was as if whatever happened here, whatever purpose this room served, that even the Republic feared it.

Outside, the sun emanates white light, the sky a brilliant crystal blue. The only sound is birdsong, the competing chirps and chimes of birds in the towering trees. She descends the steps one by one as the sun glares off the marble. With each step, she tries to imagine the Council of Light—whatever that means. How can light—like this very warmth on her skin—have power? She thinks of the tiny flint and the wax candle she used to carry into the forgotten room expeditions, how that one tiny flame could illuminate a buried world.

Now, *this* world! With colors more vibrant than she knew could ever exist, with this air like silk on her skin, and the soft morning music of birds and wind through the trees! Ahead, the Aurora's balloon floats languidly over the treeline, and she wonders if the crew is still aboard, waiting. The docks are just ahead, and she doesn't want to be seen, so Ady turns off the path and into the woods. A small path weaves between the trunks.

Sunlight beams through the boughs. Light seems to hide behind every leaf, making the forest glimmer, as though lit by some internal fire. She's read about trees like this—oak and pine and red cedar—and seen a few images that survived in books. But it's the smell she loves: grass and birch bark. And the way the birds flit overhead from branch to branch. Most of all, what catches her eye are the orbs of light that float among the branches like cupped stars.

Ady halts as a pack of deer dart through the woods just ahead. They are does with cinnamon-brown spots. A small fawn trickles behind them, her legs flimsy as twigs. Ady smiles after them, wishing they'd come back so she could embrace the baby deer. Most animals around the Citadel were long hunted for pelts and meat; the ones that remained had left for the dunes and high ground. They knew to fear people. The only animals she remembered seeing from her dorm window were the occasional basking snake or the stray cat that would visit her. But these deer seem so unafraid—they ran right by her! Gaia and Echo said that Atherians harm no creature, that the earth gives enough.

Ady smiles as she continues through the woods, toward the sound of rushing water. What would Commander Cayhill think of this place? Would the Republic want to control somewhere like Atheria, or would they simply feel wonder at the reality of floating islands and the way time seems slow, not like the steady unwinding of thread back home? The one thing she wishes, thinking back to everything her brother said last night, is that these so-called protectors of humanity had intervened before now. Why let the world descend to ruin during the Great War? Why sit back and let so many perish? If the War had never happened, there would have been no Republic, no Rebellion in the Wasteland, no cruel control in the Citadels.

The woods are thinning, the trees more sparse as she steps off the path. The water sounds are louder now, the distinct sound of waves she recognizes from arriving on the Aurora. Ady pushes back the last bough and steps upon an opening with the greatest vantage point. It's a cliff of worn silver stones, each longer than she is tall. The ledge slopes down to a creamy white beach, the edge of the island. Far below them, the ocean laps and sways, catching the morning light in glimmering streaks across its surface. Ady walks to the far edge of the cliff, and can just make out the prismatic colors of an Atherian waterfall to her left. The foam descends to the ocean, where the cascade disappears into the blue.

She sits on the largest stone and pulls her knees to her chest. She lets the soothing cadence of the water wash over her. And when she closes her eyes, it's as though all the life force in Atheria surrounds her—she can feel it. Something is around and through her, like the very wind that lifts her hair is really kissing her neck, that the very rays of the sun are holding her in some intimate embrace, encircling her waist. Her skin tingles as though she's cold. Instead, there is a warmth, warmer than the furs on the Aurora, warmer than the hottest desert night, and it moves through her arms, up her spine, into her heart. She can feel a warmth trickling through her chest. Ady opens her eyes. The water is still there. The other islands in the distance still float like gentle ships in the air. A shadow catches her attention, and she looks up to see the hawk flying overhead, closer this time. She knows this hawk without question. Is he following her? Beyond him, she notices the faintest glimmer of what looks like stardust, silver and shimmering, against the morning sky, lined in perfectly placed patterns across the sky.

The day is cloudless. But this light does not come from the sun in the east. The glimmer arcs across the entire sky, long lines that start in the ocean and cross over the islands. Intersecting with another—and another—a whole gridline of the softest silver, almost like a patchwork constellation. Like a blueprint for the world.

ATRIEL

Ady continues her journey through Atheria, further into the forest. The colors are more vibrant the deeper she roams between the trees. The orbs flicker through and among the boughs, faint in the morning light, and she feels such peace in their presence. Even though she is alone, there is a constant source of something or someone close to her. It surrounds her. Her intuition drives her deeper into the forest like a calling.

She takes in the scent of wildflowers, the freshness of the soil, and the wood's richness from the immense trees she passes. The leaves move in the warm breeze as the sun glimmers through the branches as if the trees whisper to her. The flowers meet her waist as she runs her hands atop of them. Deeper she goes.

In the distance, there is movement, the sound of bodies on the forest floor. The birds stop their morning song. Ady slows. Through a small opening in the trees, she can just make out the soft grass of a meadow—and the scuffle between a man and a wolf. She has never seen a wolf in person but recognizes it from fables: the grizzly snout and the tufty gray fur on the timber's back. Ady looks around, frantic for a tree limb, a stone, anything to help fend off this predator. Why hadn't Athos warned her there were wild beasts in Atheria?

But then she hears laughter. The man's voice is low and sweet. Ady steps closer, nearing the edge of the tree line, and watches as the man wrestles the wolf to the ground like it's a small stray dog. *Peculiar*, she thinks, as she watches in awe.

A twig behind her snaps and she jolts around. Another wolf, pure white, stands before her, not a meter away. Her eyes are blue and clear as glass. Ady takes a slow step back, but the wolf's gaze does not break. She steps back again and breathes deeply, her eyes still meeting the wolf's.

"Don't be afraid."

The man's voice comes from behind her, a whisper into her ear. His breath is hot against her cheek. Ady flinches but doesn't take her eyes off the wolf, which is almost near enough to touch. Her whiskers look delicate as thread in the morning light.

"Why not?" Ady asks, taking a breath, her voice a whisper back.

"She is an Archlight, your Archlight," he says calmly. He is warm and tall standing behind her, his shadow casts into the trees. "Her name is—"

"Shiloh," Ady says faintly. And suddenly, the wolf seems familiar, as if from a dream or a memory, as if Ady has stood here in these woods before, has reached out to touch the wolf's snow-dusted head before. She has stared into those eyes, has felt that gentle nuzzle against her cheek. She knows her name—it's as if the wolf tells her directly in husky sweet thoughts. "It's Shiloh."

The wolf perks at the mention of her name and noses up to Ady's outstretched palm. Her white tail swings behind. Ady stares at the gentle beast, breathing deeply. At last, she turns to the man behind her. He is tall and broad. His hair is dark as the trees, and there's the faintest shadow along his sharp jawline. She recognizes him instantly as the man she saw fighting with the bo staff last night.

"My name is Atriel," he says with a soft smirk.

"Ady." She smiles and feels her cheeks redden.

"I know who you are."

He's looking at her intently—too intently. That unbroken gaze of familiarity. Eagan used to look at her like that when he told her she was his North Star. Ady drops her gaze and returns to Shiloh.

"How is this possible, these wolves? How can I hear her?"

"They're spiritual messengers and protectors sent from the Council of Light," Atriel says.

Shiloh jumps up now, and the weight of her forepaws on Ady's shoulders almost sends her careening backward.

"What do you mean, messengers?"

"They can relay messages sent to you from the heavens. They're multi-dimensional. That's why you can hear her thoughts. She can hear yours. And she will also always protect you. At all costs."

The other timber wolf approaches them and burrows into Atriel's side. "And this is Skylar." He rubs the wolf's head gruffly. "My Archlight."

"It's nice to meet you, Skylar." She holds her hand out for the wolf to lick with his papery tongue. "All of you," she says to Atriel.

He studies her for a long moment. At last, he says simply, "Would you like to see more of Atheria?"

Ady nods—exploring is what she does best.

They walk along the pathway, deeper into the woods as Shiloh and Skylar trail them close behind. The sun has nearly cleared the treetops now, but the air is still cool. The breeze is soft as feathers. Ady can't help but watch the light orbs dip along the trees like small fireflies.

"What are those?" she asks lightly.

"There's so much energy in Atheria that they conjoin and make those spheres of light. It's beautiful at night. They just shine."

Ady tries to not stare, but from the corner of her eye, she can see his sharp chin and jawline. "What are you doing here in Atheria? I haven't seen any other humans besides my brother."

"I'm here the way you are," he says calmly. "Anointed."

She glances at him, unable to tell if he is being facetious or not.

"I have been studying with the Nobles and Athos. Training in combat as well."

"I think I saw you fighting the other night."

"Yes, with Thelios, my mentor. He is the leader of the Atherian army. They fight with the mind. Although they are also highly trained in other ways as well. He is teaching me their ways. They are preparing to protect Atheria against the largest war mankind has ever seen."

Ady's eyes drop down to the ground, processing what he might mean.

"He's much taller than you. Are all Atherians taller than us?" Ady asks, attempting to bring the mood back up.

"Not all Atherians. The Nobles are the oldest in Atheria. And the elderly tend to shrink," Atriel smiles.

They walk in silence for a few minutes. But even as Ady keeps her gaze on the path ahead, as they wind deeper into what appears to be a valley along the shoreline, Atriel keeps casting her side glances. They are quick and shy but noticeable. She longs to demand, "*What?*" Or to have him explain the way he seemed almost embarrassed to admit, "I know who you are." Did everyone know about this calling but her? Shiloh must sense her growing agitation because the wolf moves to walk parallel beside her. Ady keeps one hand gently atop the creature's head, her fingers buried in the silken fur.

She can hear their destination before she sees it. The drumming of water gets louder with every step. The path opens to reveal a clear ravine of water, filled by a melodious waterfall. The crashing rapids are white and lavender from where they stand on the rocks, and the sound is almost musical. The rest of the pool ripples gently, as though a million stones skid across the surface every moment.

"I love this spot," Atriel says as the wolves lower to the water and lap. "Sometimes, we swim here in the evenings before dark."

Ady stares at the blue and can't help but think of Grenn the last time they studied in the library. She sat there with her map of the Old World. She picked up a blue pastel and shaded in where the water used to be. Grenn would have loved this—these colors, the ability to freely submerge in clean water.

"It's beautiful," she sighs.

Atriel lowers to a stump and runs his hand along the reeds that rise from the shallows.

"Listen, I'm sorry about your Citadel," he says at last. "That's the hardest thing to see."

Ady starts at the mention of her home. She can only nod: "Yes, thank you."

He does not look up from the reeds when he says, "Mine fell a few months back, in Old World time. The North West."

Ady watches the way he mindlessly picks at the stems and lets them float away down the pond. Is he, too, thinking of someone he lost in his Citadel's collapse? Parents, a brother, a love? She kneels to the soft dirt and burrows her face in Shiloh's mane. The wolf smells so sweet, like ripe fruit and dewy flowers. She thinks of those she has lost.

"The Rebellion will pay for what they've done," she says.

Atriel grimaces. "But it's not the Rebellion who's to blame."

ELLINGTON FLIES

Ellington stands on the bridge of the airship and feels the wind, cool along the back of his neck. He has been on an airship only once before, with his father, on an early scouting trip to one of the decimated Old World cities. Los Angeles. Ellington couldn't have been more than eleven or twelve when they flew over the gray and ravaged buildings, still covered in a sheen of ashy dust. Large vehicles were stopped in the street, frozen in time. Everywhere: glass and debris, bones and caved-in houses. When they landed, his father led him into an abandoned market, mostly picked over, where they scavenged for canned fruit and beans.

Now, he flies again. This time, to the Wasteland. He can already see the craggy hills taking shape in the distance: the rocky dunes that hide the Rebellion's camp. Doköran will be waiting.

Commander Cayhill was the one who sent him, but Ellington would have volunteered regardless. The conversation was swift, one-sided. The Raiders of the Rebellion had captured Eagan and the other traitors. Cayhill wanted them back. All of them, alive.

"We can't have the people thinking that you can defy the Republic, steal our airships, and seek refuge among the Rebels," spat Cayhill at his desk.

But there was more he didn't say. His eyes betrayed him. They were red-rimmed from lack of sleep, and he could hardly keep his gaze on Ellington. He didn't say what they all knew: that Doköran might kill him if he returned to the Wasteland again. Rumors trickled through the guard of how Doköran had murdered one of his own in front of Cayhill, just to show he could. Now, the Chancellor was here within the walls—now, the Republic needed to show its strength.

"I trust you can retrieve them. They are, after all, your men," said Cayhill.

If he suspected Ellington had helped Tiri and Grenn escape from the officials' barracks, the Commander did not let on. He only fidgeted with the quill on his desk, distracted. His mind was clearly leaps and bounds away from the Lower West Citadel.

Ellington stared at this man for a long moment, studied the wrinkles in his face like lines on a map. It took every ounce of strength not to shout, not to demand answers, not to betray his hatred. Instead, he folded his hands behind his back. He nodded. And he said, "I will do what needs to be done."

"We're nearing the settlement!" the navigator calls from the helm. Ellington nods in the man's direction. He has the distinct and sinking feeling that something dreadful awaits him in the Wasteland, at this rendezvous. That perhaps the men are already killed, their heads severed and staked on great poles in the desert. That this is all a trap—or worse, a way for Cayhill to get rid of him.

But perhaps it's not. Perhaps his men just need him, their Captain, to find them.

The airship begins its descent. The wind warms, the sails catch a new current, and Doköran's settlement comes into view.

HALL OF KNOWLEDGE

Days pass, and soon, the palace in Atheria seems less empty. The Nobles no longer hide away in their chambers. They are present in the grand hall. They are seen roaming through the corridors, scrolls tucked under their arms as their deep blue robes flutter behind them. Sometimes, Ady awakes in the morning to the sounds echoing from within the gardens: Atriel training with his bo staff, practicing his grounded block and hook kicks. She'll sit along the steps of the garden, noticing how the sweat beads on his shoulder blades, until he must sense her eyes on him and stop. She averts her eyes to the pages of a book she brought.

Something seems to have awoken in Atheria.

On a particularly sunny day, a note from Athos arrives on her breakfast tray. *Meet me in the Hall of Knowledge at mid-day.*

By now, Ady knows her way around the palace. After dressing in one of the simple silks in her wardrobe, maroon with silver embroidery, she ventures into the central atrium and down the east fanning corridor. She passes a statue, upon which a stone angel holds a closed book, its colossal wings outstretched. Another angel holds a sword etched with symbols along its blade. Athos stands waiting for her outside the Hall. He wears his same blue robes like the Nobles, like a daily uniform.

"Good morning, sister," he says and opens the rounded wood doors for her.

She can almost smell it before they enter: old books and parchment. A library. And nothing like the old library in the Citadel, with the books all re-covered in dusky blue. These books are from floor to ceiling and are in every color of binding, different thickness and height. There are not just books, but there are scrolls with copper handles, loose parchment in smooth stacks. And between the books, there is an array of curios: a tiny globe, clocks, glass vials filled with clear liquid containing colorful prisms that float within them. Deep rich hunter green curtains cascade from the arched windows, through which light welcomes them. Brass spiral staircases with wooden railings rise toward the ceiling, at least three stories high— where Ady notices more paintings of angels. Here, it seems these angels carry swords, like leading into a battle. The swords emanate light, like a lightning bolt from the shiny metal. Their eyes are gentle but piercing as she follows this story along the ceiling. A brass telescope sits propped near the window desks, its eyepiece poised to the heavens.

Ady gasps with delight. No more forgotten rooms and scavenging for any book she can find! Here, there are more words than she could read in many lifetimes.

"The Atherian Nobles have been curating this collection for centuries. For longer than centuries," says Athos, striding in behind her. "It houses works from every major library in history. It also houses the wisdom for the New Earth."

Ady walks to the nearest case and runs a hand across the scarlet bindings. The words are raised in thick, metallic paint, but she cannot make out the language. It must be Atherian.

"Back home, in the Citadel, we only had a few books from the Old World," she says. "That, and the Republic prints. Which wasn't much."

"I remember. Here, you have everything," Athos moves to stand beside her. "Let's see, we have religious texts from around the world, the best and brightest scribes and sages. Some actually got their theories pretty close to reality, which is always nice to see. Then, down by the window, you have histories. Northeast Asia, South America, Central Africa, everything in recorded order. Which is a miracle, considering how many texts were destroyed in the war. A true loss. But here we have it all. The Nobles have spent their entire lives inscribing all of humanity's history. The good works—and the dark ones."

Here, he nods to the farthest shelf from them. Glass encases the rows, sealed with a gold padlock. From here, she can only make out the shapes of a few ominous tar-pitch scrolls.

"What's over there?"

"We'll get to that. But I don't want to tell you. I want you to see it for yourself." Athos smiles, a grin so large that, if not for his thick beard, he'd look like himself again, as a child for a minute. Not the serious scholar he's become, but the playful and wild one. "Ady," he says, almost breathless. "You see things sometimes, don't you? Things that other people don't see?"

Ady freezes. She looks back to the books and moves her hand down to one sealed in hunter green. She remembers the water, the bath, how she coughed through the night.

"How did you know that?" she says at last.

"Because it's your gift. All the anointed ones are bestowed one. Yours are visions, aren't they? That's why you'll be able to see the words in the Book of Light." She can hear the excitement in his voice, but he tries to slow his pace. Her heart pounds. "Sometimes, maybe, your visions are a fleeting moment in the daylight. Other times, dreams that feel more real than life itself. Isn't that right, Ady?"

She nods softly.

"Come, I want to show you something."

Athos turns and walks to a long table, lined with velvet-backed chairs. The sunlight lands upon the maple wood, warming the surface. The table is inset with quill pens and ink vials, nested into the wood. Ady follows, but she watches Athos with some hesitation. She has not told anyone about the dreams or visions, only Eagan. And then, only some.

She sits across from him. Athos folds his hands and nods intently.

"It may not feel like it, but you can summon these visions. Conjure them at will. Not always and not all the time. But sometimes, the moments will come to you."

"How could I even do that?" She asks softly.

"Go ahead, try it," he says. "Close your eyes. It'll come to you."

Ady does, and he continues. "I've already told you about The Council of Light, how they have wielded their efforts to save humanity. They have intervened in the past, sending rain after famines, sending peace after war. Stopping a global flood. But there is another council, a dark one, that opposes them."

Ady taps her foot against the stone. She has never been able to summon the dreams on-command, not even in the Citadel garden, where visions appeared like grass in spring. And frankly, she's tired of others knowing about her life, her gifts, more than her—First Edgar, then Eagan, now Athos. Even Atriel, with his kind eyes, knew who she was while she had been kept in ignorance. The dreams are all that have been truly hers, a secret, sacred thing. But as her brother speaks, his voice a low lull, something flickers in her mind, as though a match was struck in the far distance.

The light widens and warms, spreads like fire on oil. Her body stiffens. The hairs on her arms stand high. She can feel every nerve taut and focused as images crystallize before her. Dark shadows are whispering evil thoughts into the ears of men in power, men at war: she sees villages burning, bodies disemboweled, she sees warriors cutting off a town's water supply, she sees longships and riders on horse-back with swords held high, she sees cannons and gas chambers, war-torn cities, ruins that once held life. Prisons brim with thousands of innocents while a man is tortured with tiny metal tools. Every image is quick, a slide, then onto the next. In every one, the shadows are there, orchestrating. She sees trees burn, ocean waves filled with debris. Dark liquid moves through the clear water. A woman screams in the night, alone, afraid—a whole people wait in the bunkers for the bombs to cease, then nothingness. Then, only the shadows. They are not human, they are something much more hellish. They drag upon the earth, collecting dust into their form, absorbing it. And suddenly, she knows who they are, she can feel it. The Erlick Federation. The moment the name comes to her, the shadows seem to turn, as though they can see with their black snake eyes into the Hall of Knowledge where Ady sits across from her brother.

The vision vanishes. Ady shoves away from the table, nearly knocking the chair from behind her.

"What—in the name of whatever is unholy—was that?" she pants, sweat beads across her face.

The room spins. The bookcases seem inverted, the windows are twirling, and the light makes her dizzy. She needs water, she needs to lie down. Athos is upon her just as she lowers to the stone floor.

"What did you see?" he demands, his hands on her shoulders.

Ady presses her palms to her eyes. "I saw them, what you said, I saw what they've done." The screams of children still echo in her mind. The tears come hot and quick.

For a long moment, Athos says nothing. He only sits beside her, his arm around her now. "Maybe we should have started with something else," he says at last. "I'm sorry. I can have Gaia bring us some rose water."

Ady breathes deeply and looks out at the room again. It is still and right.

"Has Atriel seen this, what I saw?" she whispers.

"Atriel's gifts are different from yours. Every anointed one has different gifts from the Council of Light. His is that of knowledge." Athos hesitates before asking, "Do you want to be done for today, Ady?"

But she cannot end the day with that—the shadows will follow her. She needs to rid them.

"No," she says. "I'll be fine."

"I think we should be done for now," Athos kneels as if to stand, but Ady stops him.

"No," she says more firmly. "Tell me more about the Council."

A look of both concern and pride crosses his face as he settles again. "Whatever you say, *anointed one*." She brightens at the soft playfulness in his voice. "Well, thousands of years ago, there was a great war in the heavens."

This time, she wants to see. Ady presses her hands into the cold stone, remembering the stone bench in the garden back home, the one place she loved. The hawk is there, and she is alone, and Athos' words come to life. The Council of Light, they are not human. Twenty four of them sit facing one another, in a great circle, like giant pillars themselves. In the center, clouds move beneath the stars, and the world is visible. She sees vibrant colors and pathways of gold brick, and the sky above is lavender. There is music from somewhere, and lighted figures, some with wings larger than birds. There is food, too, with smells she cannot place, and someone is making wine. Everything around her, every image, seems to glow with something burnished and bright. And then, there is chaos. Someone has interrupted a feast, the shadows from before have invaded the Council, and there is a war that is not like war, more like the sun fighting not to set across the stars. Then she sees the silver, shimmering gridlines in the night sky. Sees them shatter as the dark energy attaches to them. Two iron serpents emerge along the lines. They see her, watching with piercing red eyes. There is no bloodshed, not even pain. She sees many winged creatures approach, angelic and strong, driving the darkness into an abyss. Something tingles through Ady's body as she watches one of them lift a gold-hilted sword. He then kneels over a gateway, behind which the demons rage, plunging his sword straight down and locking it. Ancient letters line the bars, a sacred language.

She opens her eyes, still on the floor beside her brother as he finishes, "And they've been banished behind the Iron Gates ever since."

"But their energy still resides here?" Ady asks.

"Yes. Through the gridlines. They have embedded into our energy fields on Earth and have corrupted the consciousness of mankind. Not all, of course, but through those who are not aligned with the Light."

"The serpents...they saw me." She breathes heavily.

"They know you're awakening."

"Awakening?"

"They know the Council of Light has been preparing for this dark time, calling on mankind's help. The anointed ones."

Ady sits in silence, staring ahead. Memories flood back from her life, as a child in the Citadel, a young girl seeing things, feeling like the world was supposed to be different. When her mother was carted away to the medical ward that night, Ady knew, even then, that this was not how life is meant to be lived.

"So, the Council of Light won?"

"They did," says Athos. "But for every human life the Erlick Federation takes, their power grows, and the Iron Gates they are banned behind weaken. Since the Great War, the Federation has almost broken free. Now, their escape is imminent. Don't you see, Ady? They have been coordinating the destruction of mankind since they came to Earth's plane. They are behind everything. Every war, the Republic, the power it seeks, all of it. What happened to your friends during the raid. They feed on that, those demons. This is much larger than us against your Citadel or even the Republic. This is us against the dark powers of the universe."

THE ATHERIAN MARKET

A long the far side of the forest, the village sits tucked within the trees along the cliff's edge. Cottages speckle the forest, made of large stones and wooden roofs. The market brims with laughter and conversation as Atherians bustle around the cobblestone pathways. Atriel leads the way along the tents and bartering vendors. She is glad to have a new friend here, someone *anointed* who can show her the ropes of this wondrous place.

As they enter the market, Ady sees Atherians with long braided hair selling every kind of tincture she could imagine. The medicine woman in the Citadel would have gawked at their wares. Rosehip oil and lavender and sage! Ginseng, milk thistle, and crushed valerian root. There are sachets with perfumed and dried rose petals—and hand-threaded wraps practically straight from the silkworm. The smells are overwhelmingly beautiful, like flowers and the richness of tea leaves.

"The Atherians live off the land," Atriel says as they walk. "They believe every plant provides a property, and each a different one. When consumed, it invigorates the body, mind, or heart in different ways. Rosemary for the mind. Goji for immunity. Eucalyptus for a cough. And it smells *amazing.*"

"Atherians can get sick?" Ady asks.

"Not usually. They are all strong and healthy. They eat well. They are very different from humans."

"I see," Ady continues walking by Atriel's side. She notices how all-knowing he is, but it is so well spirited. Not a hint of arrogance. He is kind and gentle and happy to be sharing this knowledge with her. *Knowledge*, she reminds herself of his gifts.

"The Atherians are much more advanced when it comes to how to care for the body. They are also incredibly skilled with their minds."

Ahead, Ady sees a large fountain in the market's center. It pools calmly with the softest trickle of water as a stone angel looks upon the market, his wings large and grand.

Two Atherian children play and laugh along the fountain walls.

"Let me show you," Atriel picks up a small stone from the ground. Placing it in his hand, he tosses it up and then brushes the air just before it hits his hand, sending the stone to skip across the water of the fountain. The children laugh and watch the rock skip.

Ady's eyes widen as she smiles, "How did you do that?"

"Energy. It flows and exists all around you. If you can harness it, you can move it by then moving objects. Thelios has been training me to do this. The Atherians can move much greater stones than this." Atriel pauses for only a moment, "Telekinesis is what they called it once before in the Old World."

"People from the Old World could do this?"

"No, not everyone. Not even a few. So many of the Old World forgot the ways. They always had it harnessed within them, so few really tapped in." Atriel expresses.

"That's really magical. I would love to learn." Ady then smiles.

"I would love to teach you. Thelios has been my greatest instructor. Athos had me start training immediately with him."

"Do you train with Athos?" Ady asks.

"Athos has been sent here as *your* guide. He does help tremendously, and I am forever indebted to him. He has been waiting for your safe arrival for a long time now. We all have."

Atriel offers a soft smile. Then they walk up to a tent full of beautiful clocks. Ady stops and watches them as they tick. The sound washes over her, reminding her of home, her pocket watch, Eagan. She reaches for the chain around her neck.

"Everything alright?" Atriel asks.

"Yes," she pauses, "No. I left someone behind. Many behind. My friends. And someone dear to me. His name is Eagan." Ady says somberly. "Or was."

Atriel analyzes the sadness across her face, searching for the right words. Silence seems best.

THE WASTELAND

Ellington's quarters in the Rebellion's camp is not much smaller than the Citadel outhouses. An overturned fishing boat is raised and propped on a pole. Canvas flaps hang from the stern. There is a rolled cot stuffed with alfalfa and a clay pitcher of water. Outside are the sounds of the camp at night: women laughing, weapons being sharpened by hand and flint, shouts and cheers from a wrestling match just outside Doköran's tent.

The meeting had not gone well. But at least he knows where the men are. At least, they are mostly alive.

Doköran was everything Cayhill's men had said: the raven-eye branded on his chest seemed to watch the proceedings. The longhorn skull he wore was dipped in blood and only added to his height. His teeth were dark, his face sunburnt and brown, his nails rimmed black.

Ellington's orders were simple: to pay the bounty on the Brutallion, a total of 15,000 silver coins, which was waiting on his grounded airship outside the camp. And it seemed at first that Doköran would take the money. He rubbed his hands and laughed at his spoils. He boasted about how *his men* had found the Republic's most wanted. But as he moved about the crowd of his Raiders, encircling Ellington, who stood still and unflinching, something changed. A man in black robes emerged from Doköran's tent and whispered to the leader.

Suddenly, Doköran's attitude cooled. He demanded the remaining balance owed.

"Your people owe me more."

"Give me proof the men are alive," Ellington said. "We will not pay for severed heads."

Doköran smiled and unsheathed his ax.

"Bring out the prisoners!" he cried.

From the front of the camp came a long string of them—Eagan, bloodied and bruised, his hair covered in dark and dried blood. The others staggered behind, their hands all bound in coarse rope. They tripped over each other, some foaming at the mouth. Their bodies all bore the evidence of beatings.

The Republic would not treat its prisoners of war this way, Ellington thought. But then he corrected himself. Yes, yes they would. The Brutallion had been in Cayhill's prison first.

The worst was when Eagan noticed him. Their eyes met for a fleeting second, a blend of bewilderment and terror. Ellington had seen that expression before when James Alexander died. As he was led from the Citadel prison and onto the scaffold where his noose waited, he found Ellington in the crowd. He locked his eyes with his betrayer.

Then Eagan did the same. He was his father incarnate. It took every ounce of strength for Ellington not to scream in defiance right there, not to betray himself by shouting: "I will not do what I did to your father."

Eagan looked away again as the Raiders jolted them to a halt before Doköran, who strode around like they were prized calves.

Why hadn't Cayhill sent the full remaining balance if Doköran was owed more? Wouldn't he know the Rebellion would deny the offer?

"We do not have the remaining balance with us," said Ellington, and he held Doköran's gaze. "We will send Swifts back to request reinforcements and your payment."

As the men were led away, Doköran announced that a jackal should be roasted for dinner. This was a day for celebration. The Rebellion had again proven its superiority to the Republic. Fires were lit, dances began, as the Raiders pulled out flasks of wine. Before being shown to his quarters in the camp, Ellington sent a Swift from his ship: but he did not request reinforcements. Instead, the message was blank.

But Doköran didn't know that.

Now, alone, Ellington looks up from his mat as footsteps approach. A small girl, thin as a bean pole, enters his tent. She carries a bowl of what vaguely resembles stew.

"Our Lord said to bring this to you," she says and places the bowl on the desert ground before him.

"Thank you."

But she does not leave. She stands by the opening, her dirt-smudged hands folded across her belly.

"Is there something else?" Ellington asks.

The girl does not look him in the eye as she speaks. Her gaze goes past him to the rotted wood of the boat. Her eyes are a muted thistle-green. "I am to ensure that our guest is comfortable." Delicately, her fingers move to untie the lacing across her bodice, but Ellington raises his hand.

"No, no," he says. "None of that, I'm fine. Thank you."

The girl nods, blushing, and slips out from the canvas again—but the flap is open just long enough for Ellington to see out into the camp. Corvis stands among other Raiders, his arms around a young woman, slender and small. He knows her instantly, despite the matted blonde hair and the soot streaked across her pale cheeks. There are still bandages around her leg and waist. Grenn. Something in Ellington breaks when he sees the hollow look in her eyes, however quick.

The canvas falls again, and Ellington eats in silence. He waits for darkness to fall.

Ellington moves like a ghost through the camp. The Raiders are all drunk and sleeping, some sprawled by the fires, some grunting in their tents. He walks briskly in the pale moonlight, careful not to slip on the wine spills or crunch licked bones beneath his boots. The wind is barely perceptible and warm. The air is haunted, still, by roasted meat and dying embers. In the distance, Ellington can make out the shape of his airship. The Republic sails hang limp, like fabric on a clothesline.

Voices rise from one of the tents, and Ellington pauses and holds his breath before continuing on. He passes a wooden dock, blood-strewn, where the hunters must skin their finds. As he nears the edge of the encampment, he sees, too, that there are buckets scattered in no particular order—for rainwater, he presumes. The silver moonlight illuminates the craggy dunes miles away, rising up from the desert earth.

And then the prisoners—his soldiers! As Ellington approaches, they look almost dead, their bodies heaped upon each other in a tangled mess. Their wrists are still bound. Ellington kneels by the first man he reaches, a young one he doesn't recognize, and saws at the ropes with his paring knife. The man looks up in alarm, his eyes wide and veined, and almost screams, but Ellington stops him with his palm.

"It's me—be quiet. Do as I say." Ellington takes a second knife from his belt and hands it to the boy. "Release the others."

Within minutes, the men are awake. They are cutting and coughing and struggling to stand. One, a new recruit Ellington recognizes—Ivan—cries as soon as he's released and sinks back to the sand. Ellington grabs him by the shoulders and shakes him. "Be quiet, boy. Don't you know they'll hear you? Don't you know there's more of them than us?" The boy whimpers and bites his lip.

These are *his* men. He will not leave them to die like slaves in the Wasteland or like traitors in the Citadel. He knows how Cayhill wants to see them swing.

The chaos is quiet and contained until they are all freed. Ellington doesn't know what he'd expected: his pulse has been racing ever since he left his tent. Did he expect the men to anticipate his plan and run to the airship? Or gather around Eagan, waiting for instructions? Or perhaps he'd anticipated failure, that a Raider on nightwatch would see him and sound a horned alarm. He does not expect the mad scramble for the water buckets that lay scattered across the sand. The men knock some over in their madness—they cup water into their open mouths. They cry as they taste it.

At last, Eagan reaches him through the crowds and says in a cracked voice, "Where to, Captain?"

The airship is only a few hundred yards away from the camp. At Ellington's command, Eagan takes off, but not in a run, not with his usual powerful gait. There is a partial limp to his step, but what makes Ellington marvel, as he stands back, as he takes in the prisoners' smell—sweat and excrement and blood—is how they follow him. They have followed Eagan toward and away from death so many times. James Alexander had been like that. He was a man men wanted to be.

But the luck runs out.

A shout pierces the night behind him. Ellington turns to see a Raider waving a torch in the air. The simple halo casts an orange hush over the night.

The Brutallion continues to run—some look back, others scream. But Ellington stays still. He does not join them. Instead, he only unsheathes his sword. He watches as the Raiders gather en masse around their tents. Light floods through the camp as more torches are lit. Doköran's wrath is coming. Ellington braces himself. He knows how the Raiders fight, how they match brute force with feral strength, how they will surround him with their war cries. They are running toward him faster than the coyotes that prowl the Citadel walls, weapons arched over their heads, eyes wild and crazed in the moonlight and flames. Ellington places his back foot, adjusts his weight. He holds the sword high, on guard.

He missed the last fight. He will not miss this one.

LETTERS TO EAGAN

Dear Eagan — Day 1, Atheria

There are no words to describe this place—how it feels, how it smells. How the air is so still that you can almost hear the birds from down by the water. I wish you could see Atheria, see what I'm seeing. I keep looking up to the stars at night, thinking that surely, somewhere, wherever you are, you see the same night sky. But I don't even know if that's true. The night here is different—the stars seem closer somehow, and the shapes in the constellations are clearer, as though burned into black velvet.

Most of all, I wish you could meet my brother. Even writing that is strange. Athos is alive, but I suppose you already knew that. He tells me he's been writing to you, asking you keep me safe. Eagan, you would love him. Though the strange thing is, I hardly know him now. He is not, of course, the boy I remember. Or if he is, that part of him—the adventurous and wild one—has shifted. He is serious and thoughtful, reserved and quiet. He loves Atheria, and he believes in me. Perhaps more than I believe in myself.

I love you, Ady

Dear Eagan — Day 2, Atheria

*I don't know where to begin...Last night Athos told me something.
Something I am to do, someone I am to be. I haven't quite processed
this place or his words...I wish you were here.*

Ady

Dear Eagan — Day 5, Atheria

*Atherians are much different than humans. There is a whole
world here, Eagan. A whole group of people that Athos calls "protectors of humanity." Yet they are not "people," they are more interesting to me. They are graceful, mindful, spiritual. They live
differently, too—they do not harm any living creature for any
reason. Which I think is refreshing. Why would we do that in the
Old World? And their food tastes amazing—perhaps it's because
I was so famished.*

Love, Ady

Dear Eagan — Day 6, Atheria

*I've met someone. It seems he was also brought here after his
Citadel collapsed—isn't that strange, that many others are facing the fall of their home? His name is Atriel. He is anointed as
well. I wish I could describe what that means and what it is we
are meant to do, I am still unsure of my task here. The nice thing
is, we're both outsiders here. He's been in Atheria longer than me.
He's been helping me learn my way around the island, which seems*

small from the sky, but is really quite large. And this is only one of them. There are many islands here that float in the sky. I've also met two wolves...they aren't like normal wolves we've read about in Old World texts. They are called Archlights. Spiritual beings embodied as wolves on this plane. They can deliver messages and hear our thoughts. And I can hear hers...Shiloh is sworn to protect me at all costs, though there hasn't been a need to, yet. Skylar is Atriel's Archlight. They are magnificent. I understand if none of this makes sense...I, myself, feel I am in a dream.

Much love, Ady

Dear Eagan — Day 15, Atheria

Counting the stars...Missing you...

A

Dear Eagan — Day 25, Atheria

I have been learning more about myself. My gifts. Can you believe that? I have gifts of my own that I just needed to learn how to harness. Athos has told me that I am grasping this easier than he expected. Remember all the times I told you about my dreams? Or, in some cases, my nightmares. Well, some of them were real. Visions I was having...I often close my eyes and try to go back to our first kiss, or our last, just to relive those moments with you. They stay memories. I wish you were here.

Love, A

Dear Eagan — Day 35, Atheria

I haven't really written much about the Nobles, but they've occupied a lot of my time here. At first, they gave me space. It was really just Athos and me and then Atriel. But now, they have begun including me in Atriel's lessons in the Hall of Knowledge.

The Nobles are the high officials of Atheria—except, not in any "ruling" capacity like we knew in the Citadel. They're peaceful. They're academics and scribes. They read and study the stars and pray. But their lessons! I feel in my bones that I've known the truth for years, perhaps forever. But they've been telling me about the Old World and beyond, they hold all the knowledge of the world. From before the Great War, answering every question about forgotten rooms, the underground bunkers, the bombs, the cities, the vanished oceans. The Republic is not what they claim to be.

They banned mass weapons like the bombs but kept their own stockpile in case of "traitors." And it wasn't blatant anarchy that led to the Great War. People weren't just hungry to use their weapons without cause. They were rebelling against tyrannical governments in countries all over the world. Here, and in continents from the Old World—Asia, Europe, Africa. But there weren't enough shelters for everyone. People died by the millions. Others were left exposed and sick. Those rumors, Eagan, they're true about the Rebellion—how some were cast out, deformed and ill! The Republic wants us to know about the horrors of the Old World: pandemics and violence and weapons. But they don't want us to know about the beautiful things: parks and art, literature and music, freedom.

There's so much more than I can write here. But I am brimming with the news of it all!

Love to you, Ady

Dear Eagan — Day 48, Atheria

It's heavy, thinking of the destruction of humanity. The vile and horrible things we have done to one another. To the world. To life that existed before us. Did you know how many species existed in the Old World? Millions. Animals and birds. Sealife in actual oceans...

It's heavy to me because they were voiceless, and we destroyed them all. We destroyed each other, Eagan. Mankind turned on one another. In darker ways than within our walls. I just need a minute to let this settle.

A

Dear Eagan — Day 56, Atheria

Time is passing very unusually here. I have been here for almost two months. I think. Athos told me time is different here, and I feel like I can feel it. Your pocket watch provides me with the only sense of our world's time. I can watch the second hand tick forever.

I still can't grasp what has happened to you. Last night, I dreamed you climbed through the window of my chambers and slid into my bed. I could smell the sweat and dust from the training grounds. I could feel the heat emanating off your body from exhaustion. And when you kissed me, there was the rust-taste of blood on my tongue. But then I woke up. And the room was empty, and there was only moonlight. And this morning, as I write this, as Echo brings me a tray of fruit and Enchanted Tea, I just want to throw the food on the ground. Because I'm not a fool—I know what happened that night. Forgive me. Forgive me for leaving you there to die.

A

Dear Eagan — Day 58, Atheria

Please disregard my last letter.

Ady

Dear Eagan — Day 90, Atheria

For weeks now, Athos has been giving me books to read and exercises to, as he says, "strengthen my mind." This is Athos' idea of training. Occasionally, we'd meet in the Crystal Hall and he'd ask me probing questions, either about my life before or things I've dreamed about in Atheria. I could not bear to tell him about the dreams involving you. But today, for the first time, he wanted me to spend hours in meditation alone. "You're ready," he said. But for what? He did not join me in the Crystal Hall this morning. Instead, the room was empty. There were candles and incense, and someone (Athos I presumed) had left a knee pillow on the ground. I knelt and closed my eyes. It felt like minutes—but instantly, I was back in the garden, on the stone bench, and a hawk was flying over me, its shadow cresting my cheek. I could smell the smoke from the mess hall, and I could hear the clashing weapons from the Redcoats in training. In my excitement, I looked up to search for you. And then it was gone. I was back in the Crystal Hall, and the candles had burned down to their wicks. Athos came in and said, "That's enough for today." I went to my room, shaking. It felt so real, Eagan. Not at all like dreaming.

Ady

Dear Eagan — Day 110, Atheria

I continue training my mind. My heart. Meditating. Looking inward to myself, while remaining silent. The thoughts that bound through my head keep my mind racing. My thoughts always come back to you. I will always love you.

Love, Adylyn

Dear Eagan — Day 134, Atheria

I feel as though Atheria has blossomed like a season was waiting to change until I got here. The palace is now filled with people: young Atherians who tend to the fountains and the gardens, the Nobles who always take to the Hall of Knowledge and spend hours with their texts. On the grounds, the army trains under the morning sun. Atriel tells me they are preparing for a battle greater than man could ever know. They are to protect their Kingdom. They do not train like the Redcoats. When they get into formation, their general, Thelios, leads them in some sort of meditation. The soldiers close their eyes and raise their palms. And across the expansive green, stones rise into the air, just floating like clouds. The rocks tremble as they go higher. When they open their eyes, the stones fall back to the earth. There is weaponry, too: bo staffs, spears, even swords. They are all equipped with an Atherian element. Made of Atherian alloy. Their uniforms and weapons are brighter than the silver coins I once found in the Citadel. They gleam with a vibrancy I have never seen before.

I wonder what Captain Ellington would think if he could see this: there is a whole world here, with airships and armies, whose very comprehension of life is so different from our own.

Yours, A

Dear Eagan — Day 145, Atheria

I have been riding horses! Real horses! They gleam like the sun - their bodies. Riding feels like flying. Yet, so a part of something. So connected to something.

Just wanted to let you know.

A

Dear Eagan — Day 165, Atheria

Atriel has been showing me the techniques he is learning with Thelios. Atriel practices with his bo staff: balancing and mastering his agility helps with his mental athleticism. His discernment. I feel similarly. The more I run through the woods or ride along the shoreline, the more I climb the water-smoothed rocks near the falls, *the easier I can dip into my visions. They are clearer: like muddy water becoming clean as rain.*

Ady

Dear Eagan — Day 200, Atheria

We have been preparing our next steps. I have been training, meditating, harnessing my visions. Athos has told me that a vision will lead us. Or the book... I'm sorry I never got the chance to tell you about it. I am to read it. I still haven't seen a word on a page, I know that sounds crazy. It's a lot of pressure to provide this knowledge, but in so many ways, I am feeling more ready than ever before. We are to prepare ourselves as best as we can, knowing we must leave to seek others who will join our cause. I feel like you would know what to do.

A

Dear Eagan — Day 222, Atheria

We are preparing to leave in the coming days. I am meditating on an answer from the Council of Light. I look to the stars. I look within. I close my eyes—still, nothing on the pages and no answer yet of where we must go.

Adylyn

Dear Eagan — Day 228, Atheria

I can't help but feel the wonder of Atheria. It's been almost eight months of being here. I have made friends with Atherians, specifically Echo and Gaia. I've gotten as close as I can to my brother again. He has been here for almost 17 years in Atherian time, which can change you. He is so serious, but he means so well. Thelios has taught me so much about the Angematonic element, and preparations of how to use it on our quests. Edgar and the crew have remained in Atheria, awaiting our next moves. I hear them on the Aurora joyously drinking and laughing. They love it here. And my closest friend here, Atriel. I am happy to have another with me on this journey. Another anointed one. He understands my visions, supports me to have more, can answer just about any question. So knowledgeable, well, I suppose that is his gift!

I do wish you could be here to experience this with me. And Grenn. I wish you could all be here. You are both missed terribly. But I want you to know I am okay. I am more than okay.

Much love, Adylyn

Dear Eagan — Day 243, Atheria

I think this will be my last letter. I find myself feeling guilty if I don't write to you every day. Some days, I'll wake up and won't think of you or the Citadel straight away. I'll get dressed and eat and be in the middle of a lesson with the Nobles on Old World religions. And suddenly, some word, some thought, some sound will remind me of you. I'll think of those early years when we sat in lecture together before you were recruited. How we passed notes back and forth until our knuckles were swatted by the Speaker's rod. How you rolled your eyes when I rolled my eyes. We were so in sync, and those memories flood me. But they also distract me.

I have so much to continue to learn here. Do right by my calling, by these gifts that I am still trying to navigate how to wield. And I know you wouldn't want me to be pining or stuck with one foot still firmly planted in my old life. Right? At least, that's how I would feel about you if I'd been left behind. The one who died.

I meant it when I wrote that I will always love you. I always will. You have always been and always will be my North Star and my first love.

Adylyn

WRITTEN IN THE STARS

A dy sets down her quill at the desk, finishing her letter to Eagan. She stares gently at the words. She has written to him for months, *eight months*. And never expected a returned word. Just the hope that he knew how much she loved him. Taking him along her journey made it feel more real. This place. Her calling. Her gifts. His death.

With a shiver, Ady walks onto the balcony and sees it's not yet night. There are no stars yet in the heavens—she cannot count the light like she once did with him. Dusk brings a myriad of purples and orange to the horizon. She thinks of the last words she wrote. *You wouldn't want me to be pining or stuck with one foot still firmly planted in my old life.* Her old life was beautiful in its own way: it was all she knew.

But there is a new life waiting for her, here, knocking gently at the door, gently at her heart. Calling her to something greater. To someone she is called to be. She knows she must listen fully if only she can allow it. There is so much love and light here, so much support for her newfound gifts. And is she taking it? She turns and walks back inside, fitfully trying to navigate from old to new. She knows she must tear down the walls that have been possibly holding her back from emerging into this new life.

Ady's attention snaps as a knock sounds at her large wooden door.

She opens it, and standing in the hallway is Atriel. He smiles at her gently.

"Hi," Ady says softly.

"Hi. Would you like to go riding?" he asks.

Ady smiles back and nods a *yes*.

DUSK

The air is still and calm. Salt from the sea rises to the cliffs, where Shiloh and Skylar bask in the late sun. The rocky hillside slopes into the sandy beaches. The waves are far below, lapping near the lower islands, but the wolves can hear every crashing wave. A pod of dolphins, glowing blue, crest the water. The Archlights' ears are cocked and ready, listening.

Voices dance on the wind—and laughter. The sound of horses' hooves on the wet sand. From the palace path come Atriel and Ady at a gallop. Her hair streams like a whipping pennant behind her. The wolves stand and watch the horses.

And then they run.

Along the cliffside and rushing past the trees, finally down the steep bluff and onto the beach, nearly parallel to the horses now, the pads of their paws so silent on the sand. They watch the anointed ones for every flicker of movement, every shift of the reins, and tilt of the head. They anticipate the next move as Atriel and Ady cut onto a forest trail and back toward the heartland. The horses' hooves strike hard on the leaf-strewn dirt. Still, the wolves run.

And when they reach the clearing where the trees part, where the setting sun burns orange in the western sky, they hang back among the boughs. They watch the orchestrated movements: how Atriel dismounts first, then helps Ady down. How, together, they tie the horses to a low-hanging branch. Shiloh peers closely through the leaves as Atriel's hand moves to Ady's hip. Shiloh knows what Ady knows: that no one has ever touched her this way except Eagan, who brushed his fingers against hers for the first time when they were thirteen. They were exploring a forgotten room in the darkness. One minute he was shuffling through boxes; the next, his hand was there. They were best friends, lecture-mates, tethered by a mutual love for Eagan's father—and then suddenly, with one move from Eagan, they were more. And Shiloh knows that Ady is trembling because she can feel the shiver along her fur. But there is also the sense of competing feelings—the beauty of the sky, so orange and red at dusk, and the way the floating lights shimmer in the trees, and the way he is looking at her so tenderly, not at all with the strong and stable gaze that Eagan used to give. His look is with something so much softer, like a question.

The wolves watch as he kisses her for the first time, and as she kisses him back. Gently.

And then the Archlights turn to leave. They pad back through the woods, darkening now, back to the cliffside, where they will sleep, watch, and wait.

REBUILT

The palace is empty by the time Ady and Atriel return. Sconces cast a candle glow on the marble, and the moonlight sends shapes and spirals through the central atrium. They are silent as they walk to Ady's chambers, but she can feel Atriel beside her—quiet with his soft footsteps. But his breath is heavy and warm. Is it from riding or the many stairs? Or from the kiss that still sears her mouth?

At the door, she turns to look at him. Her hair is tousled from the wind, her dress creased from hours of riding, and she can almost smell the sweat from her own skin. But here he is, looking at her. His face is dark in the shadows, but the moonlight outlines his sharp jaw, his sleek shoulders—the way his hand reaches out for hers. And suddenly, the months in Atheria have felt like years, like she's been living in this alternate plane for centuries, has known Atriel, this fellow anointed one, for most of her life. His fingers brush against her cheek.

"I'll see you in the morning?" Atriel says, his voice a whisper.

"You will," she smiles back.

He leans to kiss her again, this time on her cheek, like the softest brush of silk on her skin. And she sees so many moments from the past months: Atriel introducing her to her Archlight, explaining Atherian traditions he has learned from Thelios since before her arrival, showing her some of the best vantage points on the island. Teaching her how to use a bo staff, how she tried lunging in the garden but slipped on her first try, laughing in the grass. Trying to explain her visions, the way the Federation and the Council appeared to her, as clear as light; running with

Shiloh and Skylar through the wooded forest together, waiting for the sun to set and the stars to appear.

Atriel pulls away at last and retreats down the corridor. She closes the door softly.

The bed has been turned down for her, and a pitcher of cool spring water and mint waits on the nightstand. Her night robe and bath towel lie folded on the blankets. She smiles, thinking of Gaia and Echo. But what draws her eye is the journal, open on the chaise, filled with all those letters to Eagan.

Ady walks slowly forward. The very sight of the journal tonight sends a chill up her spine. How many hours has she spent writing to a dead man? That is her Old World, she knows. Her old life has gone up in flames, and somehow she survived. She will carry the burns forever, but it's time to heal, to stop peeling away open wounds.

She has been stripped of everything and everyone—she has been broken. But she will rebuild. Atheria has shown her that it's possible to become someone new. Her calling, her anointing, means that some gift abides within her, right? Someone or something was watching over her, all this time, from the garden to the Raiders' siege to the battle in the skies. She survived. She could cry, "Why me?" for weeks and never know the answer. She could live in grief and misery. Or she could learn to be whole again. This is about more than Eagan or Grenn or the entire Lower West Citadel—this is about something cosmic. Ady runs her hands over the soft exterior and remembers writing in the library with Grenn, in the Aurora on those fitful nights of travel. She will not forget. Sometimes, perhaps, she will allow herself to venture into those forgotten rooms—those memories—and re-live what they once had when the Citadel was their world. When Eagan was her home.

The tears come as Ady settles on the chaise. She removes Eagan's pocket watch from around her neck and lets the chain pool in a gold circle next to her. In the pale light from the stars and crescent moon, she writes on a clean page: *I needed to completely break down before I could rebuild. And I will now step into every part of who I was meant to be. Signed, Adylyn of Atheria*

THE ARRIVAL

A dy awakes to a blaring alarm through her chambers. At first, the sound enters her dreams, like the ram's horns blown on the Citadel rampart. She jolts up, panting in the morning light, and half expects to be in her dormitory, to see fire out the window and Bluecoats ransacking her room. Instead, there is her white, ivory, and gold chambers, the peace of the morning interrupted by a distant and resounding gong of a bell, which seems to emanate from the very walls of the palace.

Atriel rushes through the door, the panic clear on his face.

"What is that?" Ady cries as she throws on her dressing gown.

"The breach alarm," says Atriel. He holds out his hand for her, and she joins him, running through the corridor to the central atrium. The palace is filled with Nobles now, some shouting, some milling about aimlessly, their navy cloaks regal and luxurious. There is no sign of Athos, but through the arched windows, she can see figures filing across the grounds, shields raised high in the sun.

"Where are we going?" Ady demands.

"The Crystal Hall," says Atriel over his shoulder. "We'll be safe there."

Edgar watches from the bridge of the Aurora as the Atherian army convenes on the cliffs. They emerge in tight, ordered lines, rolling advanced cannons out to the hillside. Everywhere, across the island, the breach alarm rings clear, from the palace to the docks.

Someone—or something—has parted the clouds. Something has entered Atheria.

"Get those lines off the bow!" Edgar calls to his crew. "Prepare to fly, turn 180 toward the breach."

Members of the crew stagger from their private quarters, some still drunk with sleep. It's been months now since active duty, and some—most—have become undisciplined with the waning hours. The Boatswain twins have gained a collective twenty pounds. Only Edgar has kept to their usual schedule, up at dawn to watch the sunrise over the floating islands, content with having the ship to himself for the rare morning hours.

Ella is at his side in seconds, her ringlets wild in the wind.

"Cannons to starboard," he orders, and she nods emphatically.

The fire in the engine room starts up, and heat floods the deck as the balloon inflates to her full expanse.

Athos had warned him a breach might happen, especially since the Republic was on the verge of identifying Adylyn. He knew the alarm would sound if an unidentified ship ventured through the cloud layer. But as the months passed, it seemed impossible that they'd been followed or traced. He began to sleep without a dagger at his bedside. But had some outlier settlement seen his ship over the Forgotten Sea and sent word to the Chancellor? Or was this the plan all along—a stealth attack? The deck rocks beneath his feet as the ropes loosen from the mooring. Edgar peers into the bright morning sky and can just make out the faint shape of a ship, red sails full and round.

A Republic vessel.

But of course, he remembers. It's been only days in the main world. Time runs as slowly as honey from a pot in Atheria—it is thick and warm and prolonged. Perhaps it's been only a fortnight in the main world, while here, his men are growing fat on Atherian fruit and splendor.

Every crew member is perched at their positions, Ella and the gunners are with the cannons, prepared to fire at a moment's notice—the twins in the crow's nest, one sliding down a loose rope—Calvin carries a map of Atheria and spyglass up from below decks.

"Give me that," says Edgar, taking the spyglass.

He lifts it and blinks first at the blinding sun, then searches for the approaching ship. Why would the Republic send only one aircraft after such an important fugitive? Was this a scouting vessel, sent before the rest of the armada? The ship comes into focus now, and he can see the crimson sails, the gaudy gold on the mast, the propeller vents along the rich wooden hull. It's from the Republic all right— but as shapes appear on the deck, he sees that they are not in the Redcoats uniforms. They look more like slaves, he thinks, in under-tunics, without the Republic armed forces' distinctive cloaks.

"Captain, the Atherian army is about to fire!"

And then Edgar puts down the spyglass.

"Hold your fire!" he cries. "Stand down!"

The ropes have all but loosened. The Aurora is about to lift into the sky as Edgar drops the spyglass, runs across the deck, and jumps feet-first onto the wooden scaffold. His crew shouts from the ship, but he runs on, past the Atherian dockmasters, through the underbrush of wildflowers and low-hanging trees, toward the beaches where the cliffs rise like towers from the rocks, where he must stop the Atherians from firing. Birds screech into the air as he weaves between the trunks, waving his arms wildly and screaming with every step—"Stand down, stand down!"

They are in the Crystal Hall for what feels like hours before the breach alarm ceases. All the while, Ady sat huddled by the door, her ear cocked for any sound of the Nobles or Athos. But there was nothing more than the low hum of voices and footsteps on stone, the alarm shrieking every few seconds. Atriel paced in the center of the room, one hand running incessantly through his hair. Echo entered the room with a breakfast tray of mint tea, bread, and hard cheese, but Ady could not think of eating.

When the alarm stops, her ears still ring with the sound. Atriel stops pacing and places one hand on the amethyst pillar.

"Has this ever happened before?" Ady asks, now standing.

Atriel shakes his head. "It means someone has broken through the barrier and found us. Athos warned it was a possibility. Odd, though, that we didn't hear the cannons fire."

Ady blinks when he says this. Did that mean the breach was not from an enemy, not the Republic coming to bring her body back? Or the Rebellion seeking a bounty? Was it possible? Had Edgar told them where to come, how to find her? But surely not after all this time...She's been in Atheria now for what, eight months? Atriel's brow creases with concern as Ady rubs at her temples. She thinks she might get sick and collapse, right here in the palace's most sacred room. She must see for herself.

Ady bursts through the hall door and runs down the corridor. She passes the high-arched windows that overlook the grounds and the kitchen, which smells of herbed bread. She enters the central atrium, where the Nobles still stand clustered in hushed conversation, but they part like the sea as she rushes past. Her footsteps carry her down the grand hall where sunlight illuminates the greens and blues in the marble patchwork. Finally, she throws open the wooden doors and emerges on the palace steps.

The sky is so bright, it's almost white, with hints of the pink and dusky blue left from the dawn. Red sails float in the wind over the trees—a Republic vessel. She would know it anywhere, that blood-red canvas that always wafted in the sky over the rampart walls. Her eyes follow the path from the docks to the white stairs. Athos is leading a group of men up the steps.

Something inside her catches, and she stops. She sees the man walking beside Athos, just before the step. Steady and slow, his shoulders broad. His hair is dark from here—perhaps from dirt—but she knows it's him, she feels it beneath her skin, in the cold trickle that runs down her spine like chunks of ice. She opens her mouth to call out, but nothing comes. For the briefest moment, she thinks she might faint and tumble down the steps in a rolling mess of silk.

He is here, in Atheria.

Eagan has returned.

As if from the grave. He must have seen her because his pace quickens, and he takes the stairs two by two. With every step, she can see his features more clearly: the stark green of his eyes, the lips she has called home, and his firm jawline.

Emotions coil within her, gratitude, as her prayers are answered. Love, pouring from her heart. Guilt, because he was left behind. Betrayal, for he lied about Edgar. Grief. He was dead, but here is the ghost of the one she loved. He looks as though he's waded through mud, with dirt streaking every surface of his body and blood dried hard on his cheeks, but he is here—alive at last. Athos' words from her first days in Atheria return to her. *Time in this plane is not on our side.* She has since buried him in her mind with a wounded heart. She's been here for nearly eight months. How long has it been for Eagan?

She does not get a chance to ask before Atriel joins her, rushing beside her atop the steps.

"So they are not intruders?" he says with concern as he reaches for her hand. His palm is heavy and warm, but she grips it back tightly, still afraid she might fall, overcome with emotion.

"No. They are my people," she whispers.

The clasp is so quick, a tiny intimate moment, that she hardly has time to register who is watching. Eagan stops on the steps, and his men follow suit. Ady steals her hand back, presses her fist against her chest, realizing it's too late. Neither move toward one another, saying enough. She can see the look Eagan casts her way, the shock or confusion carved into his stone face.

He does not continue up the stairs to the palace. Instead, he turns and descends the steps.

THE GIFT

The Chancellor's stay has been long and unwelcome, though Cayhill would never breathe a word of this. For days, the Chancellor hardly set foot outside the officials' headquarters. His men stood guard while he did whatever he did. Send Swifts back to the Basilica? Oversee maps and battle strategies? Sleep? Impossible to know. Cayhill personally saw to it that the Chancellor had only the best of the Lower West Citadel's rations— seared squirrel, lizard soup, sprout salad, and barley tea—but the trays went mostly untouched outside his quarters. His mere presence cast a pall over the Citadel, like a storm cloud of dust and debris, something waiting to drop and crush them. Cayhill tried to proceed with business as usual: he filled in for Captain Ellington to ensure the remaining Redcoats did not grow soft in his absence; he made rounds to the various chore brackets, from the mess hall to the outhouses, thrilled by the way the children and women froze in his shadow; he pushed for the continued return to normalcy after the siege, whether that meant the rebuilding of broken structures or visiting the makeshift medical wards.

And yet, every day brought just the wait: for Ellington to return with the traitors. For the Chancellor to reveal his real purpose in being there.

Then, just as suddenly as he arrived, the Chancellor announced one morning via a note under Cayhill's door that he would be returning to his home at the Basilica.

There is a surprising coolness to the air as Cayhill climbs to the airship dock. A darkness in the distance, over the dunes, seems to threaten rain, an early outlier of winter storms. The Chancellor's ship sways in the breeze, and the canvas flaps violently as falcons' wings. The Chancellor himself stands at the end of the scaffold, his hands clasped behind his back, his eyes cast over the wide and rolling desert. His bondsmen scurry back and forth from the deck, lugging trunks and rations for the journey. The Basilica is a good 2,000 miles from the Citadel. Cayhill watches the work rhythm with both a rising fury and relief. Why hadn't Ellington returned already with the traitors? Cayhill had lulled himself to sleep at night with thoughts of his victory in front of the Chancellor: the scoundrels dragged back from the Wasteland, set to pay for their crimes against the Republic. Perhaps the Chancellor would have promoted him at this conquest. There would have been ceremonies and badges of honor. Perhaps that would have erased the greater failures—the girl's disappearance and how the *book* slipped through his gates.

Just as the Chancellor turns and gathers his robes to ascend the gangway, an airship appears in the distance, coming from the west. The ram's horn sounds from the rampart walls.

Cayhill can barely contain his excitement. He rushes to the far end of the scaffold and shields his eyes from the early light. The wind is strong, and his white hair blows haywire, but he watches intently as the ship grows closer and closer—as his vindication approaches—and as the black sails take shape.

He has met Corvis once before, and not in a pleasant encounter. On an early negotiation trip to see Doköran, the Skyraiders intercepted his airship and demanded a reason for invading Rebellion airspace. From across the sky, Cayhill could see the raven-like eyes and imagine the reek of death that must cling to his skin. From the bridge, he personally waved a white sheet and shouted "parley" before Corvis let him descend to the Rebellion's camp. Now, that ship is here at the Citadel, its hull encrusted with stones and scrap metal. The engine groans loud as it nears, like a thousand trapped birds cawing.

"What is the meaning of this?" The Chancellor calls from the gangway, but Cayhill has no time to speak. The ship is upon them, and the Bluecoats are shouting from the walls—*should they fight, should they fire? Is this a second attack?*

The ship lowers as if to dock, so close now that Cayhill could almost touch the stern. This is when Corvis appears on the deck, his matted tails of hair hanging over the rails.

"Doköran has a little present for you!" he cries and throws a canvas rucksack to the scaffold below. The bag lands almost at Cayhill's boots. He can smell the blood even as he sees the soaked cloth. And when he tips the bag with his toe, the head rolls out, bloated, pale, and still bleeding. Ellington.

"Play games with us again, and you're next," shouts Corvis as his ship lifts high again.

Cayhill stares blankly at the head. He can look at nothing else—not the Chancellor who's shouting from the gangway, telling the Bluecoats to fire, god-damnit, fire! Not Corvis' ship as it disappears from sight, just the head on the ground. The eyes are still open. His beard is untrimmed. Cayhill swallows the bile that rises in his stomach because he knows—it would have been him.

CONFRONTATION

Time seems to hold for a long moment as Ady watches Eagan retreat. She can feel the hot stares around her: from the Nobles in the palace, from Athos and the men frozen on the steps, stricken with immobility. And from Atriel—she can feel him assessing who this might be.

Then she takes off running, down the steps, past her brother and the men she recognizes with continued shock—Tiri and Ito, faces she thought she'd only ever meet again while dreaming. Each man looks more haggard than the one before, with scrapes and limps and hastily wrapped broken bones, but there is no time to stop. Edgar and the crew are coming up the hill from the docks now, but Ady tears past them without a word, off into the forest path where she's ridden with Atriel so many times. She knows each turn and sudden uneven patch. She knows where the branches are low enough to grab her hair—she runs nimbly through the boughs that still purr with the glowing orbs. "Eagan!" she cries, but he does not stop. His stride is long and fierce as he cuts away from the path and toward the cliffs that overlook the beach. Ady half expects the Archlights to be basking in the sun when she crashes from the forest and onto the rocky overhang—but there is no trace of Shiloh or Skylar. There is only Eagan, his back to her, hands gripped tightly.

Ady watches him for several seconds as her breath levels. His skin seems so different. She can tell even from here that there are new scars on his shoulder blades, raised like whip-ridges. He is dark, too, from the sun and thinner. Even his ribs look visible.

"I can't believe you're here." Ady's voice is a soft whisper. She takes one step forward, feeling slightly afraid of what he will do for the first time in her life.

Eagan turns, his face hard with an expression she's never seen. He is not himself. She can see that instantly. Dried blood coats the left side of his face. His hairline has been stained brown with dirt, and his shoulders are purple and green with bruises. *What have they done to you?* Ady raises a hand to her mouth in shock. Should she run to him? Shower him with kisses? Take him back to the palace and personally wash each and every wound? She closes her eyes as tears threaten to pour down her cheeks—none of this would have happened if they could have brought him to Atheria in the first place. What tortures must the Republic have inflicted upon the man she loved? But the moment she thinks this, she is grieved again. Eagan is staring at her with such anger, such revulsion. He has never once looked at her this way. There was only ever tenderness, his hand through her hair, his kisses on her neck as they watched the starlight together.

"Who is he?" Eagan says. There is a dryness to his voice like he's gone days without water.

The trees in the forest groan as if in answer. The wind picks up from the ocean; from the corner of her eye, Ady can see dolphins leaping in the distance far beneath her.

"He's no one," Ady says before she has time to think. Who is Atriel to her? Does she even know? Now that Eagan is back, that her prayers have been heard, that he has returned as if from death, why doesn't she feel more joy? Instead of just this aching regret?

"Do you know what I've been through?" He speaks slowly at first, almost coughing on his words. "To come here, to find you?"

His voice rises now, and he runs his hands through his crusted hair. He looks sleep-deprived and is slightly shaking as he begins to pace along the cliff's edge. Far below, gulls soar over the ocean waves in concentric circles. "Do you know that Cayhill wants you dead, that he blamed my men and me for your escape?"

"I didn't ask you to do that, I wanted to—"

"God—do you hear yourself? We were imprisoned, waiting to die, and then after we escaped, we got taken by the Ravens, and do you know what happened to

Grenn? Of course you don't, but you probably don't even care, do you? You've been over here in your own paradise, just what, running into another man's arms?"

"It's *not* like that, and you cannot talk to me that way." The tears are there now, and her vision blurs. Of course she cares. If only he knew how many nights she cried over him, over all of them. "What happened to Grenn?"

"It's been three weeks, Ady. *Three weeks*. We've been together for years, you and I—and my men have survived hell to come here, for me to find you, finally, and this is the welcome we come into?"

"It's been eight months for me, Eagan!"

"Oh, okay," Eagan stops pacing and laughs at this. "Of course it has. I'm sure it's felt like such a *long* time for you here. This is what you've always wanted, isn't it? Life outside the Citadel. Well, here you have it."

"You don't understand, time here is completely different than anywhere else in the world," Ady tries to explain. But her words sound hollow.

Footsteps sound from the forest and Ady turns to see Atriel emerge from the path. The concern is evident on his face as he slows his pace. Why had he followed? Hadn't he realized that he was the reason for Eagan's anger?

Ady watches the resentment register deeper on Eagan's face. She has seen such looks before: in the way he used to glare at Captain Ellington, who turned in his father. It's the look of betrayal.

"Eagan," she says with as much calm as she can muster. "You're not yourself— let's get you some food, some rest. I'll explain everything, I promise." She steps tentatively forward. A smell rises from his skin. Up close, his bruises are darker and knotted, and there's the faintest black eye on his right side. She reaches to touch him and briefly grazes his shoulder before he brushes her away.

"No. It is you who is not yourself."

Ady stands still as the ocean wind lifts the hair off her back. She watches Eagan glide past and retreat again into the forest, but not before walking by Atriel. She can barely stand watching them exchange glances. Their silence is deafening.

Her eyes drop to the ground, dotted with dandelions. Her neck is painfully bare, as she reaches for where the pocket watch had hung for many months. She can only imagine he noticed this as well.

The orb lights are dancing, and the tree limbs sway, heavy with budding flowers. At last, Ady moves to the rocky cliffs and drops to the ground, hugging her knees. The water so far below is an icy blue today, almost bright as crystal. To the left, the Aurora's balloon is visible over the tree bed—and the scarlet Republic sails wave in the wind like patriotic banners. The other islands float like clouds across the water. Tiny rainbows catch the morning sun from the waterfalls that cascade to the sea. How can it be this beautiful when she feels so dead inside, like a part of her soul she'd already buried has been killed again in front of her?

"Is there anything I can do?"

Atriel approaches from behind her, and she can almost sense his hesitation: should he touch her, say something? But his very presence only reminds her of what Eagan must have seen as he arrived from the docks, as he climbed the steps to be reunited with her—at last. And there she was, holding tight to another man.

"Please, just go," she says and buries her head in her hands.

She can feel him linger a moment longer before he, too, falls back into the forest.

ON DECK

It feels like days before the sun begins to sink, at last, over the island's treetops. The sky turns a pale lavender, then darkens to indigo, and finally, the stars appear in their silver shapes.

All afternoon, Eagan roamed through the woods—angry, then tired, then weak to exhaustion. He napped beneath a large oak tree and awoke to the floating balls of light that had descended to dance near his skin like fireflies. He found a glistening pond, filled by a small waterfall at the end of an overgrown path, and here he swam, bathing himself in the cool spring. For more than an hour, he washed away the blood, grime, and salt layers on his arms. The cuts along his back burned fresh, but then the water served as a balm. He felt the sting leave his body. And when he dressed and began the trek back to the docks, he started to feel almost like himself again. The smell of the Wasteland had clung to him like a second skin, but now that was gone. In its place, there was only numbness.

He clears the forest at dusk. The palace is lit by many candles within—from the sloping hillside, he can see the flickering shadows upon the stone. The marble steps catch the moonlight. Ady will be that way, doubtlessly dining in some fancy hall with her new man. Whatever his name is.

Eagan turns left, to the docks. The sails of his ship lap closely to the Aurora's canvas balloon; both are suspended in midair and tethered to the scaffold railing. Beneath them, the ocean pounds.

He can tell as he approaches that his ship is empty. The Brutallion must be inside the palace, he presumes, getting bathed and fed, seeking medical help. And they deserve it. But on the Aurora, lanterns swing from the deck, casting a warm glow into the night, and there is the distinct smell of roasted corn, warm cheese, and bread. Eagan strides across the dock with somber steps. How is it that he could hardly keep from bounding off the ship and toward his love just hours earlier? Now, he cannot stand to see her.

At the starboard side, Eagan walks up the gangplank. The deck, he sees, is filled with the Aurora's crew. They all sit on overturned boxes and crates, plates on their knees, and tin mugs by their boots. A basket of food is settled between them: grapes and pomegranates, rosemary biscuits and flasks of rhubarb wine, corn cobs wrapped in brown cloth and tied with twine. The crew hardly registers him as he approaches. Someone is in the middle of telling a story, and there is piercing laughter. Two males—twins, Eagan realizes—play musical instruments outside the small cluster, a dulcimer and pan flute.

"Eagan, my man!" Edgar moves from his perch by the bridge and strides to him, hand outstretched. "I'm surprised to see you join us for the evening meal. Surprised and delighted."

"I could use a familiar face right now," says Eagan. He can feel the grimace in his own features, but he tries desperately to smile.

Edgar looks at him curiously then shrugs. "Are you hungry?"

"Famished."

"The Atherians bring us food by the barrel and basket. More than we should ever eat, but don't tell that to the crew, because they'll eat what they want, believe me."

Edgar moves to the crew's huddle just as pealing laughter erupts from the circle. He stoops and gathers a brimming plateful, then nods for Eagan to join him by the helm. They kneel on the wooden step, and Eagan tears into the meal, careful not to rush and make his empty stomach sick.

"They like being here," Edgar says as Eagan sucks the last kernel from the cob, then goes for the bread. He nods at the cluster of smiling faces. "I think it's calming to them, more than anything. We've been through a lot together." Edgar smirks at Eagan with a definitive tease in his expression. "I'm sure you have, too."

"More than my share."

Eagan says nothing more until the plate is cleared. He watches the crew's raucous conversation, sees a red-haired girl stand to begin some sort of charade, waving her arms in the air like a bird as the others shoot guesses like arrows.

"So you got Ady here safely," he says at last. The very mention of her name on his lips makes him want to cry. After all he'd endured coming for her—after Cayhill's prison and their narrow escape, after being intercepted by Corvis and nearly broken to the bone, after witnessing the cruel beheading of Ellington as their ship lifted into the sky—he'd clung to the hope of the reunion. What would she say when she saw him? When they were at last together and at peace? "Thank you for that."

"Of course. I would have given my life to ensure it." After a moment's hesitation, Edgar adds: "I want you to know how glad I am to see you. I hoped you'd come, but it began to seem impossible."

"It's barely been three weeks," Eagan snaps. "Look, I'm sorry, my quarrel is not with you."

"It's been much longer than three weeks for us," says Edgar. He nods up to the sky. "The only way I know that our time here is off is because the stars aren't moving the way they should. Look, I can see Aries, Hercules, Lyra—but the sky should have turned by now." Eagan follows his gaze to the brilliant night. The stars are the same he used to chart the way here. "I think you'll find that Atheria is a more magical place than even meets the eye. I confess I was skeptical at first. Time is different here, its own dimension. That's how there are Nobles who are over 800 years old. Strange but true. The world is full of strange things."

"How did you first come here?"

"I met Athos at a trading port along the Eastern coast. He needed air travel here, we needed money. I was his way to Atheria."

How strange it was to meet Athos for the first time this morning. Eagan saw the resemblance in an instant. He had the same brown hair as Ady, the same strong jaw and rounded nose. Only his eyes were different, deeper-set and softer, and his beard made him look far older. But there was no denying he was her brother. He was the one who sent all the Swifts to Eagan. *Be vigilant. Things are not yet in motion.*

Eagan reclines back on the wooden steps and watches the Aurora's balloon bob in the air, blocking the moon from direct view. The air is just cool enough to make his skin prickle, but not cold enough to need fur. The ocean water, which seemed thunderous when they first parted through the cloud line, now seems peaceful as the waves roll below. So Ady has been here eight months without him. Doing what? And why couldn't they have come to rescue them? Perhaps Grenn would not still be in the Raiders' camp. The more he thinks this, the more the anger hardens in him. He can feel it through his muscles, tightening in his shoulder blades, so that he almost wants to kick the empty tin plate and send it skidding across the deck.

Edgar must sense this, because he places a hand on Eagan's shoulder and says, "If you're mad at anyone, be mad at me. I never even told her that I'd given you the coordinates to Atheria. That there was even a chance you might come. I was afraid of stoking a hope that seemed unfeasible."

"There is always a chance," Eagan says.

Unfinished Business

A quiet falls over the palace after the evening meal. The moon takes the place of the sun, and there is a steady retreat to bedchambers. But Ady cannot sleep.

After a good hour on the cliffside, Ady returned to the palace in search of Eagan but found only the crowded frenzy of new guests and a grand Atherian welcome. Upon arrival, Eagan's men were taken straight to the bathhouses, where they were attended to with vitamin oils, massages, and clean waffle-linens. Then the Atherians laid out a large and lavish feast in the dining hall. Not even Ady ate meals in the hall, usually reserved for the Nobles or large gatherings. Tonight, she and Atriel sat at the head of a long table and marveled at the fullness of the room—the arched ceilings and gold crown, the walls inlaid with mirrors, and the candle-lit chandeliers suspended over the hand-hewn tables. As the Atherians brought around carafes of rhubarb wine, and as the cooks delivered steaming plates of spring beans and soup, Ady watched the men eat ravenously. They reached for the food as though they'd never eaten a day in their lives. Her own appetite seemed to vanish.

Eagan was not among them. (Was he still roaming the island, fuming? Could she blame him?) But she counted more and more faces she recognized, bright and clean now. Tiri hardly looked up from his plate, and his hands remained fisted on the table all through the meal. Only Ito cast shy and questioning glances whenever Atriel laughed or leaned to tell her something. Each glare was like a dagger.

How would they ever understand?

Now, the night birds are singing outside her window, and the peaceful calm of Atheria at twilight makes Ady want to destroy the beautiful things in her room: tear books from her shelf, rip the pages from her journal—anything. Instead, she slips on her dressing gown, ties back her hair in a ribbon, and slips into the corridor. The guest rooms are near the gardens, past the central atrium. The palace is still— everyone must be asleep at last—and even the walls seem heavy with exhaustion after such a day. She moves like a shadow down the hall, into the now empty atrium, past the braided-knot on the Crystal Hall's double doors, and moves toward the garden. The guest rooms are ahead, six in a row, set off the passageway with arched and narrow entries. Ady knocks on the first. Ito answers.

She knows Ito well, through Eagan. She knows he is the fastest runner in the Redcoats, that he is from the Eastern Alliance, an orphan like her. She knows he is quieter than Eagan or Tiri; she used to see him in the library some nights after training was complete, reading alone by the window sill. Tonight, in the darkness, his slim figure looks severe. His cheekbones are sharp and rigid.

"It's you," he says. "We thought you were—"

"Is Eagan with you?" The words slip out before she can think of anything else.

"No." Ito looks over his shoulder, and Ady can just see past him, as other men pull back the sheets on their beds. Ito steps into the corridor. In the moonlight, she can see that he is wearing an Atherian robe, embroidered with silver. A deep gash, fresh and pink, slices his left cheek. "Look," he sighs, "the last we saw, you were following him into the woods. That's it."

"I was hoping he'd be back by now."

"I take it your conversation didn't go well?"

"It could have been better."

She can sense the same questions emanating from him, the same confusion and judgment. *How could she forget Eagan in just a matter of days? Who was that guy on the steps with her?* The men must hate her, all of them. Her friends, Eagan's men, this last tie to her home in the Citadel. But what was she supposed to do differently? She tried to resist coming with Edgar—she tried to stay with the man she loved. How to explain the unfolding of higher things? To Ito right now, she would surely sound demented. Or worse, heartless. A shiver runs down her spine, and Ady rubs her arms through the silken dressing gown.

Ady takes a deep breath.

"Ito, I never got a chance to thank you. That night, in the fire. I think Grenn and I would have died if you hadn't found us."

He grimaces at Grenn's name. She sees it, and her chest tightens.

"I did what any soldier would do," Ito nods.

"Yes. And a friend. So, thank you." He says nothing for a moment, and Ady ventures: "Grenn. Is she? I mean, is she *dead*?"

"I don't know."

Ady closes her eyes. Already, the hot tears are there. *Oh Grenn, oh Grenn, oh Grenn*. She looked so small and broken in the Citadel as Tiri towered over her. She was bleeding profusely, already unconscious, and the flames were so high. It seemed inevitable. Ady had anticipated this, she'd sensed the loss even as Edgar heaved her up the rampart steps. But hearing it spoken is different altogether.

"How's Tiri?" Ady asks, fear in her heart for the pain he must feel.

Ito turns back to the chambers. Ady can make out Tiri against the window, looking out into the night sky in silence.

"He hasn't said much," Ito says, turning back to Ady.

"Well, I'll leave you to rest," Ady says at last. "If Eagan comes back, would you please tell him I'm sorry? That I need to talk to him."

"Tell him yourself." Ito nods down the hallway before retreating into the guest room.

Ady turns to face the darkened hallway, lined by the smallest glow of candles within sconces along the wall.

Eagan looks so thin as he approaches. Himself but slighter. These weeks have not been kind, she knew that the moment she got a good look at him. But now, his walk is slow and somber, and his shoulders lean forward. The moonlight illuminates only one side of his face, and she can read the exhaustion in his features. New lines crease his forehead.

"You've been out all day?" Her whisper carries and echoes through the corridor.

"I got to see this place you've been calling home."

Eagan stops a few feet away from her. She can feel the distance. Usually, he would come up behind her. She'd feel his strong chest as he encircled her waist with his arms, making her feel delicate and strong all at once. Now, he leaves space.

"You must be exhausted," Ady says and musters a smile. "I'm glad you found your way back alright."

"The Nobles told me which way to go," he says. "I take it this is my room?"

"Yes, the others are in there, too. Ito. Tiri."

"They've been through a lot," Eagan sighs and runs his hand over his hair. "They deserve some rest."

She can see that he's cleaned up now. He must have bathed in one of Atheria's many streams. His hair, too, is longer than normal, curling over his ears. In the Citadel, she used to cut his hair. He'd sit on a stool in her dormitory and hold her one mirror up while she took a knife to his oat-blonde waves. She loved those intimate moments when there was silence in the room as she ran her fingers along his scalp.

He steps forward as if to pass her, but she starts again: "I need to talk to you. This morning didn't go well."

"I think that's pretty evident."

"None of this is what you think. And I just, I want you to trust me. The person you loved—still love, I hope." She speaks quickly. The desperation is evident in her voice, even she can hear it, but words stream out of her. Eagan does not maintain eye contact, and she hates this. It makes her want to shrink to the size of a tiny stone and hide. But she can't. She can feel him slipping, and now is the time to speak. "Tomorrow, let me show you this place. Please, let me help you understand. I know you knew something was coming, I knew you'd been hearing from my brother, from Edgar. So trust them. Trust me. Let me show you Atheria. Just give me that."

He straightens ever so slightly. And in the glowing light, his eyes look almost misted over. She longs to reach out and touch him, crash into his embrace, but she doubts he would hug her back.

"Tomorrow," he says, then vanishes into the guest room.

DOKÖRAN'S WRATH

For days, Doköran has hardly left his tent. The Raiders have kept a wide berth around his quarters: not even Orius has dared enter the tent uninvited. The slave girls who bring the flasks of wine and plates of dried meat tremble more than usual in his presence. They dare not meet his eyes. On the night the captives escaped, he personally executed the woman who was entertaining him. It was mindless and swift. He slit her throat with a deep blow to the jugular, and she died with a sputtering gasp. He didn't want to see her anymore. Any sight of her thick black hair across the camp would only remind him of this, his most humiliating loss. That he was here, in his tent, drunk with a girl, while his bounty slipped through his hands.

They were here. He had them within his grasp, in his camp, in his land, and they escaped. Utterly unacceptable.

He was a fool to trust that slimy weasel, that Republic scum. Oh, but how he enjoyed being the one to sever the man's head from his body. Sometimes, it was not just necessary to kill, it was *good*.

Now, it is morning, and the air is thick with dust. Doköran sits at his rough-hewn table. His longhorn helmet lies abandoned by his boots. His horn mug is empty, his plate is hardly touched. His ax is propped by the tent flap, still red from Ellington's blood. Doköran has never been angrier. He can feel the anger coarse through him, hot and heavy as brew. He wants to crush something in his hands, something soft and tender.

They were so close! There would have been more gold than his men had ever seen, enough to secure the finest ships on the black market and gun powder from the Eastern Alliance. They could have hired mercenaries to attack the Republic at its heart, at the Chancellor's Basilica. Orius had said these men would lead to the girl, but so much for that prediction. These captives made the Raiders look weak.

Doköran snatches his horned mug and throws it against the tent wall. It collides with a thud on the canvas, then falls and rolls into the camp.

And the camp is quiet. Usually, there are all the gruff and rumbling sounds of the morning rhythm. The hunters leave to scavenge; the women boil water on the fire pits and bathe the young ones; while the men sharpen their weapons, barter with each other to exchange goods or rations. The kill from the prior morning is taken from the drying rack to be skinned, cut, and salted. But for days, there has been silence. Everyone is huddled in their camps, still. Even the young ones do not run around and play, as they usually do, with pig-bladder balls and stone-carved dolls.

At least Corvis should be back soon, his delivery complete.

Doköran stands at this thought. He strides through his tent and blinks in the pale sun. Most of the wake from that disastrous night has been cleaned up, hidden from him. But he can still smell the ale, the bile and piss from the night of preemptive feasting. He moves through the camp to Orius' tent, small and covered with puma furs along the exterior.

Inside, the mage sits on his simple tri-leg stool. His knuckles are white from grasping his staff. Orius does not look up when Doköran enters. His gaze is fixed steadily on a girl, the young blonde one Corvis claimed. Her wrists are tethered with leather straps, and she is as skinny as a starving desert coyote.

"Is Corvis back?" Doköran demands. The girl does not meet his eyes, but she visibly grimaces at the man's name. She stares at the dirt and bites her lip, but Orius slowly turns his gaze. He smiles, as though nothing out of the ordinary has happened.

"Not yet. Grenn and I have just been having a little heart to heart, haven't we?" She says nothing.

"However you choose to entertain yourself is of no importance to me," groans Doköran. "But I want to hear the moment he returns. We have a response to plan for this treachery."

"Be patient, my Lord," says Orius. He leans toward Grenn and runs one finger from the nape of her neck to the soft curve of her shoulder. "I have a feeling the captives will be back. After all, they'll want their pet back. Besides, it turns out our little desert flower here knows Miss Adylyn."

Only now does she raise her eyes to his. He sees that they are blue-green but red-veined from lack of sleep. There is a plea in that gaze, desperation. Something about this look, this confirmation that yes, she knows Adylyn, makes his blood hot again. He could crush her right here. He could take her back to his tent and have his way. He could slit her throat like he did the other—he could make her yet a second example of what happens when you cross with the Raiders of the Rebellion.

Instead, he looks at Orius. The mage is pleased, and his smile only deepens the wrinkles on his sallow skin.

"All the men who were on guard that night," Doköran says slowly. "I want them killed. I want it to be bloody. And I want their bodies staked outside of camp so that when the wretches return—if they return—they will know just who they're dealing with.

VISION

Eagan awakes, numb and disoriented. The light is strong and pink in the room, cresting over the beds from the high windows. Five other members of the Brutallion are in the room with him, and they all still sleep soundly.

Last night hangs in his head like an unshakeable fog, like he'd gotten drunk on rhubarb wine or ale. But as he sits up, he knows it's just exhaustion—that, and the weariness of remembering, again, those first few moments in Atheria.

But as he stands and dresses in one of the Atherian tunics hanging from his bedpost, he finds that the bruises along his back no longer grip him with pain at every turn. And the cuts along his arms? They have healed neatly, like torn fabric stitched with simple thread. It's as though the very water and air of this place have healed him already.

When he opens the chamber door, he finds Ady waiting in the corridor. She is seated on the ground, her head against the stone wall. A thick silver book, with blank pages he notices, is open in her lap. A green dress pools around her ankles as she stands.

"How long have you been here?" he asks.

"Not long. I couldn't sleep much. Are you hungry?"

Eagan shakes his head. His stomach is still full from the small feast on the Aurora.

"So," she ventures, biting her lip. "Are you ready, then? I want to show you the Hall of Knowledge."

The thought of repeating yesterday's fight makes the pain in his body return. But Ady stands there, looking so small and perfect, her wild hair tamed back with a golden comb and braid. She tucks the book awkwardly under her arm. She has that same expression from the day he left out the West Gate with his men, that *Please come back to me* look.

"Fine, okay," he says and follows her down the hallway.

They are silent all through the corridor, past the few Nobles already at their work, past the atrium with its geometric shapes glimmering in the marble, finally past a fountain guarded by statues of angels. Ady stops at rounded wooden doors, set back in the stone.

"Do you remember, back in the Citadel, when we found the music room?" Ady smiles at Eagan, her hand on the handle. "And there were those little triangles that made a sound when we tapped them? That's one of my favorite memories, exploring with you. Atheria, for me, has been like a hundred forgotten rooms—a whole forgotten world that I've been able to explore. I know that yesterday didn't go well. I know you're angry with me. I know you've been through things I can't even imagine. But please, just let me try to show you this place. Just try to understand."

And she opens the doors.

At first glance of the Hall's towering book stacks, Eagan knows instantly why Ady must love life here. What could the Citadels, or even life outside them, offer that could compete with this? The bookcases are taller than the airships, reaching high into arched ceilings. Rolling ladders climb to their highest shelves. Cloud-white morning sun cascades through the high windows and catches the colorful book spines.

"This is my favorite place in all of Atheria," Ady says. "It houses all of the knowledge from the Old World and the wisdom for the New World." She strolls forward, "This is where I read, study, train. It's where I've learned about my place here, *why* it was so important for me to come to Atheria."

"I can see why. It's a little better than our Citadel library. Plus, it isn't burned down."

She sets the book gently down on one of the long tables.

When was the last time he'd stepped foot in the library? He quit attending lectures years ago. His whole world has been training, rampart miles, carrying sand bags for weight training. He has studied lancing, fencing, vaulting; he has learned how to subsist with little to no food, which saved his life these past three weeks. His world has been survival, not scholarship.

He snaps to attention as Ady keeps talking.

"There is a reason why this is all happening now, not years ago. Not years from now. There is a darkness in the world. Something worse than you or I could ever have imagined."

"We've always known that."

His father used to tell him about the hidden forces. Before his arrest and death, James told the most vivid and beautifully-spun stories at night, by flickering candle flames. He talked about the War and the rebuilding era, sure—but also beliefs and myths from the Old World. Stories of floods and giants, plagues and priests, back when life seemed mythic and meaningful. James had believed in something, Eagan knew, that the Republic didn't want him to: he'd believed in goodness, that there was still light in the world. And darkness, too.

"I don't just mean that evil resides in people," says Ady. "I don't even mean the Great War—at least, not *just* that." She walks to the cases and places a hand on the spines with such solemnity. Has he ever seen her so serious? His Ady used to hide away in the garden, his Ady used to sneak from the dormitories at night and explore, sending shivers of worry up his spine when he'd climb through the window to find an empty room. And yet he loved this. She was his North Star, bright and shining, and he was a ship, always chasing her. Now, here she stands, her thick brown hair braided down her back. She turns, and her eyes gleam with a secret. "This darkness is a voice that whispers inside your head, telling you to do something you shouldn't. I think they're what make Cayhill the way he is, and all of his men. I have seen this darkness, Eagan." Her voice takes on an urgent tone. "I have visions, and I've seen them. They're unspeakable, like shadow creatures, but they are real. They can corrupt even the purest soul. They can make a brother kill a brother, or a ruler annihilate his own people. These books?" She gestures to the grand shelves. "I've been studying them, what I can. The whole history of the world is here. And now that I know about the evil, about the Erlick Federation, I can see their hand in everything: every bombing, every genocide. I see what they are capable of. And all this? This is just what they've been able to do while still trapped behind the Iron Gates, where they've been for thousands of years...I can't even fathom what they could do if free. And they want something that has been entrusted to me." She nods to the silver book, which looks more sacred than a sanctuary in the whole Republic. "The Book of Light."

Eagan just blinks at her. It's as though overnight, she calmed—today, she is like a cool pearl, bright and blushing. Beautiful, earnest.

Yet what she says sounds absolutely foolish. Can she hear herself?

He crosses his arms and leans back against one of the tables.

"Proceed," he says, trying to keep the scoff from his voice.

"Please take this seriously."

"I am, try me."

Ady takes a deep breath and holds her hands against her chest. "I am an anointed one," she says at last. "Me and...others. We are called to do spiritual work by the Council of Light. We are called upon this mission to help demolish the darkness that is coming."

"And by others, you mean *him*?"

"Atriel is one of them, yes. But there will be others, too. Someday."

"Oh, others, will there? Other handsome young men? Anointed? And anointed by whom, exactly?"

He watches the color flush to her cheeks, redder than a desert sunset. "This isn't funny. This is real. You said you'd let me show you, now let me."

She explains about Atheria and the anointed ones: about time in this plane versus the outside world, about the Council of Light, the god-like guardians watching over Earth and all her people. She speaks quickly, like an oracle. Her words come faster and faster. She steps forward when describing the Archlights, the messengers from the heavens, how she's seen them, even touched them—a wolf that is called to protect her, a hawk that circles the sky. And it's not that Eagan tries to discount what she says. As he settles against the wooden table, as the warm morning light hits his face from the high windows, all he can see is that this, this is not his Ady. Her eyes have never lit up like *this* in the Citadel, not when they explored the music room; not when he first moved his hand to her hips as if to say *I love you*; not when she kissed him in the garden for the first time, on the stone bench with her legs across his; not even when he gave her the pocket watch, his father's, that beloved token, before he marched out with the Redcoats. And suddenly, as she nears him, close enough to touch, it's not so much funny or even delusional. Mostly, it is achingly sad.

Suddenly, Ady stiffens. Her head tilts as though she's listening for some sound on the wind. Eagan looks up, but there are only the arched beams in the ceiling above. Then, from the high windows, a shadow appears—a hawk. The bird catches the light before gliding into the Hall. His wingspan is almost as long as Ady, and his talons look sharper than a sword. Eagan leaps back from the table and instinctively reaches for his sheath, but there are only the tassels from his Atherian robe. Ady does not move. She watches the hawk spiral and land where Eagan was just standing, the claws gripping the table's edge.

"What are you doing?" Eagan shouts. He steps further away from the bird and collides with a velvet reading chair behind him.

Ady stays calm. She does not flinch, but only stretches out one hand. The hawk nuzzles at her touch, and Eagan could swear he sees the faintest shimmer of gold as its feathers rustle. Ady's lips move gently and silently, it's as if they are communicating in some silent language.

Eagan stumbles into the open chair, his heart pounding. The bird lifts its tail feathers now, then wings. When it lifts from the table, it flies smoothly out the window as if carried on some invisible current.

For a long moment, Ady just stares ahead of her. There is no clear emotion on her face, no fear or confusion. Eagan watches as she closes her eyes, then kneels and presses her palms against the cold stone.

"Ady?" he calls. His voice bounces between the bookcases.

She does not answer. Her body trembles slightly, as though in some sort of trance. Is she having a vision?

Eagan stands and moves in slow, cautious steps toward her. From the corner of his eye, he watches the high windows for any sign of the hawk. When he reaches Ady, still collapsed near the shelves, Eagan kneels and places a hand on her shoulder.

His touch seems to startle her awake. Ady sits back on her heels and gives Eagan a long look, laced with meaning he cannot interpret.

"That was a message from the Council," she says. "Our time is running out."

STRATEGIZING

Ady shakes with adrenaline as she runs down the palace corridor. Every sensation seems alert and alive. Her brain buzzes with activity in the aftermath of the Archlight's message and the vision that followed. She narrowly misses a Noble carrying a taper candle and sacred scroll, and she almost drops the Book of Light. Eagan is at her heels, calling for her, but she can think of only one thing: the Crystal Hall. She must find Athos and warn him. There isn't much time.

The passageway opens into the central atrium, where Athos is just coming up the garden steps with Atriel. Their heads are bent toward each other, and their voices are low. Atriel notices her waving. He grins and steps forward to greet her with an outstretched hand. She does not take it.

"I need to talk to you both," she says, practically breathless.

"We've been on the grounds for a morning lesson," says Athos. His voice is steady and calm, as though he's come out of deep meditation. His beard looks almost bronze in the morning sun.

"You look agitated. Is everything alright?" Atriel's gaze goes past Ady, and she knows he must be watching Eagan.

But there is no time for that, for their quarrel. Ady takes a deep breath.

"I received a message from the Council of Light."

"When, now?"

"Yes, it was the hawk. In the Hall of Knowledge. I've seen him many times before, but never up close. And never with a vision."

"There was a vision, too?" says Athos. He looks momentarily delighted. He'd been training Ady for months to understand visions, the Archlights, the Council, messages from the divine, and she can see the pride register on his features. Just as quickly, this is replaced by concern. "Is everything okay?"

"No." Her voice is cool and firm and resounds through the atrium. She can feel everyone stare at her—Eagan and Atriel, the Nobles who have stopped their morning walks and discussions to listen. They stand poised in the hallways like ultramarine shadows.

How to explain everything the hawk said? Shiloh, her wolf, has only ever been a gentle presence, a quiet observer. But this bird, peregrine brown, looked at her so intently with his golden eyes that he seemed almost human. And she could sense—hear—his urgency. He was firm but not afraid. She could tell by the way he did not flinch at her touch. His head moved to meet her palm. A calm flooded her whole body, like relaxing in a warm bath. Everything in the Hall of Knowledge seemed to vanish except the bird. The books, the old paper smell, even Eagan backing away in shock. It all melted away, so there were only her and the hawk and a message from the Light.

"The hawk came to me with a message from the Council. I had a vision. Of where we must go."

Athos straightens his shoulders and surveys the growing audience around them. Ito, Tiri, and a few of the others have just emerged from the guest chambers. The Nobles still watch in silence.

"Let's go to the Crystal Hall," he says. "We can talk there."

Her vision was as clear as the summer sun. She saw the desert, the dunes taller than the Citadel walls. The valleys were dark charcoal, and the sky was more gray than blue. This was from a bird's eye view—the hawk's, she knew somehow—and they were flying in wide, slow circles over the brown earth below. She saw tents, animal hide, smoke. She saw men with horned helmets, women over open-fire pits, boats staked in the ground like makeshift walls. The smoke stings her eyes, and she can smell the meat skewered over the open flames, dry to the bone. She knows it's the Raiders' camp, though she's never seen it. But from a distance, she could tell that these, these were the warriors who attacked the Citadel; these were the men who set fire to her home. She saw the Raven eye branded across his chest, and she knew this must be their leader.

And this, this is where they must go.

They settle in the Crystal Hall—Ady, Athos, Eagan, and Atriel. Athos stands tall, eagerly awaiting her news. Eagan stays by the door, his arms crossed, the confusion evident on his face. Atriel keeps one hand on the emerald column. Each of the gems around the room glistens like colors cut straight from the fabric of a rainbow.

She stands in the center of the room with the Book of Light clutched to her chest. She feels like an ancient speaker about to deliver a homily. Athos nods for her to proceed.

"When I came here," she begins. She thinks of those first early days and hours in Atheria when she was still confused by everything, shocked by the peacefulness, the bliss that seemed impossible. "You told me, Athos, that the evil ones, the darkness, is growing in power. That for every human life they take, the Iron Gates keeping them locked away, weaken. The Great War, of course, killed most of humanity. Which means, their power grew like never before."

This is old news to everyone, she knows, except Eagan. She glances at him to gauge his reaction to so much in one day, but his expression does not change. His gaze is cold, and his arms remain crossed.

"The Council of Light has informed us that the gateway has opened further. The Erlick Federation is almost free. We have even less time than we thought we did."

The gateway is opening, the hawk whispered. *They will soon escape.*

She pauses and waits for Athos or Atriel to say something, but they don't. The floor is hers, and they watch intently. Before she knows what she's doing, she opens the Book of Light to its center spine. That same glow is there, but still, the pages are blank. "The Federation is clearly feeding off the Republic's evil, their cruelty," Ady continues, closing the book solidly again. "We need to return to the Lower West Citadel and face them. But there are not enough of us to stop them alone. We need help. We need warriors, skilled fighters who know the terrain of the Old World. The Atherian army is skilled, yes, but they do not know worldly warfare like humans do. It is different."

"Nor will they fight. Their existence *must* remain silent, they cannot come forward. Not yet," Athos chimes in.

"That is why we need help." Ady continues. "And why we must go to the Rebellion in the Wasteland."

"You can't be serious." Eagan's voice bounces off the far stone wall. It's his military voice, that deep bellow that can claim the attention of a whole rank of men.

Ady gives him a long look. She knows him so well, every tick and tremble, every faint sign of emotion. She can read him. There is true fear in his eyes now and alarm, and she knows that this is for her—the way he feared when she explored forgotten rooms at night, feared that she would be caught and punished by the Bluecoats. What's strange is the spirit of calm that seemed to settle on her soul during the hawk's visit remains. Much of the fury and anguish from last night is a memory. There is only the message: time is running out. This is bigger than all of them. "I assure you," she says slowly, "that I am."

Eagan strides forward into the light. Atriel does not stir but traces a finger over the ivy designs carved into the stone.

"Do you hear yourself?" Eagan cries. "Ady, we saw what they did to the Citadel—how they killed men and women and children as if it was nothing. Human life to them was *nothing*."

Of course she remembers! Of course she knows! Does he really think she wants this to be the plan? Or that she's purposefully proposing a suicide mission? But she keeps her cool. She does not raise her voice.

"I saw it in the vision, Eagan. We will go there. And they will help us."

"I can't believe this. Me and my men were just there."

"Alright now, you can't come here and tell us how to strategize," says Atriel. He moves from the emerald pillar and places himself between Eagan and Ady. "We've been working toward this plan long before you got here."

Ady tries to interject, but the men are too quick.

"Oh, excuse me," Eagan scoffs now.

"We must trust the process, trust the Council's word. And trust in her visions," Atriel says sternly.

"And have you fought the Raiders?" Eagan asks loudly.

"No, I've been training—"

"Training. Right." It takes every ounce of strength for Ady to not roll her eyes. She glances at Athos for support, but he is still deep in thought. "Well, *Atriel*, I've actually seen them firsthand. They brutalized us—they tortured us, starved us. They beheaded our captain. I saw that myself. And Grenn?" He looks at Ady now, pleading. "Do you know what they've done to Grenn? I don't think Tiri will ever recover."

"Eagan, please."

"She's one of their war brides now, Ady. And they're not monogamous. Your best friend. And these are the so-called allies you want to turn to?"

Ady closes her eyes at the blow. She expected a bleeding out in the Citadel's medical ward; she thought, perhaps, that Grenn died during their flight to Atheria. Never this. Never something as horrible as this. But even as the panic tingles on her skin, she can feel her own rage sharpen.

"All the more reason to go. We will get her back," she says. "We *must* get her back."

The quarrel continues. Even Atriel's voice gets loud, and Ady thinks she's never heard him yell before. He is usually the gentle one, the quiet one, known for his ability to walk silently through the woods, to strike with his staff from behind. His face darkens to an even richer tan while Eagan looks flushed pink. At last, Ady shouts: "Enough!"

They stop and look at her with surprise.

"We will listen to the Council," she says, her voice low and strong. "I need you to trust me."

And this is when Athos moves. His eyes are still trained on the ground when he walks to Ady and places one hand on her shoulder. He says nothing—but for a moment, he looks even more like the male counterpart of their mother Laylia. Ady has seen this expression before as a child when she gathered wildflowers and dried them herself or when she memorized stories to decant back at dinner. It's the look of regard and a hint of tearfulness. She almost cries herself when he smiles at her and nods. "We will do as she says."

THE DUEL

Ito has never felt more simultaneously exhausted and exhilarated in his life. He slept deeper and longer than he has in days. And as he roams through the palace corridors, Tiri at his side, he can still feel the soft imprint of the Atherian quilts on his skin. Not to mention that after the heavenly steam and hot water in the bathhouses last night, he still smells of rose and jasmine and some herb he can't quite place. The tiredness still resides—still, too, the grim memories of the days before. The terror of expecting death at any moment, smelling their own piss bake in the Wasteland sun as they huddled, tied and dirty, for hours that turned into days that turned into weeks. And then, freed at last, he ran with whatever strength was still in his body for the Republic's airship. He did not look back, though he knew what must be happening to Captain Ellington, how the Raiders must have slaughtered him.

But now, there is Atheria. There is rest and food at last. After Ady runs breathless through the central atrium—after she retreats with her brother, Atriel, Eagan—he and Tiri venture to the dining hall where other members of the Brutallion have already settled at the long tables for breakfast. All through a meal of spring greens and fruit, Tiri is quiet. He hunches over his plate and hardly glances at the dazzling morning light that shimmers through the hall. But Ito can hardly get enough. They'd been living in the Citadel for how many years? All while a place like this, an Eden of floating islands, with oceans of water that had not dried up, still existed?

After breakfast, they continue to explore the palace. They poke into various chambers and dodge the Nobles, some of whom try to pin them into conversations about life in the Lower West Citadel.

But it's the grounds that capture their attention. Outside the central atrium, on the wide green landscape, they find rows of Atherians with their palms raised toward the sky, as if in deep meditation. They all wear Atheric blue cloaks, mimicking the color of their spirited eyes, more vibrant than the Bluecoats dark uniforms. Their breastplates are like lustrous mirrors, reflecting the sun. Nearby on the manicured grass, there are racks of swords and staffs, spears, shields, and large stones. The metal gleams in the morning light. They're brighter than silver, glowing—as if there is an auric field of blue light emanating off each weapon. They look like they are crafted straight from the stars.

"What would Cayhill make of that?" says Ito, nodding at the swords. The blades have intricate feathered designs running all the way to the hilt.

"What do you think they're doing?" says Tiri, staring at the Atherian soldiers. This is the first he's spoken, maybe in days, and Ito is almost startled by the deep resonance of his voice. His features have been dark and lined with fury for weeks, but now, for a fleeting moment in the morning sun, he looks engaged.

"Praying? Chanting? I don't know. Let's get a closer look."

They descend the steps. When their sandaled feet hit the grass, they can see the wildflowers that grow in every color along the grounds and the tree line leading to the forest. The sky is a shimmering blue, though still pink in the east from the sunrise. The soldiers—Atherian men and women—do not acknowledge their presence. They remain in lined formation with eyes closed and heads tilted to the clouds.

"Definitely different," says Tiri.

But Ito is onto the weapons. Usually, he fights with speed and with fists. He knows he's the fastest runner in the Brutallion. He can beat Eagan's mile time by nearly half a minute. He is better with a dagger than with any heavy sword or, like Tiri, a bludgeon. Tiri was always the brute-force one—could crush a man's skull between his fists. But these weapons are unlike anything he's ever seen: intricate with artistry, not like the rough wood and inelegant steel of the Republic's weaponry. The Redcoats' gladius was clumsy, not balanced with weight. Their arrow shafts were wooden. Everything here was that opulent, bright metal.

"Have you seen anything like this before?" Ito asks as Tiri lifts one of the spears from the rack.

"Atherian alloy," comes a voice from behind them. Ito turns to see Atriel coming down the palace steps. The man is firm and tan, with a shadow along his jawline from a forming beard. He is lean but clearly strong from where the muscle shows through his robes. "It's the strongest material known to man. Impenetrable."

Ito smiles in thanks but looks behind Atriel for any sign of the others. Was their meeting over? Had Atriel stormed out? He glimpses Eagan marching toward the central atrium. His broad figure appears in the arched open windows with every step until he stops and sees them. Ito nods in his direction, and Eagan pivots to join. Even from here, Ito can tell that something has happened. Something is wrong. Eagan's face is flushed as if he'd just completed several rounds of wall miles on the rampart. This is not just the anger from last night, from their arrival. Is it that Atriel is talking to members of the Brutallion at all? Or had something grave transpired in the conversation with Ady?

Tiri is oblivious to this, his attention only on the spear as Atriel joins him at the weapon rack. Tiri cocks his shoulder back as if about to throw, and the spear tip catches the sun like a prism.

"What is the alloy exactly?" he asks.

"It's a combination of many different metals, only found, harvested, and smithed here." Atriel reaches for the sword that Ito had been eyeing. "The properties found in this Atherian metal are so much older than anything found outside this realm. It makes the metal stronger, less malleable. Perfect for the indestructible weapon."

Ito stands back as Eagan approaches in quick and long strides.

"Did you get breakfast?" Ito asks, trying to prevent whatever is about to happen. But Eagan doesn't hear him. His focus is only on Atriel as the spear releases from Tiri's hand and soars like an attacking falcon toward the treeline.

"Showing off your toys?" Eagan snaps. Atriel looks up with a placid expression. Ito almost smiles—he knows this will only infuriate Eagan more. He is not usually known for outbursts of anger, but one thing he cannot handle is disrespect or dismissiveness. Eagan is like his father in this way.

"These are not toys," says Atriel. There is no sign of anger or even tension on his face. "These are weapons made of Atherian alloy."

"Is that so?"

"They're of superior quality to anything you'll find in the outside world." Atriel holds the sword up to the light, and the bright metal glimmers along the blade's detail.

"Superior quality," Eagan nods, hands on his hips now. "Of course."

Atriel casts him a look that is at once patronizing and cold. Ito sighs—he knows what's coming.

"I mean no offense," Atriel says. "I used to fight with those outdated weapons, too. I've seen how they break. How knives dull or spears snap. Once you try these, you'll never want to go back."

"You've been caught up in this whole madness here too, haven't you?" Eagan patronizes.

Atriel holds up his left hand. "Look, let's leave our disagreements to official meetings, shall we?"

Ito and Tiri exchange glances and slowly back away.

"No, let's take it out right now," says Eagan.

Atriel makes a half bow as if to say *As you wish then*. He holds out the sword hilt for Eagan, who takes it with one hand.

"Heavier than it looks," Eagan murmurs. He scoffs when Atriel retrieves a simple bo staff.

Ito knows better than to discount such weaponry. In the Eastern Alliances, soldiers and rogues alike could do real damage with wooden weapons, combined with hand-to-hand combat. But this, this is Atherian alloy. He and Tiri step back, quiet now, as Atriel and Eagan take their places near the palace's stone steps.

They move around each other, slinking like cats with slow steps. Until Atriel lunges first and strikes low with the staff, hitting Eagan in the shins. He cries out in pain, then lifts the sword, clearly heavier than what he's used to—Ito sees his shoulders strain—and makes contact with the staff. There is the softest sound of metal against metal. It is not like the practice duels on the Redcoats training grounds. Those, when Captain Ellington would watch from his scaffold, were like simulations. There were understood moves and protocols. Ito watches in both delight at the weapons and horror at the men.

"What do you even want with her?" Eagan shouts as his blade meets Atriel's staff, narrowly missing the man's shoulder.

"What are you talking about? I want to *support* her!" Atriel lunges back as Eagan thrusts toward his neck.

Eagan is not fighting his best, Ito can see that. He is beyond angry, into an enraged space. He takes jolting steps and brings the sword down hard. But Atriel is graceful. He leaps away like a stag each time.

"Do you know what powers exist in her?" Atriel says, taking the offensive now. "What she is capable of?" He tries an upswing that Eagan deflects.

"Of course. I've known her all my life."

"Not like this—you haven't seen her like this."

Eagan's rage is fueled again. Ito looks up to the palace and sees the wrinkled faces of the Nobles watching from the arched windows as the scene unfolds below. Is it possible that Eagan would be angry enough to kill Atriel? Or Atriel kill Eagan? After all, this is his space. He has the upper hand, and that much is clear as the bo staff meets Eagan's bicep, then his abdomen, finally the back of his neck.

This is when someone shouts, "Enough!"

It is a chilling voice and an Atherian strides from the ranks of the soldiers. The army has stopped the meditation. Their arms are lowered as they watch the duel.

The figure's face is as pale as the moon, he is tall and muscular. Long, pearlescent white hair hangs to his lower back. But Eagan and Atriel either don't hear the voice or do not register. Ito watches in amazement as the Atherian lifts both arms, palms wide open toward the sky, and then heaves his arms forward, thrusting a great force into thin air—the two men plummet backward to the ground. They begin coughing and sputtering for breath once they land on the ground.

The general's expression is grim with disappointment.

"There will be no fighting on Atherian ground. Atriel, you should know that."

"Yes, Thelios, of course I do," comes his quiet voice.

"We train to protect Atheria. Humans are so quick to fight one another over their differences and do not understand that the damage inflicted goes beyond the pain in the body."

Ito and Tiri listen intently to the general and stay silent as the duelers stand, shake the grass from their clothes, and discard their weapons. But Ito can tell by their expressions—the fierce anger in Eagan and the cold hardness in Atriel—that this is far from over.

PREPARATIONS

For Ady, the next few hours and days are a blur of exhaustion and elation. After strategizing in the Crystal Hall, preparations are made. First, Ady shares the news with Edgar and the crew, all of whom are practically thrilled to be traveling again. Then she convenes with Gaia and Echo when they bring the evening meal. They are more stoic and somber, but they are also wholly unsurprised by the news, and Ady can almost sense pride in their gleaming blue eyes.

"We knew you'd come only to leave," says Echo. "That's the point of a calling. It calls you elsewhere."

It doesn't take long for word to ripple throughout the palace, then throughout the island, that there has been a vision from the Council of Light. That the anointed ones are leaving.

Atherian airships from the other floating islands begin to appear on the horizon. Crates of fresh fruit—every color, size, and shape—appear at the palace steps. Warm loaves of bread and hand-sewn Atherian silks, shorter robes with high-leg slits tailor-made for war, and smooth staffs built of Atherian alloy. They bring small white birds and rose oils, ribbons, rhubarb wines, blown glass, things they would never need in the Wasteland. Still, the gifts pile high like offerings left on an altar.

Inside the palace, the Nobles still keep their distance, but Ady sometimes sees them hover in the corridors as if striving to overhear snippets of her conversations with Athos. *What airships will we take? Can we all fit in two ships? Who are your best pilots?* She and Athos will be moving through the palace, in between meetings and preparations, between packing and overseeing the food supply, and the Nobles will emerge from their study chambers. They will stand and watch and whisper. At night, she can sometimes see the faintest glow from their Atherian skin outside her chamber doors. And in the morning, she finds scrolls from the high shelves, selects books from the Hall of Knowledge propped against the passage walls. Their titles are varied and even, sometimes, humorous: *Sun Tzu's The Art of War* and *Summa Logicae* and even the Icelandic *Edda*, brimming with religious verse. Ady stores each of these parchments away in her trunks tucked safely beside The Book of Light. She knows they are gifts from the Nobles—their way of saying, *Be safe. We are with you.*

Atriel and Thelios prepare an array of weapons, forged with Atherian alloy, knowing their strength will be indispensable to the mission. Damages to be fixed on the Republic airship were underway. Edgar wouldn't allow such repairs on his vessel, as the Aurora was his, a hardknock beauty in all her splendor in his eyes. Apart from a few Atherian upgrades.

Gaia and Echo, too, help Ady prepare. Echo abandons the most recent embroidery project—a depiction of an archangel with outstretched wings—to finish a dress and cloak for Ady's departure. "It is threaded with Atherian silks, and within it, the angematonic element. It is impenetrable from any human weapon. It will protect you," Echo tells her. Gaia travels to one of the furthest Atherian islands to gather tea leaves from a cool spring. "This Enchanted Tea," says Gaia upon return, placing long leaf-like stems in Ady's palm, "can make anyone fall asleep. Its aura is blue, dark blue like night. And this one—" Gaia retrieves a handful of dried golden leaves from a small silk bag."—This one will give you vitality. These leaves are only found in the cool, dark soil near my home's quarry. They will bless you."

But there are so many other considerations: how will they negotiate for Grenn's release? What if the Rebellion opens fire on the airships? Or worse, what if they followed in their own Ravens' fleet, traced them back to Atheria?

But Athos does not seem fazed by these concerns.

"We'll load the weapons Thelios and Atriel have prepared for us onto the Aurora and the Republic airship," says Athos during the morning meal one day. The dining hall is full of the Brutallion occupying many long tables, but they are alone, sequestered to the back under one of the low-hanging chandeliers. "I have a crew working on the Republic airship now, sprucing it up, mending a few patches on the hull. It will fly a new sail, Atherian silk. Obviously, we hope to avoid military contact with the Rebellion, but we can't be unprepared."

"So we'll have just the two ships?" Ady asks.

Athos smiles, clearly excited. "Both are now fully equipped with the angematonic element. I hear you already saw this in action on the way here? It can aid the ships in traveling fast *and* cloaking. I think you will find it will come in handy in many different scenarios. Thelios will join us to help guide the crew in using these elements. You will fly cloaked, hidden until you need to be seen. Do not fear. The ships will be ready. All prior damage from the journey here will be healed."

She smiles at the sound of that. Even as the worries arise, the closer they get to leaving, Ady knows deep within her that this is right, that everything is falling into place—finally. The vision from the hawk circles in her mind like the bird's steady flight pattern. She sees the Wasteland, the Rebellion from her vision, she hears the Archlight's urgent warning that *Time is running out. The gateway is closer than ever to unlocking.* Never has she felt so sure of anything. It's the kind of knowledge that infiltrates dreams, that she feels in her subconscious. Ady pulls a grape off a stem, and as she eats, she catches sight of the hawk's faint silhouette through the high arched windows.

The Brutallion gathers at sunset on the grounds. Thelios and the Atherian army have finished their meditations and rituals for the day; Atriel, Athos, and Ady are out of sight, likely busying themselves with last-minute arrangements on the ships. Eagan stands on the rough stone steps. The sky is warmer than a navel orange as the sun lowers in the west. The trees in the distance are just beginning to glisten with the glowing light orbs. His men stand at attention, some with their hands clasped before them.

They have recovered well, every one of them.

"My brothers," Eagan begins. He has not addressed them this way in what feels like ages. Was it that fateful meeting in the Citadel before they marched out the

West Gate? Oh, what hell they'd been through since that evening. Would these men still have joined him if they'd known the cost? Eagan struggles to keep his voice even. "You have fought hard. I know the sacrifices you have made. I have made them, too. You have fulfilled your purpose in protecting our people. You fought valiantly alongside one another against not one enemy but two. The Rebellion and the Republic. But there is a greater war before us, something much larger than both of those."

At first, Eagan tried to ignore the preparations. He tried to cloister himself to the guest chambers and simply enjoy Atheria. He took long walks in the woods, swam in the waterfall pools at dusk. But on his daily walks, as he witnessed the Atherians load weapons, food, medical supplies, linens, and canteens aboard the ships, something in him softened. And he kept replaying that moment from the Crystal Hall. Ady stood tall and calm. Her shoulders were rolled back, her chin was raised. Had he ever seen her like this before? He doesn't think so. Her voice was so measured as she said, "I saw it in a vision, Eagan. We will go there. And they will help us." Such assurance! Her eyes bored into him, pleading but sure. And as the days passed, as that moment tapped away at his conscience, he knew what he would do.

Now he looks out at his men, at every face and precious life. Tiri and Ito stand near the front, and they nod for him to continue.

"Our fight continues. I am sure this is no surprise to you now. You've heard it for days, you've seen the planning, the measures, the supplies. You know that two ships are leaving for the Wasteland any day. That they are heading back to the Rebellion."

Here, he halts. He looks fiercely in the men's eyes, lingering on each gaze sometimes so long that the man looked away first. But there is no outcry. No one turns to leave. Is it possible that these men who'd just been beaten, stripped, humiliated, left to burn in the sun and bleed without care, forced to witness the bloody slaughter of their former Captain, would choose to go back?

Eagan steps off the stairs so that he stands on even ground with them. "I don't expect you to go back. I don't. Your allegiance to this brotherhood is over if you want it to be. I will not judge you. I cannot. Because I also cannot ask you to return to the very place you barely survived. But our new battle begins there."

This is when Tiri thrusts his fist into the air and releases a guttural cry. The others follow suit. Clenched fists of every color and size punch toward the sky as their shouts ring out. Eagan joins them as they all move their fists to their hearts. One by one, they begin beating their chests. Faster and faster, letting out barbaric cries. He moves through the throng of men as they group tighter and tighter around each other like one pulsating, angry, ready riot. They will go to the Wasteland, Eagan knows then. They will follow Ady, and maybe this time, maybe later, they will have their revenge.

THE EASTERN DRIFT

The island is still and calm, heavy with anticipatory silence. Tonight, the night seems darker, the stars seem brighter. There is even something more, something Ady's never seen before in Atheria. Colors of pink, green, yellow, blue, and violet dance along the night sky, like an ethereal river through the darkness. She watches as it prances across the sky. And the gridlines thread between the constellations in silvery streaks. She stops and takes in the breathtaking sea of colors before noticing how strangely quiet it is. Usually, the night birds sing.

Ady could not sleep. Adrenaline pulsed through her veins all day, as she watched the Aurora's crew load the final baskets of food onboard. Tomorrow, they leave.

But something called Ady out of her chambers tonight. As she laid out Echo's silks for the morning—cloud white—and drained a mug of Gaia's tea, some small voice tugged at her, saying to leave the palace. Explore Atheria one more time: there was more, yet, to see. She did, but not down the palace's marble steps. Instead, she left by the back steps and walked across the grounds to the far line of trees on the other end of the island.

Now, she stands on the eastern banks, far from the docks and the cliffs that precipice over the beaches. One of the many waterfalls flows here, but this one is small, gentle. There is no thick white foam and no roar. Instead, the water's flow is serpentine and crests on rock ledges that break its surge. The small fed creek weaves through the Atherian earth and trickles south to where, she suspects, it will grow strong with currents again, become another cascade. The floating light orbs hug closer to the ground, dancing just off the wildflowers and dandelions, the grass sprouts and reeds along the pool of water. Most beautiful of all, gnarled roots rise in and out of the pool, connected to the largest tree Ady has ever seen. Its branches are thick and wide like open arms, and the trunk itself is nearly as wide as the palace's central atrium.

Ady leans against the tree's mossy bark. She breathes in the warm and earthy scent of the water here. For a moment, she feels like herself in the Citadel, exploring alone, at night. She felt desperate in those days to escape the confines of her dormitory, the Republic. And then, how quickly she was desperate to get back, just return to what she loved and knew. Didn't she spend every day aboard the Aurora practically sulking in her room, grieving the loss of her loved ones? Only at night did she attempt to explore the ship alone. She thinks of what she wrote in her final letter to Eagan: "I needed to completely break down before I could rebuild."

The floating lights reflect across the creek's surface. They dance and bob in the air, as carefree as butterflies. Ady can't help but smile at the sight of them.

She'd signed her name that night, *Adylyn of Atheria*. And is that who she is now? Not *Adylyn of the North East Citadel, Torn from Her Brother*? Not *Adylyn of the Lower West, Stripped from Her Love*? As if in response to these thoughts, one of the floating lights rises from the nearby reeds and coasts near her face. Little purple flutters appear within the light's core like feathers, and when she grazes the orb's surface, she finds that it's heated like warm honey.

She knows she is rebuilding. That her gifts are getting stronger.

Even as the week passed with steady and diligent preparations, even as Athos and Atriel supported her decision, even as she watched the natives arrive with freshly forged weapons of Atherian alloy, there was the smallest tingle of doubt. Eagan did not side with her. The one who knew her best. He'd been in her life longer than her mother Laylia, longer than her brother, much longer than Atriel. Eagan had always been her dearest friend, her soul companion. And in the Crystal Hall, he looked at her as if she were a madwoman, leading them all to their deaths. Is she wrong to follow this vision and listen to the Archlight? Is she jeopardizing anyone by returning to a place of danger? And what of Grenn? If they don't go to the Wasteland, are they simply leaving her to die?

Ady rustles the high grass with her feet, and a few stems fall into the creek.

Perhaps the Council of Light is watching, from wherever—whoever—they are. Or perhaps the hawk even now glides through the night sky, coaxing her to listen. Follow. The vision could not have been clearer. The whole Rebellion's camp was laid out like a map. The smell of their smoked meat stung her nostrils, made her want to gag. She could feel it in her subconscious, feel it deep within her heart, that this was where they were to go. The Rebellion would help them. And wasn't it wrong to ignore her gifts and dismiss a message from the Council?

A stick cracks behind her, just a stone's throw away. Ady turns. It can't be Shiloh; she would have sensed the wolf padding through the woods toward her.

Eagan steps through the brush. His frame is outlined only by the stars that gleam through the boughs and the floating orbs that cast a candle-like warmth. His face looks soft tonight, and she almost expects him to come right up and kiss her, or at least brush her hair behind her ear. He has not looked at her like this since the Citadel, all those months before. She smiles at the memories. She used to be able to discern his presence simply by smell.

"Hello," Ady speaks first.

"Hello." He stops near the creek and surveys the grand tree, the waterfall. There is only the sound of the water meeting the stone ledges before it trickles into the brook.

"I've never been here before," Ady returns her gaze to the tree and traces a finger down a strip of bark. "East of the palace, along the drift. And I've never seen a tree like this on Atheria before. Most are slender, taller than our trees, but small enough to move in the wind. Not this one." She follows its trunk to the sky, where the branches become thick and braided together. "It's older than all the Nobles here, older than the palace. Perhaps the oldest living thing on the island."

When she looks back, Eagan has stepped closer. He wears his Atherian robes with a gilded silver belt, and his hair has been cropped back to its usual length. His face has become full once again, a healthy glow has returned, and the scars and bruises along his skin have all but vanished. But it's his eyes—Ady can sense how much he longs to hold her.

"How did you find me?" she says at last.

"I just knew," he shrugs. "Like intuition. An unknowing knowing."

"I understand that feeling." Still, he approaches. Ady stands unmoving with her shoulders back. She cannot melt into him, cannot go weak, not when they leave tomorrow, not when the lives of so many rest on her vision. But Eagan's gaze is steady and unwavering. The lights lift to enclose around him, too, but he ignores them.

"Ady," he says, close enough to touch her. "I have to ask this. Are you sure you're making the right decision?"

A sigh escapes her lips, and she sits back on one of the arched roots. Eagan joins her. Ady stares into the woods for a moment. The root is warm beneath her, as though the tree is charged with something powerful. Atheria has shaded everything with its beautiful colors. This is where she's discovered her calling, her purpose, where she's grown in her gifts, and learned truths about the world! It feels already as though she's lived several years in Atheria and gleaned a whole lifetime's worth of experience. Still, she doesn't know if this is the right decision. But she must trust that small and quiet sense, that feeling in her heart that called to her soul when the hawk first soared through the Hall of Knowledge. How to explain that feeling?

How to explain that feeling?

"Ady, don't move," Eagan says cautiously. He slowly reaches for his sword and is once again tripped up in the tassels of his robe, with no sheath, no weapon.

"It's okay, Eagan," Ady says with solemnity, without turning towards the cracking branches behind her. "Her name is Shiloh."

"You've named her?"

"She told me."

Eagan looks on with utter confusion.

"She is—"

"Your Archlight, I remember," Eagan says in the softest tone.

Shiloh approaches Eagan slowly as he extends his palm towards her. She nuzzles her head against his hand. Light emanates off her fur as Eagan's furrowed look softens with a smile. Shiloh looks deep into his eyes as if speaking to his soul. Ady can hear her thoughts. *Trust that unknowing knowing.* A gentle reminder for her *own* heart.

They sit close and quiet together for several minutes as Eagan continues to stroke the wolf's white fur. The gentlest breeze flows down from the waterfall and rustles the leaves on the great ancient tree. *The Tree of Life.* Ady hears through the warm wind within Shiloh's thoughts.

"I only want to hear you say it again," Eagan offers. His voice is low and has lost all the vitriol from earlier. "I want to know that I'm bringing my men back in good conscience. That you believe we're doing the right thing."

"When Edgar said I was to go with him," Ady begins, remembering the first time she saw that strange shadowed figure in the lecture hall. "What made you trust him? What made you decide to say, yes, I will send the girl I love with you."

"Because of the letters from your brother."

But by the slight rise in his tone, she knows that even he finds this unconvincing. There was something more at work.

"You just knew, didn't you? You sensed that something beyond us was happening. And you took a risk. I'm sure that must have been difficult, watching me leave like that, dragged away in the middle of a fight. Not knowing if you'd ever see me again."

"You have no idea how much so," he whispers. His voice cracks as though he might cry.

"The world is not risk-less, and I'm learning this. Because I want it to be. Grenn was always like that," Ady smiles, thinking of those days in the library as Grenn filled in her maps, rehearsed her speeches, read from the Republic's tomes. "She wanted to know without a doubt what would happen today and tomorrow and the next day. She liked order. But that doesn't always work, does it? Sometimes, there are no guarantees."

"Except when there are visions," he smiles.

Ady turns on the root and lets her foot glide along the creek's shallow end.

"You know you never told me about Edgar," she says and looks directly at him. She's needed to ask this for days now. "Or the Brutallion. Why?"

Eagan takes a deep breath and leans over his knees, hands clasped. "It was safer for you not to know," he says and shakes his head. "If you knew, you could be in danger. You know how the Bluecoats are, how Cayhill is. He wanted nothing more than to root out men like us. It could have threatened our mission."

"I thought we weren't keeping secrets from one another."

"And all the found things you thought I didn't know about?" He casts her a sidelong glance. "You kept secrets from me too, you know? The Book of Light? This, Ady, was a brotherhood vow, and I had to take it. My father was one of them. He founded the Brutallion."

Ady says nothing.

"Look," he sighs deeply. "Our ship is loaded. My men are ready to leave at dawn. And I want to believe what you say, what you see. I really do. But I'm having a hard time. I've known you forever Ady, and now here you are claiming to have received a gift from the heavens? Just understand what it's like for me. Especially when so much rides on this vision. Can you explain to me more of what you see when these visions come? Of course, I saw you in the Hall with the hawk, and when you collapsed afterward. I see Shiloh for myself."

Ady shakes her head. She sees the hawk's golden eyes again, hears that voice enter her mind, feels the warmth that cloaked her all through the message and vision, as though every sensation in her body was alert and alive. She reaches for Shiloh and feels the warmth and calmness she offers, her fingers run along her fur.

"You just have to believe me," she says. "Trust that unknowing knowing."

They're so close now that their foreheads almost meet. In the warm glow of the night, his eyes are lit with warmth, with hope, with a question. She can read all of it: his worries about his men, fear of returning to the Wasteland, the lingering questions about Atriel. But there is also love there, still. She is still his North Star.

DEPARTURE

The morning is cloudless. The sky is so blue that it nears white. Below, the ocean is gentle, with no strong winds to make the waves choppy.

The sun has just begun to crest over the water and the farthest eastern islands when the voyagers board the airships. Ady, Athos, and Atriel join Edgar and his crew; Thelios and Eagan take the Brutallion aboard the remodeled Republic vessel, now christened the Brotherhood in Atherian script. They wear a new uniform, deep navy-blue tunics threaded with the angematonic element, providing an indestructible shield across their bodies. Atherian alloy metal adornments hang across their chests, catching the gleaming sun.

The ships shine in the morning light as the sun reflects off the alloy plated along the hulls. The boats' steerage is full of every type of food, wine, and tea, with silks and hand-pressed paper, with Atherian swords, staffs, daggers, and tipped arrows. On deck, there is no sense that a fight might await them. The energy is one of cautious excitement aboard the Aurora. The Boatswain twins play some music, and Ella braids her curls back like Ady's. On the Brotherhood, there is more apprehension. The men are quiet, fidgety. Ito climbs to the crow's nest and settles in the wooden basket while Tiri stakes his position at the bow. All look to the water, the sky.

The Aurora's balloon swells to full capacity as the fire burns in the heating room. The rotor on the Brotherhood starts up along the ship's sides, and the sails flutter in the wind, pearly white. Along the scaffold, the Nobles and Atherian natives stand to watch the departure. They are a cluster of navy robes and long white hair, and their bodies look more luminescent than usual. Echo and Gaia nod, then bow, when Ady sees and waves back.

Ady stands at the helm of the Aurora. She hardly slept after seeing Eagan, but her heart is calm. They are headed southeast, across the dried ocean beds, across the sunken ship vessels and concave graveyards where cities once stood; they will fly over decimated forest beds, life long gone from the evergreens and redwoods; they will soar into the desert, where the dunes reflect the sun, where every plant is wild and prickly and dangerous. But this is right—it must be. From the bridge, she can feel the heat of others' eyes upon her. With one hand, she shields the blinding sun and stares across the water, toward the thick and viscous cloud layer they will soon pass through. The tiny beads of rain will meet her skin again. The fog will be thick as though laced with diamonds that send rainbows in every direction. There will be this final enchanting moment of beauty before returning to the world and what awaits them.

"Go before us," she whispers as Athos and Atriel join her.

A piercing cry sounds above them. The hawk flies over the Aurora's canvas balloon and toward the cloud line, quick as a shooting star. Within a matter of seconds, he has vanished through the rosying clouds. Ady smiles after him as the Atherian groundsmen cut the ropes, and the ships lift into the air.

ENEMIES MEET

It's always hot in the desert—but today at noon, the air is unseasonably warm. No wind moves through the Wasteland. Even the tumbleweeds don't shift in the dry dust. There is a stillness throughout the Raiders camp, a drowsiness that makes Doköran seethe. Women lounge outside their tents and fan themselves with canvas. His men sit stupefied, some pouring trickles from their flasks down their necks to cool off. The camp is still encircled by the rotting corpses of his failed guards, and the smell of baked bodies clings to the air.

Doköran sits by the doused fire pit. His whittling wood lays abandoned by his blood-soaked boots. It's too hot today for even that. He can feel the sweat carve lines down his dirt-smeared face.

Orius has stood beside him for the past hour. His eyes have been trained on the sky, waiting for a rain cloud to appear in the distance. The mage grips his staff with both hands.

Doköran almost jumps from his stump when Orius says in his rasping voice: "She's here."

But the sky is only grayish-white in that desert haze. There are no round clouds to shield them from the sun, only faint wisps like smoke tendrils.

"There's nothing," Doköran groans. He almost adds, *"You crazy old man,"* but thinks better of it. One dark look from Orius, the knuckle-bones chiming around his neck, and a shiver will run down Doköran's spine, no matter how hot the day.

But Orius does not tear his gaze from the northern sky. Doköran follows his stare—and this is when he catches it, the first bright shimmer of light within the sky. One minute there is only the dusty blue, and next a glimmering, as though tiny mirrors are held up to the sun—like a fire erupting in the sky. Then the bow of an airship appears, not half a mile away. Doköran stands watching in disbelief, just as a second ship materializes from thin air. First, the rounded wooden hull, then the deck, then sails whiter than bone. Both continue to crest into sight as light dapples along the ships' exteriors in a slow unveiling, appearing from nothingness.

"It is her," Orius says, smiling now. "She has come."

Doköran stands still—both stricken and delighted—he shoves the animal skull over his own, then yells loudly to get his Raiders to attention. Their eyes are already to the skies. His men then retrieve their axes, clubs, spears. A small cluster encircles him just as the ships, fully visible now, lower in a small dust cloud to the desert floor. Through the tents and stakes of corpses, Doköran can make out the lowering of a gangplank. A small band disembarks from both ships.

Doköran sits back again on his tree stump as they approach his camp.

There are only a handful of men, most dressed in deep blue tunics belted with silver, gilded with metals and adornments. Some faces look familiar. There is the blonde one built like a swordsman, his face still faintly scarred from Rebellion weapons. Orius must have been right that the captives would return. One is much taller than the others, and his skin has an almost luminescent hue under the sun, with hair that falls in one white stream. There are others, too, all men and all silent. The girl leads them all, the girl with the bounty on her head. As she nears, the Raiders part like a tide of waves. Some clutch their weapons tighter, others let their hatchets hang loose beside them. Women slip back into their tents and stare out through the canvas flaps. All eyes remain on the girl.

Not ten yards from the fire pit, the air shimmers again, this time around the girl as she approaches. She is unfazed and keeps walking as two beasts appear, one on each side of her. Wolves. Out of thin air. One is gray and timber; the other is a pure white, both with piercing blue eyes.

Doköran tries not to show his surprise at this sorcery. He must not betray any ground. He feels Orius fidget next to him at this sight.

When they enter the circle around the fire pit, he counts only eight in their party. They do not carry weapons, not even shields. Around them, the camp is dead silent. There is only the sound of the flies that still buzz around the camp perimeter.

"So," Doköran starts. He stays seated—this is his throne, his camp. He will not deign to rise for a child. "You have come to turn yourself in?"

"Not in the slightest," she says. "I am Adylyn of Atheria. And I have come to talk terms. I have a proposition for you."

"For me? Well, how forward." Around him, his men snicker at this, but she seems unfazed. "Look, I don't have a need for little girls. Unless they'd make a good war bride, or their head a good bounty."

He watches to see how this lands, but again she does not grimace. The men with her do, though. One in particular stands in the back of the entourage, thicker and huskier than the others. The man takes a quick step forward but is stopped by one of the others, a smaller man, slender like a runner. Doköran smirks at this—Corvis had told him that his prize girl had belonged to some other man before. Perhaps this was him.

"You men look familiar," Doköran nods behind Adylyn. "Or should I call you sheep? Like stupid sheep, come back to the slaughter?"

Adylyn steps closer now. Cayhill had called her a girl, and she certainly looks young. She is not tall, but neither is she frail like most women in the camp. She has lean muscle and a strong jaw. Her crystal blue eyes are fierce against her tanned skin. As the noon sun strikes her face, she looks older than Doköran had anticipated. There is no fear in her eyes.

"My people have long lived in fear of the Raiders," declares Adylyn. "But I suspect you have long lived in fear—or perhaps just hatred—of the Republic."

"You know who I am, don't you?" Doköran places his hands on his knees and stands heavily. He towers over the girl, and his horned skull helmet only adds to his presence. Still, she does not flinch. "I am the Lord of the Wasteland. I fear no one. We raided your Citadel like mercenaries because they paid us to." He does not mention the debt that is still owed him, but his eyes flicker over the men he recognizes as his captives. Perhaps there is still a fine sum for each of their heads, too. "Your Commander Cayhill told us how to find the tunnels left over from the war. He showed us how to get in."

Adylyn's eyes narrow here. Does she not believe him? Honestly, does she think that he raided the Citadel for no reason, not even staking a claim to the fort itself?

"So then you are a puppet," she says. Doköran freezes at this. How dare she speak to him this way? His battle ax rests beside his tent, just a grasp away, and he could hurl this toward her throat if he wanted to. Does she know to whom she speaks?

"I am no puppet," he growls through clenched jaws. "I simply do what it takes to preserve my people."

"So do I. Which is why we've come to ask you to join our cause in taking down the Republic."

"Your cause?" Doköran laughs now. His men laugh with him, as though waiting for his cue. "You sound like a foolish revolutionary from the Old World."

Something hot mists his cheek, and Doköran almost punches Orius in the gut before realizing the mage has leaned in to whisper. His words are soft but quick. Doköran studies Adylyn's face: she looks so grim, so certain.

"What do you want?" he says at last.

"We want you to march with us to the Lower West Citadel. We want to take back what is ours and set our people, and yours, free."

"My people are already free."

"The Lower West Citadel has turned its back on its citizens and on your ancestors. We must make it right."

"You won't find what you're looking for there," Orius says, and Adylyn's gaze shifts to him. He steps slowly forward, and his black cloak slithers behind him. His staff strikes the ground with every pace. "You will find only death and debris. Agony. Tears."

"And why should I believe you?" says Adylyn.

"You hunger for a place where there is only hunger now." Orius stops in front of Adylyn and reaches a wrinkled hand for the white wolf. The wolf bares its teeth for the first time, and the bristles on her mane stand high. Orius shrivels back. "I've never seen one up close before," he says. "Even beauty can be ferocious."

Adylyn places a hand on the wolf, who nuzzles against her. Doköran could swear he sees the faintest sheen hidden in the wolf's thick coat.

"There is a greater power at war," Adylyn says, her fingers still deep in the wolf's pelt. "It starts here. Something worse than the Republic is coming—far worse. You either join us or die in the Wastelands."

"So you want my men to fight with you," Doköran says slowly. "And that is all?" He knows it's not all, and he knows what she will say.

"No. We also want Grenn."

Again, the man in the back looks ready to tear from the others and attack the nearest Raider he can reach. Doköran has seen that expression of pure rage on his men before; he felt it himself the night the captives escaped, as he slit that woman's throat. He can't even remember her name.

"Ah, so you want two things then? Well, it seems like I'm getting the lower end of the bargain."

"You get to keep all these lands. The Citadel itself if you want it," Adylyn says, but her tone has quickened. They've reached a fever pitch, he can tell. And he, Doköran, has the upper hand. The lots today are in his favor.

There is nothing he wants from this child, no matter what Orius might say about what is foretold. He does not need the Citadel, has no desire to live like his enemies. Despite the heat, the constant search for water, the desert suits him with its wildness. There is only one thing he wants so badly that he dreams about it, that he imagines the scenario a thousand different ways: with his ax, with a sword, with an arrow through the gullet. He wants to kill Cayhill. He wants his revenge.

"I will return the girl on one condition," he says, a smile already creeping onto his face. "That when the time comes, Cayhill is mine."

Adylyn hesitates ever so softly. The men behind her shuffle and exchange glances and whispers.

"We need to know she's alive," Adylyn says after a heavy silence.

Gladly, Doköran thinks and snaps his fingers. He keeps his eyes on the man in the back, the strong one. He watches the terror cross his face, watches the warrior bite his lip, grasping the arm of the man beside him. Poor fool. A true fighter should never show his weakness so clearly. He is melting like wax by a flame—and then Grenn is brought into the circle.

Her hair is matted and looks almost brown now. She is burnt from the sun, and her lips are covered in sores from dehydration. It's not a pretty sight, even Doköran knows that. But war brides must be broken in; they must learn who is in control and who is not. Grenn's hands are tethered behind her back, but when she sees Adylyn and the others, she tries to run to them, letting out a barbaric scream with what energy she has left. Corvis holds the ropes, and he pulls back sharply. She falls to the ground with a dusty thud.

"Release her!" The warrior calls out in a panic. He breaks through the throng of his men and past Adylyn toward the girl but is stopped immediately by multiple Raiders with drawn weapons pointed right at his throat. "Release her," he says as he stares into Doköran's eyes.

"Tiri!" Grenn cries, pulling at her ropes.

"I knew she once belonged to you," Doköran says as he approaches, slowly speaking his name, "Tiri." He stops before him, close enough to kill with a dull blade. "And now she belongs to the Wastelands."

Corvis pulls back on her ropes once again. "She is mine," he says, seething through his teeth.

"She belongs to me!" Doköran yells back to Corvis. "I own you as well, you scavenging fool."

"She belongs to no one!" Tiri cries. "She is to be set free and you will take me instead."

Doköran stares into his eyes in silence. "I kill for sport, boy. You're nothing to me. She is nothing to me."

"Then let her go."

"No one tells me what to do," he pauses for a long moment, "Take him."

The surrounding Raiders grab his arms and tie them behind his back, as Tiri doesn't flinch or fight. His eyes stay trained onto Doköran's.

There is a stunned silence from the entourage. For the first time, Adylyn looks shocked enough to cry. The wolves tense again, their teeth bare and gleaming.

"We will keep Tiri, and you will return Grenn to us now," Adylyn says as her gaze returns to Doköran. There is a new sternness on her face.

"That's not how this works, child," Doköran smiles. "Because it seems to me like you need my help more than I need yours. We keep them both."

Grenn attempts to stand and run toward Tiri, but her ropes pull so tightly that she hits the ground hard as Corvis drags her away. Her heels dig into the brown earth, and one of the Raiders ties a canvas gag around her mouth to stop the screams. Tiri begins pulling at his ropes, screaming Grenn's name, trying to get to her, and is pulled away in a different direction. Adylyn closes her eyes for a long moment.

This whole proposition, this whole exchange—something about it does not feel right. If it wasn't for Orius's steady gaze from the side, burning into him, Doköran would send his Raiders on them all right now. The blood bath would be quick. And he'd be none the worse. Why should he risk returning to the Citadel? Why put his men in danger? Then again—he warms at the thought of feeling Cayhill's blood between his palms. That traitor, that bastard! Tiri could be used for ransom. Grenn, he will forget about in a matter of days. Grenn, he can live without. Killing Cayhill? That, he cannot. Besides, what better way to destroy the enemy than by siding with his most wanted?

"Then Cayhill is yours," Adylyn says. "If and only if they are *both* kept alive and well. Unharmed." She shades her eyes from the sun before returning her gaze to Doköran. "Tomorrow morning, we will be ten miles outside the West Gate, just behind the dunes," she says. "Meet us there if you are joining us. We will march together."

FIRE AND WATER

The airships fly as low to the ground as they can without scraping the hulls on the crags and cacti. They fly east now as the sun falls behind them—so quickly, it seems, outside Atherian time. The sky is pale blue one minute as sweat drips down the crew's faces. Then there are the pinks and yellows of summer sunsets. As they near the Citadel, they pass more ruins of the Old World: bent and rusted street signs, a few abandoned tires, the hull of vehicles with the metal armor long stripped by scavengers. And then the dunes. Ady used to see these rockfaces in the distance as the furthest point of the world. She knew every shadow from her dormitory window. Now, as night falls, the ships anchor here, hidden by the high mounds. Aboard the Aurora, Edgar schedules a full night watch to scout for attack from the east (the Republic) or the west (the Rebellion). Atriel volunteers first and stakes by the bow with his staff, Skylar by his side.

Ady retreats to her quarters, the same wooden room where she'd spent those first nights outside the Citadel, after the fire. Shiloh has already made herself comfortable when Ady arrives, exhausted, and darkened from the sun. The wolf yawns and stretches, rolling to her side on the mattress in greeting. She brushes the wind from her hair, changes in a dressing gown, and rinses the dust from her face.

The meeting with Doköran hadn't gone as well as she'd dared to hope. It had taken every ounce of strength. The doubt struck with a new fury as they neared the camp. She could see the bodies skewered through the poles. Atriel coughed into his tunic; Athos held his breath; only Eagan, Ito, and Tiri were unfazed by the flies that hung in thick black shrouds around the dead. Worse of all was the smell of corpses cooking in the sun. But she could not let any sign of this show to the others or the Raiders. That would mean weakness, and then the entire mission could be shattered. Still, she gagged as they entered the camp, almost cried from the stinging rot, and yet, she held her head high. And when she saw him—Doköran—she stared him down and tried to ignore the raven's eye branded across his chest, that third pupil staring at her. She held his gaze. She kept her trembling to a minimum, bit her lip to keep from screaming when Grenn emerged, dirty and bruised, her eyes wild with desperation. She kept from crying when they took both Grenn and now Tiri away. The Archlights stood by her for strength, and the men stood behind her—even though she could feel their tension grow as their brother was dragged away. Eagan, who she knew from his silence on the walk from the camp to the gangway, he was still anxious with trepidation and now laced with anger.

Ady moves to the porthole window and looks at the Brotherhood ship, floating just a few yards away. She cannot make out any faces in the dark. Both ships have turned off all lanterns and candles tonight. But she knows Eagan must be over there, probably still awake with too much adrenaline to sleep. Has he lost *all* trust and hope in her? Was he right to not have trust in her plan? In the eastern drift, it seemed like the canyon between them had lessened. And yet there was still distance, still questions. Now it feels like there could be mountains between them. A never-ending path of distance and anger. And yet, he is right there aboard the second ship floating quietly in the night sky. So close, and so far. As they boarded the ships to leave Atheria, she could sense his irritation that Atriel was flying with her while he was not. If only Eagan could truly understand, she'd needed Atriel as a companion, a friend to help her explore Atheria and this new side of herself. He was an anointed one, too, and he understood the high calling. Today, he'd provided the calm she needed. He held her hands as they took deep breaths as the ships lowered into the Wasteland.

Shiloh whines from the bed, hearing coyotes in the distance, as Ady leans against the window for a minute. The night air seeps through the small opening.

When Athos first told her about her calling as an anointed one, she had not expected this path to be so lonely. How could she have anticipated the agony of watching her dearest friend be dragged away to more horrors in the Raiders' camp, unable to rescue her? Or the sacrifice Tiri made for his love? Perhaps she should have sacrificed herself as the mission felt failed? Or the crushing torment of seeing the man she loved looking at her with such suspicion and even, at times, disgust? The pain throbs in her heart and disperses into her body.

Will they ever be able to recover what was lost? What they once shared, before life took its twists and turns? Will they all ever be the same?

Ady turns away from the porthole and joins Shiloh on the bed. It is consoling to have her near, while feeling so alone. Safeguarding, especially at night. The wolf must sense her complete fatigue and defeat because she gently licks at Ady's palm until her eyelids flutter to sleep.

The vision comes almost as soon as she reclines upon the mattress.

There is the water, the cavern. This place has begun to feel comforting in its familiarity. She is again in the pale white tunic, and the fabric clings to her frame as she steps deeper and deeper into the pool. The ground is cool like the stones near Atherian waterfalls, and yet she does not slip. Ahead of her, there is an unknown void. The cavern walls feel wide and unreachable, and she can sense that the ceiling is arched high above her head. Light still spills from behind. Then, that sweet lyrical voice returns: "I am with you, Adylyn." This time, Ady does not sputter awake—this time, she turns toward the light. The figure in the light is tall and graceful, with hair that curls gently against her breast. She seems to be clothed in light itself, with a golden pearly sheer down her arms. Even like this, transformed and angelic, Ady would know her anywhere: Laylia.

"Mother," Ady whispers. It's the first time she's ever spoken in the cavern, and her voice sounds faint in the large space.

Laylia speaks with command. She hovers over the water, almost too bright for Ady to look at directly, and says: "I have been watching over you, my dear girl. My fierce and sweet Adylyn. This road is not easy. But you know your chosen path. This calling is embedded deep in your soul."

"But Mother, I don't. I'm trying..."

"Your power grows. Your gifts grow."

"But how can I be sure?"

"Trust in yourself and trust in knowing your gifts were given to you for a reason. Follow your visions. Lead with your intuition. You are not alone. I am here with you—in your heart and within the waters." Laylia raises her hand over the cavern's pool, illuminating the smooth rock wall and the dark ripples around Ady. And then, she shrinks, drawn away from Ady and the cavern, back toward the light that pulses far in the distance.

Ady wakes to find the room still dark and unchanged. Shiloh sleeps soundly beside her with thick and heavy breathing. A handful of stars show through the round window and bring a translucent light into the chambers.

Had her mother been with her through every vision? Every time she stepped into the pool and felt that cold water around her ankles and the light upon her back, was Laylia behind her, waiting to say something? That voice when she dreamt in the bathtub, back when she first arrived in Atheria—that was her mother, too?

Ady's bare feet hit the wooden floor. She needs fresh air, a moment above deck.

Outside her chambers, there is only quiet. All of the doors are closed and dark. Ady walks silently down the passage and up the stairs to the now-empty deck. The Aurora's balloon casts a shadow over much of the ship, shielding them from the moon's fierce light. Most of the crew must be fast asleep by now—even the Boatswain twins, who'd begged Ady and Atriel for details about the Raiders after the meeting finished. Atriel pacified them with a description of the encounter as the ships rose again.

Ady wonders if Atriel is still on night watch. But as she approaches the front of the ship, she makes out the tall bearded figure. Athos stands at the bow.

He turns only when she is just behind him.

"You're up late," he quietly states.

"I can't sleep." She leans across the railing and smells in that desert air she's known all her life. It's dry in her nostrils.

"Thankfully, you're the only living thing I've seen since I took over the watch." Athos tilts his head toward her, intending to be light-hearted. But Ady doesn't laugh. She just gazes out toward the Wasteland, then back to the dunes on her right. They are far less steep than she'd imagined—less mountainous, more rocky sand. "Is there anything you want to talk about?" he asks.

Ady shakes her head. The night wind twists through her freshly brushed hair. "Mother just came to me. In a vision."

She feels him staring at her, waiting to say more. But she cannot—this one feels sacred.

"I can't talk about it," she says in almost a whisper. "But it happened. And it was her."

Above them are the stars she's known and traced all her life. She knew from reading in the library that there were named shapes in the sky, stories hidden in the constellations from ancient times. The Old World had loved the stars, too. But she and Eagan used to lay back in her dormitory, his arms around hers, and make up their own silhouettes in the stars. They told their own stories. Now, everything feels different, shaded by Atheria and the reality of being anointed. Her long lost mother has been watching her. A spiritual council has chosen her. Even the birds are not just birds. Her whole world has shifted.

"You were very brave today," Athos breaks the silence. He wraps his arm over Ady's shoulder and pulls her close.

Ady's eyes flicker again to the Brotherhood. The Atherian sails are lowered, so as not to reflect the moon and stars with their shimmering fabric. Perhaps Eagan is asleep now, at last—but will his dreams be fitful? Memories of what he endured in the Wasteland? What their friends could be enduring now? Or perhaps he's still reeling from the knowledge that the Republic *hired* the Raiders, that the attack on the Citadel was planned. That revelation took Ady by surprise. She had not felt brave then, not even with the wolves on either side of her. As Doköran stared her down, towered with his blood-painted skull, she felt that flicker of fear return. *The Rebellion had been working with the Republic. Was it a mistake to believe they could earn their allegiance? Had she put her people at risk?* The ships hang suspended in the night, vulnerable to attack. They told the Raiders where they'd be and when. Perhaps she'd been a fool to trust that Doköran would join.

"Athos," Ady says, so softly that she wonders if he hears. "Do you think the Rebellion will come? That they will help us?"

For a long minute, she says nothing. She just watches the Brotherhood ship sway gently in the wind and traces its silvery outline in her mind.

And then Athos squeezes her arm. "I believe they will," he says. "Because you do."

DAYBREAK

The morning air is hot and coarse. Dust blows up from the desert ground and lands on the crews' sweaty skin. Ady is back at the bow—she's hardly slept. All night after conversing with Athos, she tossed and turned, replaying the vision of Laylia. The light, the water, that voice emerging from the warm glow. *"Trust your gifts were given to you for a reason. I am here with you—in your heart and within the waters."* But now, as Ady stands at the bow, as the morning sun is already strong and cruel, this doesn't seem true. There is no water here, no mother. The ships are ghost quiet. On the Aurora, the crew silently shuffles across the deck with mugs of Enchanted Tea and plates of Atherian fruit. Even the twins are still this morning, instead of swinging between the robes that hang from the canvas balloon.

Ady stares toward the Wasteland. She strains her eyes on the horizon.

They will come, won't they? They must. Everything about her plan depends on them joining the cause, agreeing to hand over Grenn and now Tiri. And yet, there is only dry brown in the distance. There is no sign of Doköran and his men. Even the sky above is empty. She'd hoped to catch the shadow of the hawk flying over them, like a sign of blessing from the Council. But there is only the endless blue.

The hawk had appeared to her so clearly in the Hall of Knowledge. She looked into his golden eyes and felt what Eagan described so beautifully: an *unknowing knowing*. And she saw the camp exactly as it was when they descended in the Aurora. That couldn't be a coincidence, could it?

"What do you want to do?"

She starts at the sound of Athos' voice as he joins her by the railing.

— 248 —

"We'll wait," she says.

But already that doubt has returned. Doköran had promised nothing, but she'd left with the belief that he intended to follow through. As the sun becomes steeper in the sky, she moves to the port side and continues to scan the desert. The only sound is the wind coasting off the dunes—the Brotherhood sails are full now and ready to fly. On the Aurora, there is the gentle undulation of the balloon. Most of the crew hover beneath it in the shade. Ady breathes deeply as the sun warms the top of her braid, her neck, her face. She has not felt heat like this, like home, since arriving in Atheria, and in a way, it's a comfort.

The vision comes quickly—so quickly that she almost loses her balance on the deck. There is no Archlight messenger this time and no dream. Just her and the sun on her skin. And the sight: she sees the Citadel's inner courtyard. She knows the stone walls so well, the alleys, the marketplace tarps, each makeshift building. But it is not as she remembers. It is in ruins, decimated. Destroyed, still, from the siege. Carts overturned and wares smashed and food supply low, rations down to a dwindle. The rampart walk is empty, not a Bluecoat in sight. She sees children huddled, dirty, in the corner of their dormitories. She can feel their hunger acutely like a physical spearing through her gut. And the screams! She tries to cover her ears to block out the anguished cries.

When she comes to, her head throbs as though she's been struck with Atherian alloy. Atriel is already upon her, concerned, he asks, "Are you okay? Are you hurt?" Athos runs from the bow as the crew encircles her, but all Ady can see is the Citadel—the children.

Atriel helps her stand. The horizon is still clear, with no dust cloud of approaching men on the march. But Ady looks to Athos and Atriel saying as calmly as she can: "The Citadel. I saw them, the people. They're alone. We must go to them." Suddenly, Orius' words come back: *You hunger for a place where there is only hunger now.* Had he been telling the truth? That there was starvation within the city, quite literally?

Confusion shadows Athos' face as Ady stumbles to the bridge of the ship where Edgar has been watching from the helm. He wears a smirk as she approaches as if to say, *What now?*

"Pull the anchors," she says. "We're leaving."

He stands up straight and tugs at his black vest. "We're not waiting for the Raiders?"

Her assurance surprises even her. But she knows it deeply, that sense that they must go—that something is desperately wrong within the Citadel.

"No, we are waiting," Athos interjects, coming up behind Ady. He gives her a cool look, almost stern. She's never seen him like this—adult Athos, afraid. His thick beard only adds to the severity. "We wait for the Rebellion, for their numbers. Or we turn back to Atheria. That's it."

"No," she says with fervor. "We must go and quickly."

Athos strokes his beard for a moment, and his eyes scan the entire ship, from Ella to the twins to the gunners, every life aboard. Then his eyes land back on Ady.

"You heard what that sorcerer said back in the camp." His voice is hushed but urgent. "That only death and destruction await us there. What if he was telling the truth?"

"I think he was," she nods. "That's just it, but not *ours*."

Atriel's hand meets the small of her back as he steps onto the bridge. "We should do what Ady says. She's been right this whole time."

Athos shakes his head adamantly. "This was not the plan. We could be walking into an ambush. The Rebellion could have just set us up. You heard that they've been working with the Republic. That was news to all of us."

Ady's gaze turns to the starboard side of the ship. The dunes still conceal them from the Citadel's walled fortress, but just beyond this rock face is her home, if it could even still be called that. Those walls housed every place she once loved. The garden, the library, her dormitory, the forgotten rooms. Something tightens in her chest as that sharp phantom pain returns to her belly.

"We can cloak the ship and fly over," she says, eyes still toward the dunes. "We'll at least go see."

Ito is the one who notices the anchors rise from the Aurora. Eagan is at the helm with Thelios, who instructs him on how to properly balance a bo staff in the palm of his hand, when Ito shouts down from the crow's nest. All eyes turn to the Aurora. Sure enough, the anchor shuffles along the desert ground, sending up a drudge of dirt before it winds aboard the ship. And then the cloaking: that magnetic shimmer that covers the ship inch by inch, foot by foot, until the Aurora is only a floating and invisible mass.

"What are they doing?" Eagan asks.

Thelios, like all Atherians Eagan has met, is usually so collected and hard to read. Today, Thelios frowns, white hair knotting in the wind.

"They're leaving," says the Atherian in that crisp voice.

"Back to Atheria?"

Eagan feels a mix of emotion, relief, and worry. Had Ady realized the Rebellion wasn't joining after all? Were they going back to demand the release of Grenn and Tiri? The plan was to wait for Doköran and his Raiders, but after hours of panic-inducing searches, after Ito refused to come down from the mast, after an empty horizon, they were finally giving up! They wouldn't press onto the Citadel without reinforcements, right? But then Thelios orders for the crew to raise their own anchors and trigger the cloaking device.

"Set our course east," Thelios shouts as members of the Brutallion snap to attention. Thelios then turns to Eagan and says with an unreadable expression in those sky-blue eyes: "The plan has changed. I can feel it from the Archlights aboard. We're heading to the Citadel."

THE FALLEN

Nothing could have prepared Ady for the destruction within the Citadel. As the Aurora approaches the walls, still cloaked in invisibility, Ady stands starboard—chilled and pensive.

The rampart walls are empty. There are no signs of the Bluecoats on their morning rounds; no crimson flags are waving from the four columns. All the gates are closed, except the West Gate. There is an eerie quiet. And when the Aurora crests the high walls, Ady peers into the courtyard, the market, the garden, and gasps at the sight. The fires destroyed most of the infrastructure, that much is clear immediately. The library where she spent countless hours doing homework for lectures and rifling through the Republic's scant collection is burned to the foundation. Several of the dormitories have fallen in, concave. It's as though a dust storm blew through and overturned everything—sending barrels into the streets and coating the remains in a layer of soot. But it's the smell that gets to her the most. She's smelled it only once, as they marched past the rotting bodies and into the Wasteland camp. Like dry death.

Where are all the remaining people? Where is the Republic?

Ady scans the ground, frantic for a sign of life.

The Aurora's crew is silent as the ship coasts over the ghost town below. The gunners poise near the cannons they'd rolled on deck as an emergency measure; the twins are suspended midair beneath the balloon; even Edgar looks steely as he maneuvers the ship's wheel and directs them toward the airship scaffolding dock on the north side. The Republic's airships are all gone.

Ady struggles to breathe as she clutches the Book of Light to her chest.

The instant the ships took up anchor, Ady ran down the deck steps and to her chambers. The Book of Light was packed along the Nobles' parchments and manuscripts, tucked beside Gaia's pressed tea. As Doköran's taunt replayed in her mind, Ady had suddenly remembered what Grenn said that night in the fire. *"They were in your room! I went looking—and they were there."* It was a Bluecoat who'd gashed her stomach, sliced her body, not a Raider. One of their own.

The Republic had orchestrated this all to happen. They were looking for her and for the book. Doköran's violent warriors had been hired by the Republic all along, which meant that Cayhill *wanted* an attack to happen.

Ady turns to see Athos and Atriel beside her, unmoving and dumbfounded— had they been there this whole time? She hadn't felt their presence.

Edgar calls, "Bartholomew, we have the all-clear!"

Ady recognizes him by the goggles and leather vest. Bartholomew nods and fumbles along the helm. Onboard, the uncloaking doesn't feel like much—only the faintest sparkle of light that runs along the ship's exterior, which Ady can catch if she looks for it. But she keeps her eye trained on the Citadel ground below. They're nearing the training grounds now, just as the ship's shadow appears, first as a small tip of the bow, then the hull, and then the entirety. Behind them, the Brotherhood unveils as Thelios uncloaks them.

The air is grim as the ships dock, and they all descend into what appears to be a mass grave. Everyone is quiet, somber. A heaviness settles on Ady's shoulders as she climbs down the rampart with the book in her satchel. She steps again—perhaps for the last time—into the Citadel. The walls don't seem as tall anymore, not after the high trees of Atheria and the islands that hang suspended in the sky. It's as though Atheria is all color and light, where this is all gray and dim.

Dust rises from the ground with every step she makes.

"My God," says Atriel, joining her. He is blank-faced as she's never seen him before. Numb by the sight.

There are bodies everywhere. They are lying in the street and propped against rotted timber. Some are in canvas bags, waiting for burial outside the walls. Some bear wounds from Rebellion weapons; others, she discovers upon hearing a stray cough, are still alive—but barely. All look thinner than she thought possible.

The crew disseminates to hunt for survivors. Eagan and the Brutallion branch left toward the training ground; Thelios scouts through the rubble of the market-place; Athos goes off in search of the underground tunnels Doköran mentioned.

Ady roams as if in a trance through all the places she once knew as well as her palm, but that now feel mangled and wrong. Atriel follows just a step behind. She hugs the wall and practically retraces her steps from that last night, remembering the screams as the Raiders infiltrated the courtyard and the way the smoke made her eyes and nose burn.

She stops just feet away from where the library used to be. Only weeks ago in Earth-time, she ran out of this building with the book that would change her life. Was she standing at this very spot when she witnessed a Bluecoat about to punish a small boy for thievery? Now, there is only charred wood and the faint fluttering of burnt pages in the dilapidation.

"I can't describe what this feels like," Ady says. "It's all just gone."

"I know," Atriel nods, with such meaning that she knows he means it. After all, his North West Citadel fell, too. What horrors must he have seen?

"It's like seeing someone you love dead," Ady says in a whisper. The sky above is cloudless and hawk-free, but she senses that the bird is near. "Just being here, I mean. When my mother died, and they brought her back for Athos and me to bury, she looked like stone. Like pure white stone. She was so cold. It feels like that. Like, it's not what you remember, but also is. She looked like herself but also didn't."

From a nearby tumble of fallen wood and broken glass, she can hear Thelios call for any survivors.

"My Citadel looked like this at the end," he says softly. "But it was not from any attack. Everyone got sick. And we were all walled in." His voice breaks, but he clears his throat and straightens. "Look, if I've learned anything from my studies in Atheria, it's that an ordinary person's life can have a lot of meaning. And you, Ady, have proven yourself. Your visions have been true. I know this—my gifts have helped me to understand."

One bead of sweat drips down his sharp nose, and his face looks noticeably tanner after a few days in the sun aboard the ships.

"I just feel like we're here too late." Voicing this lifts the heaviness from her shoulders, but only slightly.

"But at least we came at all," he says.

A cry interrupts them—Athos' voice, coming from the courtyard. Ady runs in his direction. The satchel bounces along her hip. But as she rounds a fallen market tent and cart, she sees people, a slow teeming crowd, straggle into the open courtyard.

Athos must have found the tunnels. The people all stream from a forgotten door she'd never opened, not far from the old music room. They appear by the tens, then twenties, all tiny and ragged. They blink blindly in the sun. Have they been underground for days? Ady stands stricken as women collapse from exhaustion on the stone ground.

And then she runs toward them, exhilaration burning through her with every heel-strike. She recognizes their faces as she weaves through the throng—cooks and classmates, women she shared chores brackets with, a kind merchant who sold her charcoal pencils for lectures. The old filament peddler! Marta, that boy's mother, and the young boy! They are alive. Even the youngest look twig-thin, with skin pulled tight over hollow features. Two children run toward her with sunken cheeks and widened eyes, as though they'd been stripped of their humanness. They show no sign of recognition—though she recalls them as some of the Citadel orphans. Still, they throw their arms around her waist. She can hardly make out what they say through their tears, but she calls for someone to bring food and water from the ship, and within seconds, Ella appears and escorts the children herself.

Soon, Edgar forms an assembly line as the baskets and crates from the Atherian islands are ushered into the Citadel.

"Bring the tea!" Ady cries to a crew member as he makes a return trip. She's so numb that the sound of her voice feels far and foreign. "Gaia's tea—bring it for them! It will restore them."

The people brighten as the smell of sweet food slowly overtakes the lingering cloud of ash and decay. Ella brings by plates of yellow fruit, and the twins take turns pouring the restorative rainbow-hued tea, causing small groups to gather around them with every step.

Meanwhile, Athos gets the story bit by bit as the survivors take to the food ravenously, clawing at the different pieces of bread and cheese. After Captain Ellington was found dead—and the rumor was that he was beheaded by the Rebellion—Commander Cayhill and the Chancellor retreated to the Basilica. They took all the rations, most of the water supply—what books were left and medicine. It happened swiftly, practically overnight, so that when the people awoke, the Citadel was abandoned, and they were alone in the desert. Trapped to starve and die. Some had ventured beyond the walls to hunt what game they could but must have died of thirst or the elements because they never returned. Others retreated to the tunnels to escape the unrelenting sun.

"Two babies died," Athos told her as he held back his tears. "Their mothers couldn't feed them."

Ady closes her eyes at the horror. Had she known this would happen? She had dreams of such things—people digging for water, the Citadel wells gone dry. *"I am here with you—in your heart and within the waters,"* Laylia said in the cavern, as the pool rippled around Ady's legs. Perhaps it was the calling to come here and bring water to her people—to bring them home.

"Call the Atherian ships. We need them to come here. Now," Ady says.

"You know we cannot do that. We cannot reveal them," Athos advises.

Ady gives him a long look. Doesn't he understand? There is no room for all of these people on their two ships. They cannot—will not—abandon them as the Republic did. These people need the medical attention that Gaia can provide with the tinctures and herbs and teas; they need to be clothed in Echo's warm robes. They need hot baths and food, a place to restore.

She sternly says, "Do it."

BROKEN GLASS

Ady climbs over fallen beams and crumbled cinderblocks to enter the dormitory. The stairwell is cluttered with debris, and the hallway of rooms is dark with shadows. The dormitories were never much more than small squares of stone. But as she creeps down the passageway, she walked so many times before, a new sadness comes over her. That death smell is strong here, and she wonders how many died on their bunks, shriveled and starving.

The roof has fallen in several patches, creating small mounds to clamber over. Her room is at the end of the hall, one down from Grenn's. She can already see the door ajar, swinging softly with a low squeak.

Ady stops in the doorway and takes in the chaos. The damage is not from the fires. The flames must not have reached this far—but the room is covered in ash and has been completely inverted. The mattress lies against the wall with a deep slit down its belly; floorboards have been pried up, revealing torn pages from her found-books; the desk is smashed and splintered. All her belongings, everything she once cherished, lie littered on the ground: her *Big Bang Theory* mug and milk saucer for the stray cat, her silver coins and rings. Even the barley tea spills from its bag on the floor. A small mouse nibbles at one of the pods. The Bluecoats left nothing unturned as they searched for the Book of Light, invading every aspect of her private life. She can see that, as glass shards break into smaller pieces beneath her shoes. Her Old World has been eradicated along with her old self.

Ady fumbles in the dim light for anything to salvage of this life. Her flint and wax candle are nowhere to be found. Perhaps one of the Citadel survivors had already scavenged this place and taken it. But when she kneels to search under the bunk bed frame, she sees that slender book of poems by e.e. cummings.

This must have been the book that Eagan found one night and read. Lyrics about the stars, calling her his *North Star*. She thumbs through the pages a moment before placing it in her satchel.

Standing, she then sees a streak of red along the cinderblock walls where her drawers once stood. Ady moves toward it, realizing something as she nears—the streaks are blood. It must be Grenn's. She can almost hear the penetrating screams of Grenn, stabbed by their own people of the Republic, for witnessing what was happening and being punished for it.

Ady wraps her arms around her stomach and slides to the floor. The tears come quickly, hot down her cheeks.

"How could they do this to you?" she whispers.

So much horror has been enacted on her account. Eagan and his men were brutalized by the Raiders. That would never have happened if the Republic hadn't wanted her and the book. Her friends and fellow citizens were murdered in the siege's bloodbath. Captain Ellington was beheaded. Survivors were left to starve and rot in the streets. And Grenn—her dearest Grenn. Her fate was the worst of them all. *Unharmed*, Ady demanded to Doköran. They needed her, and Tiri, *unharmed*. But she could tell in his twisted smile that he had no way to guarantee this. Everyone watching the meeting in the Raiders' camp knew what reality faced Grenn as they dragged her away, still bound. What wicked things were happening to her even now? Did her screams still pierce the Wasteland, or had she become numb, taking whatever pain with a steeled endurance. Was Tiri still alive?

But no, this is *not* on her account. Not her fault. This is the Republic's doing. The Erlick Federation has orchestrated all of this, haven't they? She'd seen them in her vision, those shadow creatures that lurked upon the earth with their black snake eyes, tormenting souls and luring minds to darkness. They used the Republic as pawns. What kind of leader turns on their own people? Who coordinates an attack on their own fortress, standing back to watch innocents slaughtered? Who leaves orphans and widows to die, while retreating to higher ground? Ady can feel it course within her veins—less sadness now and more of righteous rage. This is different from learning about the Great War, learning of their treacherous acts throughout history in Atheria, or even witnessing its effects ripple through her past life. This is personal. The bodies. The emptiness. The death. In a place that was once her home. Grenn. The Brutallion. Her people. James Alexander. Her Mother. How much more evil could they wreak upon the world? That knowing feeling burns in her core. They must be stopped.

Ady stands from the ash and debris. Something tugs at her spirit as she continues these thoughts of rage, turning them, transmuting them into something greater. She knows the will of her spirit, that she has been called for such a time as this. She knows what she must do, that she must continue to set out, find the other anointed ones. Build from this place inside her being, build a revolution toward a new world. She will not stop until they are stopped. The Republic. The Erlick Federation. The evil of this world. She breathes deeply, closing her eyes a moment, the tightness of her balled fists relaxing.

Ady snaps to attention as the familiar sound trickles from the windowsill, followed by Eagan's boots landing on the window ledge, as he slowly emerges into the dorm.

They stand in silence. He takes in the debris with deadened shock.

"I can't believe they did this," Ady says at last. Her voice does not come out like a whisper as she intends—she sounds strong and firm.

"I feel like my father expected it," he says. "Maybe not this bad. Definitely not this bad, but something. He knew the Republic could turn on their own people at any moment. My men and I, we were supposed to prevent that."

"This isn't your fault," she says with vehemence. "It's only theirs. They did this, the darkness."

"I want to confess," Eagan approaches her closer, "I was so angry with you when Tiri was taken away. We not only lost Grenn but now also my brother. I can't stop thinking about their fate. I know the Raider's way, Doköran's way. I still don't know if they will join your cause."

"It's our cause." Ady affirmatively says. "And I had no idea he would do that. That he would step up and sacrifice himself like that."

"Of course, he was going to do that. He would never have left her behind, not again on his watch. He thought she was on the ship, Ady, and we couldn't turn back and risk the entire Brutallion. We set our course for Atheria. Our vows go beyond our brotherhood. They are also for those we love." Eagan looks down, fighting back the tears. "Don't you understand? I would follow you anywhere, even if it doesn't make sense and even if it hurts like hell."

Ady's gaze stays fixed on him, waiting for his eyes to meet hers once again. They don't.

"I didn't want to go to the Wasteland in the first place and felt like this was just another way I was putting my men in danger. I could see their shocked faces. But not one stayed behind. Not one. When I saw your anchor rise today in the dunes, the ship cloak, I thought we were heading back to the Raiders or Atheria to re-group. I never thought of coming here. Thelios said you set a course for the Citadel. So we all gathered our weapons, lined the deck. I was expecting this big fight when we arrived. We braced ourselves for an uneven battle. But then," he shrugs, "the ramparts were empty. The Citadel. Empty." When he looks up at her, his eyes are sheened with tears. In the shadows, he appears like himself in the old days—chiseled jaw and earnest face, slipping in the window to kiss her. "You knew to come here. You saw a vision, didn't you? This morning?"

Ady nods, silent.

"We would have left," he says this in a soft whisper, more to himself than her. "We'd have gone back to Atheria, made new plans. They would have all died, Ady. All of these people...the people I thought *I* was supposed to protect. But you're the one protecting them."

Ady stares at him intently, a piercing yet soft gaze. Eagan nears closer as glass cracks beneath his boots.

"I never thought I'd see this dorm again. And for a while, I never thought I'd see you again." His hand reaches for her cheek.

"I never thought I'd see you again either," she says and offers as warm a smile as she can muster.

"I want you to know that I believe...I believe what you see, I believe in whatever force is guiding you."

As he says this, that knowing feeling returns. She felt it when the hawk delivered its message. She felt it in the Wasteland as the wolves manifested beside her like gifts from the Council. She felt it when her mother appeared like a shimmering angel. And now, finally, the man she's always loved is looking at her with confidence and conviction. She was his North Star, he always said, which was endearing in its hyperbole—but he'd come for her. He'd followed whatever light had led him to Atheria; he'd followed her back to this hellish place. And now, she sensed, he would follow still.

"Do you need more time here?" he asks after a moment. "I can leave you alone."

She surveys the room one last time, picturing everything as it was in her memory: her neatly-made bunk, the found things, her hidden books, the drawers filled with wool and flint, silver treasures secretly kept underneath, and the small window to the world, her one square view of what lay beyond.

"No," Ady says with a deep sigh. "There's nothing more for me here."

HORIZONS

Eagan stands on the rampart where he's run so many wall miles, last heard his father speak. He was right about everything: to start an allegiance of brothers to protect the people. To make him promise to protect Ady, as if he knew her destiny before she did.

The sun now lowers to the west, and the sky has already warmed from blue to orange. Ady leans against the battlements beside him and radiates with a quiet fury. In the courtyard, the people sleep on makeshift sheets and mattresses, whatever they can find, lulled at last by food and tea.

The afternoon passed quickly. Athos sent an Archlight to summon the Atherian fleet. Atriel served more food to the survivors. Thelios led a moment of silence and blessing for the departed souls within the Citadel. Ito and the Brutallion searched for any weapons to bring onboard but gave up when nothing proved good enough to rival the alloy.

Now, they are a small crew on the rampart. Athos and Atriel both shield their eyes as they await the Atherian ships from the north. Edgar's gaze is trained west toward the Raider's camp. (Could they still come? Eagan wonders. Is it possible that they will join after all? That Doköran will seek his revenge freeing Tiri and Grenn? They will find them no matter what.) Ito sits along the rampart with his legs dangling over the outside wall, dropping stones to the desert floor and counting how long it takes before a dust cloud appears. Eagan can only watch Ady. He sees how the light graces her round nose and soft neck, the way the wind tugs loose strands of dark hair from her braid. There was a change in her whole demeanor back in the dorm. A new assurance. She was right, back in the eastern drift, when she asked why he'd trusted the letters or Edgar. He'd known somehow that something beyond them was happening. His father had always treated Ady like someone to be protected—and not because of her fragility, but because he could sense her strength. Now Eagan can, too.

As the sun turns a deeper red, Ady takes a book from her satchel. He recognizes it as the Book of Light. The cover looked like what the swords of Atheria were made of—Atherian alloy. Slowly, she unlocks the metal clasp and opens the book to the middle. Closing her eyes, she runs her hands along the pages, which are blank, a creamy white parchment. Perhaps it's really a journal, Eagan thinks, and not a book at all. But when Ady opens her eyes, they land onto the pages, as though she has read something. Eagan sees nothing. Ady gasps ever so slightly. A whisper escapes her lips as she moves a finger across the page.

"What did you say?" Eagan asks.

"The Unfallen Kingdom," she says in the softest whisper.

His last school lectures were years ago, but he can swear he's never heard that name. Could it be beyond the Eastern Alliance or one of the other realms divided after the Trinity Convention? Eagan steadies himself against the stone battlement and waits for her to say more. But Ady is in a trance. Wonder explodes on her face as she murmurs over and over to herself. *The Unfallen Kingdom. The Unfallen Kingdom.* A smile widens.

"Is that somewhere outside of the Republic?" Eagan ventures. "I've never heard of it."

At last, she looks at him, her face bright and hopeful. "I can read it. I can read it! It was only shimmers of light before, but now?"

Eagan glances at the pages, which are still empty and unmarked. This is when Atriel looks away from his post and joins them.

"Did you read something?" he says, but he answers his own question when his eyes drop to the open Book of Light.

"I don't know where the Unfallen Kingdom is," Ady says, her gaze back on the pages. She touches the parchment tenderly and speaks as if to herself and no one else. "But this is where we must go."

Atriel is immediately ecstatic. He says the Council has revealed this, that the journey must continue. He moves around Eagan to peer over Ady's shoulder at the open book. Eagan just stays still against the warm stone wall. He has a barrage of questions. Where is this Unfallen Kingdom? What will they find there—and why? Shouldn't they follow the plan and return to Atheria, see these survivors back to safety? But he watches as Ady turns the pages with great care, as Atriel reaches a hand to brush the parchment, too.

Before he can say anything, Edgar's voice interrupts them. All heads turn to follow Edgar's outstretched arm. Above, the hawk screeches in the sky, its golden feathers catching the last light. The sun sinks behind the dunes, back toward the Wasteland, where heat emanates from the ground. That is where they appear, silhouetted in the hazy distance of the horizon—the marching line of the Rebellion.

ACKNOWLEDGMENTS
JENNY McCLAIN MILLER

As I begin my first ever acknowledgment in my very first published book, I can't help but reflect. It is spring, and the sun is shining after a very long winter in Michigan. The seasons of change are such a parallel to the journey Ady is on, ever-changing, ever-evolving. The waves outside my opened window, crashing along the shoreline of the St. Clair River along the Great Lakes remind me of the waves crashing in the Pacific along the ocean when Ady first came to me. Where the hawk flew high above Skylar and I during the first stroke of my pen as this story took shape in my journal. In Little River, California, one of my favorite places, *Age of Atheria* was born. I sat along the cliffs, closed my eyes, and meditated on the answers in which this story would construct. It was a time when I needed to be my own hero – to myself, for myself. Ady is that to me – a hero in her own right. Harnessing mystical powers she didn't know she possessed, continuously finding her way through trials and triumphs, making waves of impact. And it is just beginning.

The journey, oh the journey. I created this story eight years ago as a television series pitch while I worked on the development of new content. It started with continuous worldbuilding, the creation of characters, their storylines, their *why*. I spent days on set and nights until 2 or 3 o'clock in the morning working on this project. I'd choose to miss events or nights out with my friends to stay in with these characters and write. After pitch meetings with agents and production houses, I would continue to build because I needed to tell more of the story. I knew my job wasn't complete. That idea of starting this story as a novel beckoned at my heart and ultimately became the path this story would first take.

This journey would not be possible without so many, and I want to take this time to thank them, as you have each been such a champion of my dreams, and the dreams I share with Greg. And each one of you has impacted me at such a deep level.

My parents, thank you for always believing in me and supporting my dreams. I have so much gratitude for you both. Thank you for your love of music and fantasy, as well as the movies we would watch as a family that led to many of my inspirations. Thank you for every road trip and adventure in which I gained deeper levels of imagination as we saw the world; each trip I'd pack my journals or five-subject notebooks, writing new "movies" and "books" in each subject section in hopes it would one day hit the big screen or bookshelves. There may still be some pretty good ideas in those.

Dad, my guide, my hero. You have always made it possible to go after my goals – with your support and unwavering belief in me. I thank you for the endless conversations about this story, about life, and helping me navigate through literally everything. Thank you for being someone to bounce ideas off of and never thinking anything is too crazy. For your wisdom and the best Dad advice that I always turn to. For every adventure. For your mastery in so many things I am so fortunate to learn from. For your gift of naming people, places, and things just right. For always believing in my vision and my goals. For lifting me up, always, and knowing before I did, that I could do this. To remember to go at this four rows at a time. Thumbs up, we did it!

Mom, thank you for being a teacher in my life. For knowing I could achieve anything and making sure I believed that, too. For supporting my dreams as a little girl and to the woman I am today. Thank you for every dance party and concert of ours in the living room, learning the ability to express myself through other mediums. For all the laughs. For all the travels. For being the best Momager. Thank you for conducting the tedious planning required in my life from the pageant and dance days. And, thankfully, how that carried over into my own innate need to plan and organize the details. Thank you for raising me to be the Mommy I am today, and for all of the magic you always created for us as kids. Thank you for helping my dreams become a reality.

To my Grandparents, who each believed in my dreams and told me to write. To not stop. I will forever thank you for the level in which you believed in me. Thank you for showing me the tablets.

To my in-laws, or as I prefer to call them – my in-loves – thank you for jumping into this crazy idea headfirst and always believing in both of us. Your love for this project gives me so much gratitude, as you have always had open arms to this story and to me. Maria, I love your calls when you have an idea, and we talk through ideation together. We can always talk for hours! Gene, your professor and mentor mentality have been immeasurably helpful as we have gone through this process. Katie, you were the first Miller family member we spoke to about the book, and I will never forget your level of enthusiasm and love from the get-go on that call! Both you and Zach, thank you for loving fantasy and our story to read through the early drafts with excitement and support. Kristin, Greg, and the boys – thank you for always checking in on our process and knowing how important this is to us. To my whole Miller family, I am the luckiest because I married into the absolute best. And you all mean so much to me.

Carmine, thank you for the long talks, the spiritual directions in life, singing bowls, and animal guides. For hearing out my own spiritual journeys with no judgment and all love, the openness of our conversations. Supporting my dreams to such a high degree, reminding me I can do it. Reading through every early draft so quickly and passionately. Always ready for the next chapters and expressing your excitement to read more of the story.

Aunt Jeannie and Uncle Paul – thank you for being you. You're so special to me. The level of love and support you provide is unmatched and I am forever grateful. My Uncle Jim, for your love of history, maps, and castles – and the many talks about those. Sara, for always being so supportive of me. Thank you to my cousins Heidi, Gracie, and Sophie for being some of the first to read our story, for your insight and love. Marc, Molly, and Todd, for all your support, always. The Tasler clan for always loving and supporting me. My brother, John, for the help in understanding war-torn societies and how they operate, the answered questions about wars and battles, and our love for *The Lord of the Rings*. And thank you to the rest of my extended family for all of your love and support. I love you all so much.

To my hometown friends, you all never cease to amaze me with your support *all* of these years. It means so much and I am so happy we champion one another and have always remained close, no matter the miles apart. Many teachers of mine throughout the years, I don't know if you know the impact you had on my creative writing. To those who have supported us along the way, your friendship means everything to us. You know who you are. Thank you to you all.

To Tina, for being one of the first I shared this story with many years ago, you have been there since the beginning. Thank you for letting me present mood boards to you and share these characters and their storylines during late nights as roommates. You have always supported this journey, no matter where it would take me. Thank you for every coffee. Every cry. Every laugh. To Molly, for always knowing where I was going with my hopes and dreams, sometimes before I did, and pushing me to go – for being a true friend for the past 25 years. To Brooke, my fellow queen, thank you for always supporting my vision, and for always driving while I wrote more of this story and other stories from the passenger seat on our long-distance desert trips. To Carter, thank you for all of your support, the many laughs, and friendship all of these years. To Michelle, for being my entrepreneurial baddie. To bounce ideas off of together as we always remain inspired. To Ryan, thank you for your expertise of the writing process. You're a genius. Thank you for reading through the drafts and providing the best insight. To Paul, thank you for your friendship with Greg, and now with me, you're like family, and your support is eternal. To Jason, thank you for your unconditional support for us. You've been there for us since the beginning, the very beginning. To Solenn, thank you for your beautiful hand-drawn rendition of Atheria at night. We are blessed with your artistic vision. To Jaida, thank you for capturing the essence of us in the place it all started, you're such an empowered creator and photographer. You're all sisters and brothers to me and hold a special place in my heart.

To Marissa, I have many thanks – thank you for being the first to complete our final draft and read it with such conviction and care. To talk for hours about our story with me, with us. Thank you for being such a pivotal part of the *soul work*, my sister. To create with us is to know us. We have such a blessed friendship, and one of the most unique and epic friendships in life. My greatest thanks to you is for Greg. You were the vessel that led me to my husband. And I will thank you for that for the rest of my life.

To my Atherian sword and shield – my writing partner, my life partner, my husband Greg. You are my North Star. My fiercest protector of our hearts and home. My creational partner in life. I love your mind, our deep conversations, and perspectives on life, every memory made, and plans for the future. I know and love your heart. I knew it was you when we took our first trip together. My forever. When I introduced this project to you, you understood it in a way that I did, as an author of this story. I always knew I wouldn't do this alone, and I knew then – I found you. The teammate to elevate this story to the next level to new places I hadn't imagined. You grew to love these characters as I did. We grew together, and we built. We built our own path and brought this story to new heights and places. The direction in which our life is going is thanks to our teamwork, mentality, and belief in ourselves. I thank you for that belief. For saying yes to ourselves over and over again. For picking up our lives and driving across the country together to go after our dreams. To continue to create this story, and now a legacy of our own with our two little boys. I thank you for pouring your heart and soul into our journey. It has been quite the ride. And I am so grateful that it is with you. It is an honor to be your wife. I love you forever, my love.

To River and Ryder, my sweet boys. Our brave, independent, loving, adventurous explorers. Being your Mommy is the greatest gift and favorite paths of my life. I love watching you experience your many firsts in this world with such joy, guiding you as you grow, and all of your snuggles, laughs, and love. It was a beautiful journey to be creating both this story, and life, simultaneously with each of you. You both evoke so much inspiration and have taught me so much. That I can be both a Mommy *and* go after attaining my goals. With vision, determination, patience, and drive. My greatest hope is that you boys are proud of Mommy and Daddy, and that we may teach you by putting your heart and mind to something, you can achieve anything. I love you both so much, throughout all of space and time.

To Ciera, our editor. Thank you for working on this project with us. It was such a unique time to be working together during a global pandemic, both pregnant, and due one week apart with our holiday babies! Going through edits and morning sickness together is an experience I will never forget. Thank you for your understanding to our project and for being such a pivotal working relationship of ours, and now a friend. Cassy, thank you for your love of YA Fantasy, and working through our book so tediously and tirelessly. You were an influential set of eyes on this book. To our beta and sensitivity readers, thank you. It was an arduous ask, and you all jumped in delightfully and were so supportive and timely. Mike Weiss, thank you for being such an incredible source of support and protection for me, and for us always. You are the best in the game. We appreciate you so much. To our incredible PR team and the entire staff at Otter—you all are rockstars! Brittany, Gaby, and Chan, thank you for helping our story see the world with such dedicated and enthusiastic care and for being the "Dream Team!" To our entire team at Palmetto Publishing, to Kelly, Jackie, and Erin - We know our book is in the greatest of hands, with such consideration and care to make it the best it can possibly be. Thank you for answering hundreds of questions and guiding us gracefully. We thank each and every one of you, as you all have had such a pivotal role during the journey and launch of our book, and you all mean the world to us!

Thank you to Audiomachine, M83, Zack Hemsey, and my Pandora playlists that helped formulate this story with the constant replays and inspiration to set the backdrop and tone. Thank you to California – LA, the Redwoods, and Joshua Tree. To Michigan, the place where this story was brought to the pages of a manuscript, was completed, and now published out into the world. From the ocean to the river, I thank the journey.

Thank you to the hawk for soaring through my life, placing reminders on my heart to keep going.

Thank you to Skylar, you were the absolute first. You were there for the very beginning of the journey in Little River, just you and I in our little cottage by the sea along the cliffs where this story began. You were my hug while I cried. You were my listening ear. You were my rock. You were my protector. You were my consistent throughout every up and down. You are so many beautiful memories. You ride with me through the realms. And I finish this entire series in your memory, my great guardian angel. I am blessed to know and love your soul.

Thank You to God. For placing this story on my heart, and onto Greg's. For this soul contract to do our very best to share this story. Thank You for walking through doors with us while we continue to be of action. Thank You for showing us the way.

ACKNOWLEDGEMENTS
GREGORY JOHN MILLER

It's interesting to be writing acknowledgments for a project that I never knew would be in my life. As I sat across the table from my future wife five years ago for a chemistry read, I'd have never guessed it would all play out this way. A couple of months after the chemistry read, we had a picnic in the park somewhere in West Hollywood. Jenny and I started sharing our stories, interests, goals, family, and everything in between the cracks of time. There was something magical, something divine at work, and we both had this unknowing knowing that there was something there, something beyond the chemistry for a TV series.

So, one night I invited her and a couple of friends to Redondo Beach where I was living. We went out dancing in Hermosa Beach. We took pictures in the photobooth where time became irrelevant, and our energies danced through the rest of the night like the Aurora Borealis. It was a short time later that Jenny invited me to go to Joshua Tree. It was in Joshua Tree that Jenny introduced me to her baby, her project she had been working on for a couple of years now as a television series. It was called *Rise of the Legion* at the time. I never related so much to a story as I did this one. I instantly loved Jenny's mind and had already adored her heart, but what also happened in Joshua Tree was the intertwining of two human spirits. She was the one. I thought I left New Jersey to get my own story out to the world and inspire others, but here I was guided by a divine source to meet my beautiful wife, the mother of our two amazing little boys.

Now we have finally finished the first book of a series that she introduced me to five years ago. A story that is now called *Age of Atheria*.

Jenny, my love, my rock.... I want to thank you first and tell you how proud I am of you, how honored I am to be your husband and partner in not only life, but creation, whether books or babies! I am so proud of the woman you have become and are still becoming. I am so proud that you took this vision that blossomed from the ashes of another and believed in yourself enough to spread your wings all alone in Little River, CA with just you and Skylar. It's truly inspiring my love. Thank you for entrusting me with your project, your baby, and allowing me the space to tap into creative energy I didn't know I had. I love you forever and am so excited to write book two, and three, and four... And just continue to build on our foundation of love and loyalty and provide our boys the best life we possibly can. I love you my forever cupcake.

To my Mom and Dad...where do I even begin? You've loved and supported me for my entire life, and nothing has changed even throughout our whole publishing process. Thank you so much for all of your great feedback on our story; it means the world. You two taught me what it means to work hard and follow-through, whether it was in life, school, or sports. You've always been so selfless, supporting my goals and dreams of being a professional baseball player, sacrificing your time and resources to come and watch me play whether it was in our backyard, or in tournaments across the country. You sacrificed your nights, weekends, summers, etc. just to support me and my dreams. I honor you for that. It means everything.

Dad, you have always been there for me. To me, you're not just my dad, but my coach, my friend, my hero. You've always pushed me to be my best whether in sports, school, or life in general. You challenged me to challenge myself. I'll never forget the words, "There's always someone out there willing to work harder." That has stuck with me until this day in everything I do, and I thank you for that. Mom, my Viking warrior mother! You have always been the heart of our home, loving us with your beautiful and kind spirit. Your love and understanding has gotten me through some of my worst days, and your support has always been there to lift me up even higher on my best days. I couldn't do this life without your love and support. I love you mom.

To my late Grandmothers, Joan (aka Mom Mom) and Jeanette (aka Grandma)...I miss you and love you both so much. Thank you for always loving me even in times when I didn't know how to love myself. I can still hear your voice,

Grandma, when you used to say, "My Gregory... I love you, my Gregory." I love you, too, Grandma. Mom Mom, thank you for all your love and support throughout the years. You always checked in on us, your grandsons, and how Jenny and I are doing with the book. We did it! It's finally ready, and I know you both would be so proud. God gained the most incredible angels. You're both forever embedded in my heart, mind, and spirit. Until we meet again...

To Kristin, Greg, and the boys, thank you for always being there. Thank you for your love and support no matter where life has taken us. Kristin, thanks for being the best big sister a brother could ask for. I also want to thank you for being one of my biggest cheerleaders while I traveled and played baseball around the country. Your support has and always will mean so much to me. Jon, Declan, and Cole, always chase your dreams. If you work hard and stay persistent, you'll eventually catch them. I love you guys.

Katie and Zach, you have been two of the biggest advocates for our story, given in-depth feedback, and really taken it to heart. Thank you so much for that and for always supporting us and our story. Katie, my amazing little sister...I love you so much and thank you for all of your support throughout the years. I still have all of the letters you sent to me and they have been a large part of my motivation and inspiration. Thank you for being you and I can't wait to meet our little niece!

To my in-laws. Mark, thank you for believing in us and providing us the support to fulfill our goals of making this dream a reality. Thank you for every lesson from fixing things, to brewing beer, to planting gardens, and tapping maple sap. Thank you for the early morning to late night life talks, advice, and your words of wisdom. Thank you for being the grill master and kitchen king. I am so grateful to call you my Father-in-law. Carmine, thank you for all of your love and kindness, and for always being there to support our goals and dreams. You're the kitchen queen! And one of the punniest people I know, second to only me. It's no fun with no pun! Grateful to have you in my life. You both mean the world to me.

Lonnie, thank you for being such an amazing Grandmother to our two little boys, and always supporting our family with your love and guidance. You always make holidays so special and help remind us to keep our childlike spirit. Your humor is unmatched, and I love all of our laughs together. I am so thankful that you are my Mother-in-law. John, you're such an intelligent guy, and we admire your strengths and skills you bring to the world brother. To the Havnen's, Tasler's and entire extended family, thank you for your love and support.

To my entire extended family in Iceland and in the states, thank you for your love and support.

To Zeke, Paul, and Matt; I want to thank each of you for our friendship and brotherhood. All of you have helped shape me into who I am in so many different and awesome ways. I am eternally grateful to call you my friends and ultimately my brothers. Thank you for all your support and for being my accountability partners throughout the years, whether in baseball, work, or life. Many of our conversations have sparked thoughts and creations within this story, and I thank you for that.

Finally, to my beautiful baby boys and our greatest creations. You are the light of my life, and being your father has been the greatest gift I could ever ask for. Every day I get to wake up to your smiling little faces, and it instantly brightens my day and brings me ultimate joy. I want you to know that I love you for the rest of time, and anything you choose to put your mind to, you can and will, achieve. River, my bold and courageous little boy...You are stronger than you even know. Your will and tenacity are something special, and I know that you will harness those gifts into something magnificent. Ryder, my sweet soul of a boy. Thank you for your smiles and laughs. Thank you for your calming energy and always wanting to snuggle and spread love. I hope that you both always go after your dreams.

I'll leave you with three things... Every obstacle is an opportunity to learn and grow. The summit of one mountain is the bottom of the next, just keep climbing. And lastly, if you fall down seven times, stand up eight.

Photography by Jaida Bentley

Jenny McClain Miller grew up in Iowa and spent over ten years working in Los Angeles as a content creator, writer, producer, and actress. She holds four degrees in Marketing, Product Development, International Manufacturing, and Business Management. She continues to work as an author, screenwriter, and producer.

Gregory John Miller is a former professional baseball player originally from South Jersey. He was drafted out of Seton Hall University as a pitcher in the 10th round of the 2008 MLB draft. While documenting his journey after baseball, he discovered a passion for writing. He is currently working on a motivational book to help others unlock their potential.

Jenny and Greg are married and have two young boys. They love being partners in entertainment and in life. They enjoy spending time together as a family, exploring the world, the ocean, and being in nature. *Age of Atheria* is the first in the series and the couple's debut novel together.

www.ageofatheria.com

Follow along on social media. @JennyMcClainMiller @GregoryJohnMiller